Praise for Soul Mates

"I was captivated from the opening paragraph as Jeane magically wove the story of financial opposites. With the help of her masterfully crafted characters, the principles of Law of Attraction are introduced and artfully explained. Jeane creatively dances between pure captivating fiction and lessons of living from a place of love, trust, and faith. This book is well worth reading."

—L. Neil Thrussell: Best selling author, personal coach and workshop facilitator

"Soul Mates is dynamic, passionate, and full of surprises. Interwoven principles of the Law of Attraction are the building blocks of this lively, engaging and satisfying tale of human relationships. They make one pause to think, and entice the reader toward advancing his own personal evolution. A great novel for our times!"

—Helena Kalivoda, Author of Awaken! and Purposeful Mind Series

"Within this classic romantic tale, there is an authentic pull that develops over the course of the chapters, personal growth in each of the characters that makes the story resonate richly. There is food for the soul, the mind, and the heart—ideas to consider for one's own life in terms of focus and the energy that fuels our minds, the emotional rush that comes from feeling the spark between two characters, and the gifts that each of these characters shine onto the world. While at times the story can feel a bit like a soap opera, there is something quite real to each character that caused me to cheer for things to work out and justice to be served."

—John King, Research Assistant

SOUL MATES

Jamel ~
Your vibration is
everything!
J Waters

Other Books by Jeane Watier

LAW OF ATTRACTION TRILOGY:

Life's Song
A Song of the Heart
Hearts Reunited

A Brief Moment in Time

COMING SOON:

InSight

For more information go to:

www.jeanewatier.com

Soul Mates

JEANE WATIER

Copyright © 2013 by Jeane Watier
All rights reserved.
No part of this book may be reproduced or transmitted in any form or by any means, electronic or mechanical, including photocopying, recording, or by any information storage and retrieval system, without the written permission of the publisher, except where permitted by law.

Library and Archives Canada Cataloguing in Publication
Watier, Jeane, 1963-
Soul Mates / Jeane Watier.
ISBN 978-0-9877179-5-5
I. Title.
PS8645.A846S68 2013 C813'.6 C2013-900701-6

All characters, events, and locations portrayed in this book are fictitious. Any similarity to real persons, places, or events is coincidental and not intended by the author.

Published by: Novel Ink, Calgary, AB
www.novel-ink.com

Cover design and layout by: Serenity Design Concepts
Original photos/artwork: "Swirls" (Image for chapter headings) by Ivan Prole, "Romantic couple" by Yuri Arcurs (Shutterstock 87748423), "Abstract Background" by Viktor Vector (Shutterstock 121151329)

For more information on this and other books by Jeane Watier please visit: **www.jeanewatier.com**

Dedication

While the story is a product of my active imagination, the truths contained in this book are based on the teachings of Abraham, channelled by Esther Hicks. It is my desire to share the understanding that I have gained from Abraham, and point others to the wonderful nonphysical teacher that I have come to know and love.

www.abraham-hicks.com

Thank you, Esther, for allowing Abraham (and now Jerry) to speak through you, addressing the questions on so many minds, for helping us stand on the leading edge with confidence and knowing, for preparing us to be the teachers and uplifters we came here to be.

Continuing thanks to my husband, Ron, and many friends and family members whose love and support means more to me than words can convey.

Jeane Watier

"Everything is energy and that's all there is to it. Match the frequency of the reality you want and you cannot help but get that reality. It can be no other way. It is not philosophy, it is physics."
---Albert Einstein.

Chapter 1

Jace climbed the steps to his apartment building, his arms full of groceries. Shifting the bags awkwardly, he pulled open the front door as Chad called out his name. Jace turned to see his friend crossing the street toward him.

"Hey, buddy," Chad grinned. "You're gonna love me."

"In your dreams," Jace retorted absently, holding the door with his foot while he readjusted his load.

"You're gonna bow down and worship me."

"Do you mind helping me?" Jace asked, ignoring the last comment. A bag was slipping, and he hoped it wasn't the one with the eggs.

Chad caught it before it fell, then followed Jace up two flights of stairs. In his apartment, Jace set the groceries on the counter and took the third bag from his friend. Finally his curiosity got the better of him. "Okay, what is it? What's so great?"

"I got us tickets for tomorrow night's game."

"Seriously?" Jace beamed. "How'd you score those? I heard people were paying as much as five hundred bucks for playoff tickets."

"Carla's dad," Chad replied matter-of-factly as he helped himself to a beer from Jace's refrigerator. "A guy he works with owed him a favor or something. Her dad was planning to go, but he was called out of town at the last minute."

"Sweet."

"I'm gonna need cash up front, though."

"What?" Jace grimaced, suddenly knowing it was too good to be true. "How much?"

"They were a steal—a hundred bucks apiece. Said he had people offering him two."

"I don't know, man," Jace sighed. "I'm tapped out till payday."

"You can't be serious!" Chad exclaimed. "I mean, I can sell your ticket easy and make a tidy profit, but you don't want to miss this. If they win tonight, tomorrow night's game could be the final. We'd have prime seats."

"You think I don't know that?" Jace couldn't hide his frustration.

"Hey, chill. Just get a payday loan. It's easy."

Easy for you, Jace vented silently. *Your parents bail you out every time you get in over your head.* As he turned away, pretending to arrange items in the fridge, he exhaled heavily. He didn't like feeling jealous. It wasn't Chad's fault. Life had thrown Jace unexpected curves. His parents had spent all their savings when his dad was sick, and Jace had had to quit school. Now that his dad was gone, his mom lived on a meager income. Jace helped her as much as he could; he couldn't stand to see her do without. But it meant he didn't have money for extras, and his debt was starting to escalate. His bank account was overdrawn. The groceries he was putting away had been bought on credit.

He did his best to ignore the growing anxiety in the pit of his stomach. He hated being broke. He was tired of living paycheck to paycheck and going deeper into debt every month. He had big dreams, but lately he hadn't let himself think about them, they were too unrealistic.

Jace had never hidden his circumstances from Chad. They'd been friends since childhood. Nevertheless, Chad didn't understand. He couldn't relate to the financial bondage, the ever-increasing weight on Jace's shoulders.

As his friend stood waiting for a response, Jace knew what he needed to do. Like it or not, it was the responsible thing to do. He turned down the ticket.

"Okay, pal. Whatever," Chad shrugged. "You still coming by to watch the game tonight?"

"Yeah," Jace nodded, feeling defeated. "See you later."

After Chad left, Jace finished putting the groceries away. He opened a beer for himself and paced back and forth in his small kitchen, trying to justify his decision. *I can always watch the game on TV. The crowds would be nuts, anyway. If they win, it'll be pandemonium in the stadium, and if they lose, there'll be thousands of disgruntled fans.*

It was no use. No amount of justifying would ease his frustration and disappointment. He wanted to go.

It wasn't simply the chance to see the big game live; it was much more than that. It represented all that he wanted in life, all that seemed to be just beyond reach.

Suddenly frustration turned to anger. "Damn it!" He slammed his fist down on the counter. "I deserve to go. I work hard, and what the hell do I have to show for it?" The anger edged him on, challenging him to action. "What's a little more debt?" he sighed, knowing he'd probably regret his decision. Before he could change his mind, he grabbed the phone and dialed Chad's cell, hoping it wasn't too late.

CASSANDRA TURNED to her friend, beaming. "They're absolutely perfect! I wanted a pair in this color. They'll match the dress I bought in Paris last month. I haven't worn it yet because none of my shoes were just right."

"They're fabulous," Tanisha agreed. "Why don't you wear the dress to the club, Friday? Wow all the guys and make Nick jealous."

"I don't want to make him jealous. We're done. I don't want anything to do with him. I was the one who broke up with him. Remember?"

"Yes, because he's a lying, cheating son of a bitch," Tanisha pointed out.

"Thanks for reminding me."

"That's why you need to show up looking like a million bucks and flirt with everyone but him," Tanisha insisted. "He'll realize what he lost—maybe even come crawling back to you, sniveling and apologetic. You'll have the satisfaction of blowing him off in front of his friends."

"As appealing as that sounds," Cassandra responded dryly, "I think I'll pass." She was angry with Nick; he'd hurt her deeply, but revenge wasn't her style. Neither was going to the club to flirt. None of the guys there interested her. She was tired of the dating scene. All men were alike, it seemed—at least the ones she'd met. Rich, handsome, successful yet so into themselves, their money, and their toys that they had no room for anyone else in their lives.

"I'm thinking about getting away this weekend," Cassandra informed her friend. "It's been months since I've been home. A quiet, relaxing weekend in Port Hayden would do me a world of good."

"Your parents are still there? I thought they'd be at the summer house already."

"No, they haven't left yet. I talked to my dad last weekend. He sounded worried about Aunt Sophia."

"Is she sick?"

"Apparently she blacked out, and someone took her to the hospital. She wasn't admitted, though, and she claims she's okay now. The woman is eighty-seven and still living on her own. Daddy wants her to move in with them, but Mother says she'd be better off in a care home. The problem is, Aunt Sophia doesn't want to move; she's very strong willed."

"She's always been eccentric, too, hasn't she? Wasn't she married to a Count?"

"He was a British Lord. I never really knew him; he died when I was young. You're right, though. She's always been a little different. Ahead of her time, really. Drove her own car at fifteen. Got her pilot's license when she was twenty-one. She was an activist, too, marching in political demonstrations, joining hunger strikes. She even went to jail once."

"Really?"

"Just overnight, but it caused quite a stir in the social circles. Lady Sophia Langdon in jail!" Cassandra smiled at the thought. Her aunt was one of the wealthiest women in Port Hayden, yet you wouldn't know it to look at her. She lived in an older apartment building in the city's eclectic downtown core, and although she'd driven a car for most of her life, now insisted on walking or taking public transit. The family had tried to persuade her to hire a driver, but she'd scoffed at the idea. Cassandra didn't know whether it was a dislike for money or simply what money stood for that caused her to live the way she did. She had to admit, however, that her aunt seemed genuinely happy.

Cassandra couldn't imagine not enjoying the comforts money provided. She'd always had all a girl could want. Growing up in a city that was home to some of the oldest wealth on the East Coast, she'd gone to private schools, spent summers at the beach, traveled, ate, and shopped as her heart desired.

Her mother's life was a minuet, an elegant social dance, complete with fashionable charity work, endless society functions, and the responsibility of running a large household with servants. Her father, a powerful and well-respected man, sat at the helm of a multinational corporation, a company his grandfather had single-handedly built after emigrating from Europe and settling in what was now Port Hayden.

Cassandra had opted for a career, as did the majority of women her age. For most, it was about status. It gave the older generation something to brag about, something with which to compare their children. For Cassandra, it was about passion. She'd always loved writing. Once she got her journalism degree, she'd set her sights on one of the biggest magazines in the country. Her father had used his influence to get her the job, but her talent and zeal were responsible for her advancement in the company. She'd worked hard to prove herself. Now she was an assistant editor and loving it.

She paid for her shoes, and the two women began to walk. It was a beautiful evening. They were headed to their favorite French restaurant to meet several other friends. Cassandra couldn't wait to show off her purchase, yet her happiness went beyond her fashion acquisition. Breathing deeply, she was filled with the awareness that life was very good—something she had taken for granted for twenty-six years. As she consciously acknowledged the fact, it occurred to her that she was glad Nick Hagen was no longer in her life. Breaking up with him had been long overdue.

I don't need him—or any man, for that matter—to complete me. The thought was liberating. Having no desire to get into another relationship anytime soon,

Cassandra was at a pivotal place in her life. It was time to discover what she really wanted, maybe set new goals. A weekend in Port Hayden would be the perfect opportunity to begin doing just that.

JACE ATTEMPTED to quiet the discordant thoughts. As he focused on chores that needed doing, he tried to get excited about the game. *I should be thankful. This is an opportunity that doesn't come around every day. Besides, a hundred bucks is hardly a reason to get bent out of shape.*

He bagged some garbage and took it to the trash bin. As he returned, he had to move to one side of the narrow stairwell to allow a woman to pass. Recognizing the old lady who lived on the top floor, he greeted her politely. He was about to continue up the stairs when she placed a small, wrinkled hand on his arm

"You can have anything you want, you know."

"Excuse me?"

"You think life is dealing you a bad hand. It's not. You get to choose. It's up to you."

He stared at her, not quite sure what to do. She seemed like a sweet little old lady, reminding him of his grandmother whose mind had started to fail the year before she passed away. As he debated whether to say something or simply smile and nod, she took her hand off his arm and turned to go down the stairs.

"It's a nice evening for a walk."

Jace returned to his apartment, feeling uneasy. He'd assumed that she was confused, that she'd mistaken him for someone else. Yet, as he replayed her words, he sensed they were meant for him. *It's a coincidence, that's all,* he assured himself. *I must remind her of a grandson or a nephew—someone who looks like me, who's going through a hard time.*

Regardless of who her advice was meant for, it affected Jace deeply. *I can have anything I want? I get to choose? I wish that were true,* he sighed.

His mind drifted to dreams he'd once held of being a commercial pilot. As a young boy, his walls had been covered with posters of airplanes. Model planes sat on his desk and hung from his ceiling. He'd held to that dream through high school and wasn't daunted when his parents persuaded him to get a business degree at the local college—something to fall back on if he didn't make it as a pilot, they said.

He'd given in to their wishes. They were, after all, paying for his education. When his father had gotten sick during Jace's first year of college and their insurance covered little of the cost, Jace had dropped out to work full time so he could help with the bills. That was six years ago. Since then he'd kept his dreams carefully tucked away. Now he realized why. They were painful. When he looked at them, all he could see was the huge crevasse between the dream and the reality he lived in.

Jace quickly finished his tasks, grabbed a six pack from the fridge, and headed to Chad's to watch the game. As he descended the front steps of his building, the old woman's words remained etched in his mind. They may have been meant to comfort someone else, yet they taunted him, reminding him he wasn't living the life he wanted.

As if events were conspiring to torture him further, a plane went by overhead. It appeared to be making its descent toward the local airport, though not on a usual flight path. Jace watched intently as the landing gear was deployed and the wing flaps were lowered to slow the plane as it neared the ground. He stood a moment longer, paying tribute to the dreams of his childhood. Then he turned resolutely and walked away, not only from the sight of the plane but from the dream of ever flying one.

Chapter 2

Cassandra buckled her seatbelt and put her chair-back in the upright position. Looking around her in first class, she smiled at Mrs. Charlebois who was returning from visiting her daughter in California. Two seats ahead were Mr. and Mrs. Edmonds. They had been touring Europe for several months. The Davises were on the flight as well.

The social circle in Port Hayden was small but elite. Not much happened that everyone didn't know about. Cassandra's mother was always up to date on gossip and had filled her in on the phone the evening before.

As Cassandra rode the escalator down to the meeting area, her eyes scanned the small airport. Not much had changed in the eight years since she'd moved away. The routine was the same every time she came home. She smiled warmly at the man who had been the family's chauffeur for as long as she could remember.

"Good evening, Miss Cassandra." Wallace reached to take her shoulder bag. "Did you have a good flight?"

"Yes, Wallace, thank you," she replied as she accompanied him to the car. A porter followed and placed her Louis Vuitton in the trunk of the vintage Rolls Royce.

They chatted as they made their way to the Town House, so named to distinguish it from their summer home at Walden Beach. Her grandfather had had the house built nearly seventy-five years earlier. He was one of the first to settle in the Port Hayden area, and he'd chosen the nicest piece of real estate available. The family home sat high on a rocky hillside overlooking the town and the port itself. From the dormer window in her bedroom, Cassandra had spent many contented hours watching fishing boats coming into the harbor and sailboats and yachts setting out to navigate the islands off the jagged coast.

They rounded the last curve on the driveway, and Cassandra smiled as the house came into view. It was a four thousand square-foot, two story, chateau-style house with seven bedrooms and as many bathrooms. The manicured grounds were expansive. When she was younger, she'd loved roaming the property with the dogs by her side.

No sooner had they come to mind, when two Great Danes trotted up to meet the car. Cassandra laughed as she reached to embrace the old dogs. Nearly twelve, they looked as strong and healthy as ever. They were pure steel blue in color and stood thirty inches at the shoulders. "Hello, Samson," she cooed. "Hello, my lovely

Delilah." After reuniting with the gentle giants, she heard barking in the distance and watched a younger dog bound toward them. Her father had kept one of Delilah's last pups. Marrakesh had grown considerably since Cassandra had been home last. At a year old, he stood nearly as tall as his parents, but had yet to fill out. He was already a regal-looking dog.

"Welcome home, darling." Her mother greeted her as she walked up the marble steps.

"Hello, Mother," Cassandra smiled, taking in the familiar front entry. It was always good to be home; she felt it every time. It made her question why the lure of the big city and the demands of her job kept her away for such long periods of time.

Her father walked up and before any words were spoken, embraced his daughter. "Hi, kitten," he grinned.

"Hi, Daddy." She kissed her father's cheek, breathing in his familiar cologne. "Marrakesh has really grown. He's such a handsome dog."

"He'll sire some nice pups. I've already had inquiries about him."

They continued talking about the dogs, her mother's latest charity fundraiser, and Cassandra's work. She noted that nearly fifteen minutes had passed, and her mother had yet to ask about Nick. She hadn't told them about the breakup. However, since Nick's parents also lived in Port Hayden, Cassandra suspected she might already know.

Her suspicions were correct; her mother admitted having heard a rumor. When translated that likely meant she'd called Nick's mother, and the two had discussed the situation at length. Cassandra gave her parents the necessary details and then tried to change the subject, but her mother was persistent.

"I'm sure it was just a lover's quarrel, darling. Give it a day or two. These things always sort themselves out. Nick's a nice boy. I talked to his mother just the other day. She's so proud of Nicholas. He's taking the bar exam next month. After that he'll be moving back here to join his father's law firm."

The picture she painted was different from the one Cassandra was familiar with. *A nice boy?* Nick would become a successful lawyer; she had no doubt of that. However, she couldn't see him moving back to Port Hayden and settling down anytime soon. She was deciding how much to tell her mother, when her father intervened.

"Helen," he said firmly. "Cass is a grown woman; she knows what she's doing. Maybe Nick isn't the right man for her."

Cassandra beamed a thank-you to her father. He was a man of few words, but when he spoke, people listened. Her mother always backed down—at least in front of others. Relieved that the subject had been changed, she inquired about her Aunt Sophia. "I'd hoped to see her this weekend. Will you be having her out to the house?"

"We invite her all the time," Helen replied tersely. "She rarely comes."

"She doesn't go out much anymore." Richard Van Broden came to his aunt's defense. "She might appreciate a visit, though."

Cassandra was glad for the reprieve as she went upstairs. Breathing deeply, she surveyed her bedroom. Within its walls, life was less complicated. Though it seemed she had everything, she realized for the first time that her relationships were lacking. Even the relationship with her parents wasn't as simple and easy as it once was.

Mulling it over, she curled up on the window seat and gazed out at the harbor. The sun was low, causing long shadows to reach down the rocky slopes and drape the city in a velvety grey as they made their way into the dark waters of the Atlantic. Off the coast, several small islands were still lit up by the sun's fading light. Cassandra watched mesmerized as the shadows slowly consumed them. Her reverie was interrupted by a knock at the door.

"Excuse me, miss." A woman poked her head in Cassandra's bedroom. "Dinner is ready."

"Thank you . . . " Cassandra hesitated. "I'm sorry; I don't know your name." Her mother hadn't mentioned that she'd hired a new housekeeper.

"It's Sarah," the woman smiled politely.

"Thank you, Sarah. Tell Mother and Daddy I'll be right down."

Traditions were honored in their home, and that meant the formal evening meal required a change of clothes. Although Cassandra was familiar with the routine, she found it unnecessary and old fashioned. Her father shared her views. Whenever her mother was away, the two of them dressed in casual clothes and enjoyed their evening meal outside on the terrace or curled up in front of the television. Cassandra smiled at the fond memories, then quickly changed her clothes and hurried down to join her parents at the dinner table.

NEXT MORNING, Jace applied for a two-hundred-dollar advance on his paycheck. Chad was right; it was easy enough. Still, he had a hard time coming to terms with the extra money he'd be spending. They would inevitably go to parties after the game. By the time the night was over, the cash would likely be gone.

He hated the way money controlled his life. He longed to go out and enjoy himself like his friends did. Even with money for the ticket and cash in his pocket to spend that evening, he didn't feel free to have fun. *How ironic,* he grumbled. *I borrow money so I can have a good time, and I'm more miserable than ever.*

When he returned to his apartment, an envelope was lying by his door. Picking it up, he saw that it was addressed to the old woman upstairs. It wasn't the first time he'd received her mail by mistake, yet it seemed odd to see the letter outside his door and not in the mailbox, especially since there was no mail delivery on Saturdays.

Maybe someone else received it and misread the number as well, he speculated as he went up the stairs to deliver the envelope to its proper owner. *Or maybe someone dropped it off.* He paused when he noticed her door was open a crack. Tapping lightly, he listened for a reply. When no one answered, he knocked louder.

As the door opened further, Jace could see into the old woman's living room. It was generously filled with furniture that looked as though it had once belonged in a much grander home. The antiquated pieces had rich fabrics and delicate wood detailing.

Standing in her doorway, Jace debated whether to leave the letter and go, or stay and investigate. *Living alone at her age, she could have fallen or something. Who knows if she has family to check on her.* He knocked again. "Hello?"

"Hello, there."

The voice came from the stairwell. He turned to see the old woman climbing the stairs with a bag of groceries in one arm.

"I have to bring the bags up one at a time," she explained. "I'm not as spry as I used to be."

Jace quickly met her halfway down and took the bag from her. He waited for her to enter the apartment and followed with her groceries. "I got your mail by mistake," he informed her, setting the bag on the counter. "My name's Jace," he added. "I live downstairs, in 202."

"Yes. Hello, Jace," she responded jovially. "You'll stay for a cup of tea?"

"I... um..." Jace stammered, not sure how to respond when her invitation was more of an assumption. Having tea with an old woman on a Saturday morning was the last thing he wanted to do, but he couldn't come up with an excuse quickly enough. She'd already put the kettle on the stove. As she set out two delicate china teacups, he sighed. *I guess it won't kill me. She probably doesn't get many visitors.* "Sure," he shrugged.

As they waited for the kettle to boil, she addressed him. "I meant what I said the other day."

"The other day?" He assumed she was referring to her odd statement in the stairwell the day before. *Then again, maybe she's thinking of a different conversation with someone else altogether.* Jace began to feel uneasy.

"Oh, that was just yesterday, wasn't it," she shook her head, laughing.

"I didn't know if you were talking to me or not. I mean, I thought maybe you had me confused for someone else."

"I'm old, but I haven't totally lost my mind," she smiled. "Not yet, anyway."

"Then I'm the one who's confused," Jace admitted. "You said that life hasn't handed me a bad deal. What did you mean by that? It sounded like you knew me."

"We're all the same, deep down. We like to look for something or someone to blame when life doesn't turn out the way we want. Take some advice from an old woman. There's more to the equation. We get to have a say in how our lives turn out. It was never meant to be a struggle."

"Maybe so, but that doesn't mean it's easy for everybody. Some people have an unfair advantage." His defenses rose as he thought of those who got everything handed to them on a silver platter. Port Hayden had more than its share of rich, snobbish families. His mom had spent the last five years working as a housekeeper for some of the city's wealthiest. He hated that she'd been reduced to a servant after his father passed away. She was better than that and deserved to be treated as they were—waited on and pampered. He felt guilty for not being able to make life easier for her.

"Do you really want what they have?" she asked, seeming to know who he was talking about.

"Of course," he asserted. "Who wouldn't?"

"I've had all that," she replied nonchalantly. "It's not as satisfying as you might think."

"Thanks, but I'd like a chance to decide for myself." Jace sipped his tea. It was strong and sweet, but not unpleasant. In the silence that followed, he pondered her words. *Did she really have it all at one time?* The furniture spoke of wealth. The teacups appeared to be fine china. *I wonder what happened.*

"If you look beneath the posh and glamour, the expensive toys with all the bells and whistles, you'd see people just like us. We're the same underneath. The only difference is what we focus on."

"What do you mean?"

"You get what you focus on," she replied, taking a sip of her tea, then setting it down and staring wistfully into the cup. "You get what you expect from life. It took me many years to understand that."

Jace frowned. The explanation was too simple; it didn't account for the way life took such sharp twists and turns. He liked a good debate, however, and sensed the old bird was up to it. “It can’t be that simple,” he argued. “There are so many variables—things we have no control over.”

“It seems that way,” she went on in her sweet, even tone. “But you do have control over one aspect, and that makes all the difference.”

“What’s that?”

“Control…yes, it’s what we all want, don’t we?” she mused, appearing lost in her thoughts for a moment. “Think about it. You want money—and there’s nothing wrong with that. The problem is that when you get some, it’s not long before you want more. And if you do happen to get a lot of money, you deal with the fear of losing it. You have no assurance of where and when and how the money is going to come; therefore, you have no peace of mind. What you want even more than money is peace of mind, that feeling of control over your money.

“You don’t just want love,” she continued, pouring him another cup of tea before he had time to object. “You want the security of knowing that you’re in control of who and how much. It’s the same with health. A healthy body today won’t do you much good if you live in fear of dying tomorrow.”

“Well, yeah,” Jace agreed. “Everyone would like that control, but life doesn’t offer us those assurances.”

“You can have that assurance . . . once you understand how the Universe works.”

Jace frowned again. Though he wanted to believe the old woman had nothing of value to offer him, her words challenged his thinking. *Is it that I want so badly to believe my life could be different, that it could be better?* He sighed. "So you've figured it out? You know how the Universe works?"

"Like I said before," she explained, "it's all about focus. You can have anything you want, anything you choose. You're in control."

Suddenly Jace was frustrated. They'd come full circle, back to where they'd started the day before. *Maybe the old lady is crazy after all. Maybe she gets her kicks from believing she has the answers to life's questions. If what she says is true, how come it took her this long to figure it out? And if she's in control of her life, why is she living alone in an apartment building that has seen better days?*

Jace looked at his watch. He'd been at her place for almost an hour. He still had to fix a broken tap for his mom before he and Chad left for the game, so he thanked the old woman for the tea and said goodbye, letting himself out. As he walked to his car he breathed a disgruntled sigh, trying to shake off the uncomfortable feelings. The conversation had again left him deep in thought about the hows and whys of life. The problem was, it stirred up questions but did little to answer them.

His elderly neighbor seemed confident as she talked about focus, control, assurance, and understanding the

Universe. Jace had never thought of life in those terms. The ideas intrigued him as much as they disturbed him, and he almost hoped they'd have a chance to talk again. Part of him was curious to hear more.

Then again, he argued, *maybe it's better to leave it alone. She may have gained some wisdom over the years, but I doubt she has the answers to any of my questions.* The thought didn't satisfy him; a voice inside told him the opposite was true. He shook his head, refusing to give those thoughts any more of his attention. He had a big day ahead of him and wanted to get on with it.

Chapter 3

When Cassandra pulled up in front of the apartment building, she noticed a young man leaving. She immediately assessed him, wondering what kind of people lived in the same building as her aunt. Dressed in blue jeans and a leather jacket, he looked respectable enough. The car he got into was an older model but not in bad shape. Cassandra silently questioned whether he knew her aunt, whether Sophia Langdon associated with the people in her building, in her neighborhood.

She couldn't understand why her great aunt lived the way she did, why anyone would choose not to enjoy the benefits money could provide. The building was old. Though it wasn't run down, it lacked the conveniences of the newer high-rise apartments being built around it—a lobby, a concierge, an elevator, to name a few. As she walked up the narrow staircase, she continued her appraisal. The walls had a decent coat of paint. The carpet underfoot was in good shape. Still, it was far from the luxury her aunt had once enjoyed. *At least I assume she enjoyed it,* Cassandra mused. *How could she not?*

Her evaluation of the place and subsequent hesitation as she stood outside her aunt's apartment made her aware of her growing apprehension. It was more than a year since she'd seen her aunt Sophia, and that had been at the Town House. She had only been to her apartment once before, many years earlier. The building seemed much smaller than she remembered. Not only that, but Cassandra had to admit she wasn't comfortable visiting her wealthy aunt in such a humble environment.

The old woman answered on the first knock. A smile lit up her face as she recognized her grandniece. "Cassandra, my dear, how lovely to see you!"

Cassandra was instantly drawn to the loving warmth that radiated from her great aunt. Her apprehension gone, she opened her arms to hug the woman. At five-foot-seven, Cassandra was considerably taller, though a quality about Sophia Langdon had always made up for her small stature. Cassandra was happy to see that her favorite aunt still exuded an air of grandeur, a stately presence undiminished by her simplistic lifestyle.

"It's good to see you, too, Aunt Sophia," Cassandra replied. "I'm in town for the weekend and thought I'd stop by. Daddy said you don't go out much lately. He's been worried..."

"Worry...," Sophia interjected, shaking her head. "It's so pointless."

"But Aunt Sophia, he cares about you. You're getting older and living alone here."

Sophia patted her niece's hand. "Let's have some tea, dear."

Cassandra had to smile. Her aunt's outlook was as simplistic as her lifestyle. A cup of tea was the immediate answer to all life's problems. She watched the old woman in her kitchen, humming as she moved about the small space, boiling the kettle, filling the teapot, setting out cups—perfectly happy as if it were the most important task in the world at that moment.

"You don't need to worry about me, either." Sophia handed Cassandra her tea. "I still have some things to do before I go."

Cassandra frowned. *She's obviously referring to her own passing, but what kinds of things is she talking about?*

"You have a full life ahead of you. You'll marry and have children." Sophia paused and appeared to look right through her. "There's something else... something bigger you want to do. You're a writer, aren't you?"

"Um... yes," Cassandra stumbled, not sure what else to say. *Was that some sort of prediction?* she questioned silently. *Is Aunt Sophia psychic? Could she possibly know what's ahead for me?*

"You'll figure it out," her aunt smiled sweetly, waving her hand to dismiss the subject. "We tend to get too caught up in the details. Details don't really matter; it's how you feel that's important."

How I feel? Cassandra had concluded that she was at a pivotal place in her life and wanted to spend time in her childhood home to sort her thoughts, possibly make some decisions. Now she realized that breaking up with Nick, coming to Port Hayden, and visiting her aunt were not random events. Sophia's words sent chills up her spine.

There *was* something bigger; she'd been feeling it for months, and it seemed all that was happening was somehow leading her to it. It had to do with her writing. As much as she loved her job, a new idea was trying to get her attention, though she wasn't sure what it was. "Aunt Sophia, how could you possibly know there's something bigger I want to do? I've been feeling it, but I've never mentioned it to anyone. I don't even know what it is, exactly."

"We're all connected, dear." The old woman patted her hand again. "Once you learn to listen, you can hear a lot. People convey much more than what they say with words."

"But how?" Cassandra wasn't satisfied. She wanted to understand how her aunt could perceive a desire she was barely aware of herself, a mysterious inner longing she'd only recently acknowledged. "What do you see or hear that others don't?"

"It's possible to see with more than your eyes and hear with more than your ears," Sophia explained. "You can learn to sense what's going on with others and feel things . . . inside." She tapped her chest. "Some call it a knowing."

"So . . . you could sense that about me in the short time we've been visiting here?"

"Young people are often the easiest to read. So much enthusiasm for life. So many dreams. It's like a bright light shining around them."

"What else can you see? You said I'll marry and have children. I guess that's a common desire for someone my age, but do you know details? I mean, I don't see it happening anytime soon; I just broke up with my boyfriend."

"Yes, and I can tell that was a good decision. But someone new isn't far away."

"Not far away?" Cassandra questioned. "Are you talking about time or distance?"

"I'm not sure," Sophia laughed. "It could mean either, or both. Don't get too caught up in the details; you'll find him easiest when you're not looking."

Cassandra was dumbfounded. *She was right about me wanting to do something bigger with my life, and now she tells me I'm going to meet someone. Could that be true as well?*

"We still have time," Sophia remarked casually. "I have some things I'd like to tell you. Maybe you could write them down."

"Sure." Cassandra had no idea what her aunt was referring to or why time was an issue, but she was happy to help. "Do you have paper, a writing pad?"

"No, dear," the old woman shook her head. "We've covered enough for today. We'll begin tomorrow. Why don't you come here in the morning?" She looked right through Cassandra again and nodded. "Around ten o'clock."

"All right," Cassandra agreed. "My plane doesn't leave until six. Mother's having a garden party in the afternoon, but I could come by in the morning."

Sensing that their visit was complete, she stood up to leave. Sophia walked her to the door and hugged her affectionately. As Cassandra went down the stairs, her mind replayed their conversation. Her aunt's uncanny knowing had left her strangely elated. She felt something significant was about to happen, yet she had no idea what it could be.

As she reached for the handle of the heavy outer door, someone came running up the front steps and burst through from the other side. She had just enough time to step back and avoid being hit.

"Oh, sorry," a man said. "I didn't see you."

It was the same young man she'd seen leaving the building when she arrived. "Do you always move this fast?" Cassandra asked, annoyed. She couldn't help but wonder what might have happened had her aunt been in his way. "There are elderly people in this building. Someone less agile might not have been able to get out of the way as quickly as I did."

"I said I was sorry," the man responded with a definite edge to his voice. "Besides, you were on the wrong side. Anyone who lives here knows to open the right hand door, not the left."

Cassandra walked away without replying. Whether she'd been in the wrong or not, there was no excuse for his rude behavior. She could picture him treating her aunt the same way and immediately began worrying about the older woman's safety. Then she remembered Sophia's comment about worry. Although unconventional, her aunt's way of thinking made sense. Cassandra had to admit it was refreshing.

As her thoughts returned to her aunt, she softened. She'd always held the woman in high esteem, admiring her convictions even though she couldn't relate to her choices. Sophia Langdon had lived a long, full, interesting life, and Cassandra's curiosity rose as she tried to imagine what she wanted her to write down. Whatever it was, it seemed important to her, and Cassandra was glad to be part of it. On top of that, she was eager to spend more time with her perceptive old aunt.

JACE SCOWLED at the woman walking away from him. *Who does she think she is, coming around here, dressed to the nines in her designer clothes with her designer bag? She looks like she stepped out of a fashion magazine. Boy, is she in the wrong neighborhood.*

Had he seen her in a magazine, he might have noticed how good looking she was or how her long sweater fit the curves of her body. All he could see in the moment was a rich bitch who had the nerve to come into his building and tell him how he should act. He did, however, notice the sleek, silver Aston Martin she walked up to. But instead of appreciation for the prestigious vehicle, he felt disgust for a woman who had the nerve to parade her obvious wealth in front of others—others she was well aware didn't have the opportunities she'd been given in life.

Jace turned away, suddenly remembering why he'd been running in the first place. It had taken him longer than anticipated to replace the broken tap at his mom's. He sprinted up the stairs, changed quickly, and took off to meet Chad.

During the two-hour train ride into the city, Jace described the morning's encounter to his friend. The two began discussing how the rich controlled Port Hayden, how the middle class was disappearing, and how trying to get ahead in life was an exercise in futility. Chad liked to play devil's advocate, and they often ended up debating topics they'd initially agreed upon. It frustrated Jace. Chad didn't take life seriously; he stumbled his way through by chance. Ironically, the haphazard lifestyle worked for him. Luck was on his side more often than not. Jace couldn't understand that. It didn't seem fair.

The topic of the woman at Jace's apartment came up again as they sat in the crowded stadium, drinking beer and eating spicy nachos. "You should have heard her, though," Jace stressed, disgust evident in his tone. "She acted like she owned the place."

"Maybe she does," Chad shrugged. "Either that, or she represents the company that owns it."

"No, it's privately owned. I met the guy once, last year. He manages it himself."

"Maybe she's looking at buying it," Chad offered.

Jace hadn't considered that. It was a possibility, and it explained why someone like her would be in his neighborhood. His frustration grew as he contemplated it. She was obviously interested in the land. Real estate in that area was being bought up and developed at an alarming rate. His building would no doubt be torn down to make room for yet another high rise.

Inwardly, Jace seethed. He had no use for the aristocracy who believed they owned the city and were free to do with it as they pleased, regardless of the impact on its citizens. His anger was directed toward the woman who'd been in his building that morning, largely because of what she represented, and now he wished he'd given her a piece of his mind.

CASSANDRA SPENT a contented afternoon walking in the gardens, playing with the dogs, and swimming laps in the pool. When her mother had to run out to an emergency meeting for one of her charity organizations, Cassandra suggested to her father that they have a casual evening meal together.

"My thoughts exactly, kitten," he winked. "And the timing couldn't be better. The game's on. Come and see the theatre I had installed last month."

She followed her father to the back of the house where the family room she'd known as a child had been transformed into a sophisticated home theatre. She gazed in awe at the mammoth screen, cinematic decor, and luxurious leather recliners. The window had been removed and the walls covered with panels to absorb and diffuse the sound. Soft lighting on the floor and walls gave the room an authentic movie theater feel.

"Wow! How'd you manage this?" Cassandra shook her head, laughing. "Mother was adamant about making this into a conservatory. She had plans drawn up and everything. How did you get her to change her mind?"

"I finally agreed to accompany her to Europe," he grinned sheepishly. "It will mean three months of her dragging me into boutiques, eating ridiculous foods I despise in restaurants smaller than this room, and worst of all, visiting her uptight friends and their boring husbands. But wait till you hear the sound in here," he added with sudden enthusiasm.

"Oh Daddy," Cassandra chuckled, giving her father a kiss on the cheek. "You never cease to amaze me."

They settled into the comfortable chairs to watch hockey, enjoying the meal delivered to them by the kitchen staff. Cassandra was familiar with the game, having watched many times with her father over the years, so she followed the play with interest. During commercial breaks, they picked up conversation where they'd last left it.

"I had an interesting visit with Aunt Sophia this morning."

"How so?"

"Well . . . ," she hesitated, not quite sure how to describe the unusual exchange. "She told me some things."

"What kinds of things?" The game was on again, but he remained focused on his daughter.

"About my future . . . it was weird. She told me I was going to meet my husband soon. I don't know about that," Cassandra added wryly. "But she also told me there's something bigger I want to do with my life." Laying a hand on her father's arm, she looked him in the eye. "She's right, Daddy, I've been feeling it. I just don't know what it is."

"Give it time, kitten." Her father stroked her cheek lovingly. "It'll reveal itself. I'd listen to what she has to say if I were you. Sophia has an uncanny way of knowing." He shook his head. "A few years ago she told me that a partnership I was involved in was about to go sour. I took her advice and pulled out. Saved me a lot of money and probably some legal battles as well."

"She said she has more to tell me. Even suggested I write it down."

"About what? Did she say?"

"No, she asked me to come by tomorrow," Cassandra replied. "And Daddy, she said not to worry about her because she still has things to do before she goes."

"Hmm . . . ," her father frowned. "I wonder what she meant by that."

"Do you think she actually knows when she's going to die?" Cassandra asked, not expecting an answer. "Do you think anyone can know that?"

"Hard to say, kitten," he mumbled. His attention was on the screen in front of them. Their team had scored to tie the game with less than a minute remaining.

Cassandra smiled. He was right; her future would reveal itself; her questions would be answered. She sat back, content to enjoy the cozy evening with her father as she joined him in cheering for their favorite team.

THE CROWD STOOD to its feet. The game was tied three-three, and the teams were facing off in sudden-death overtime. Jace drank in the excitement, the rush of adrenaline. The atmosphere was electric. Throughout the stadium, fans in home-team colors cheered in unison at every move their players made. Surrounding him were comrades with a single desire—seeing their team win.

Then it happened. Less than a minute into the overtime period, their team's star player got a breakaway and rifled a shot at the top right-hand corner of the net. Jace held his breath. The puck went in; the players' hands went up in victory; the crowd went wild.

Jace let himself get caught up in the euphoria. He'd never before been that close to victory, and he liked the heady feeling it evoked. Nothing had happened to him, yet his world had for the moment become bigger and brighter. Even the future seemed to offer more hope than before. He was tempted to question it, to analyze it, but quickly let that go. Life was too unpredictable. A feeling like that didn't come along every day, and he wanted to make the most of it.

Chapter 4

Cassandra awoke, eager for the day ahead. Her curiosity had been building, and she couldn't wait to learn what her aunt wanted her to write down. She and her father had concluded that it must be Sophia's life story. If that were so, Cassandra was touched that her aunt wanted her to document it. Lady Sophia Langdon had certainly led an interesting life. Regardless of who wrote her memoirs, it would be a compelling read. *But is that to be my great work?* she pondered. *It's an honor for sure, and yet . . .* She shook her head. It didn't quite match the "something bigger" that had been calling her. *No, it's more than that; I can feel it.*

She opted to borrow her father's laptop and a small voice recorder, which she slipped into her pocket. The items helped her feel prepared as she left for her aunt's place. Only one parking spot was available on the street near the apartment building, and Cassandra pulled in with ease. She enjoyed driving her father's Aston

Martin. It was an impressive vehicle, and it handled like a dream. A custom order, the paint color changed from luminous silver to fiery copper depending on the direction a person looked at it. The interior was luxurious with hand-stitched leather and oil-finished African mahogany.

As she walked up the steps to the main doors, she was reminded of the fellow she'd run into the previous day and sincerely hoped she wouldn't see him again. She considered herself easygoing, but occasionally she came across a person who, like that man, pushed her patience to the limit—someone whom she suspected was capable of good manners when it served him yet made a habit of being impolite and disrespectful. She hoped he would treat her aunt with more courtesy.

Taking a moment to breathe deeply, she swept the unpleasant thoughts from her mind. It was ten o'clock, and she knocked on her aunt's door, excited to begin.

"Cassandra, my dear." Sophia sounded surprised. "How lovely to see you."

"Aunt Sophia," Cassandra frowned. "You asked me to come by this morning. You said you had something you wanted to tell me. I've brought a computer so I can take notes."

"Yes. Yes, of course," Sophia shook her head. "Shall we have a cup of tea?"

"Sure . . ." Cassandra began to wonder whether her aunt was as clear about what she wanted her to write as she had been the day before. *She's eighty-seven, after all. Maybe she's starting to lose her memory. I hope not.*

It'll be a shame if she can't recall her past clearly. With that, Cassandra began to think how she might fill in missing details. I could interview people that knew her, look up articles about her in newspaper archives, maybe see what information the local library has on Port Hayden and its residents.

Sophia poured their tea and invited her grandniece to join her in the living room. Once seated, she looked Cassandra in the eye. "I haven't always had an easy life."

Not wanting to miss anything, Cassandra reached into her jacket pocket and discreetly turned on the voice recorder.

"I always believed that my life was what I made it," Sophia continued. "But I thought the making of it involved hard work, pain, and sacrifice."

"Should I be taking notes?"

"Oh, no dear." Sophia sat back and sipped her tea. "I'm just telling you what not to do." She laughed softly and turned away for a moment, her eyes gazing upward. "But you'll make your own mistakes. That's how we learn, how we know what we want in life. My mistake was to fight against what I didn't want. I didn't know that pushing against problems only makes them bigger. I was an activist—that's what they called me. It sounds virtuous and valiant, but it was just me trying to change the world by my own puny efforts. There's a better way." She smiled at Cassandra. "Write this down."

Opening the computer, Cassandra felt a tingle as her hands hovered over the keys, poised and eager to begin typing.

"We're all part of a great big universe. It's an organized system, a well-oiled machine with perfection and order at the heart of it." She nodded as if to affirm her own statement and then added, "The only reason people run around helter-skelter is that they believe they're separate, and they're trying to control their life or change their environment by hard work."

Cassandra was glad she could type fast; she didn't want to ask her aunt to slow down or repeat herself. It wasn't what she'd been expecting to hear, yet she was spellbound as she listened.

Sophia explained that the universe was governed by basic principles. "The first is that all things are one. Everything originates from a powerful Source, is made of the same substance, and reacts the same way. Each of us is part of that Source, and all that we do is regulated by that power."

Cassandra stopped typing. She didn't want to interrupt, but she was curious. It was obvious her aunt wasn't talking about a traditional God or organized religion. "Aunt Sophia, I don't understand. If a power like that exists, why are so many unaware of it?"

"More people are aware of it than you may think, dear," Sophia replied. "In fact, anyone who asks receives the answer. That's how the system works." She went on to tell Cassandra about the energy that connects all and the positive nature of it. She spoke again of order and harmony.

"I remember learning about energy in school," Cassandra said, recalling that everything when broken down to its smallest form was essentially energy. "But how do you know there's perfection and harmony at the heart of it? It's a nice thought, but . . . " She shook her head.

"Some things can't be proved by science . . . or maybe they can," Sophia chuckled. "They just haven't been yet. Sometimes things need to be believed to be seen."

Cassandra was quick to correct her elderly aunt. "You mean they need to be seen to be believed, don't you, Aunt Sophia?"

"No, dear," Sophia stressed. "That's where we've had it wrong. You have to believe first. Once you believe, you'll start to see life differently."

Cassandra felt a comforting connection to what she was hearing. Her aunt's views, unconventional though they were, resonated deeply. "Go on," she encouraged when the older woman didn't continue. "This is interesting; I'd like to hear more."

Sophia sat back with a contented sigh. "I think that's enough for today." She took another sip of her tea and looked at Cassandra indirectly, the way she had the day before. "Don't overlook the obvious, my dear. Sometimes what you're looking for is right in front of you."

"But what am I looking for?" Cassandra responded, hoping for wisdom from her insightful, old aunt.

"Your dreams, your desires," Sophia explained. "You've been asking. The Universe has already answered. You just have to let them in."

"Let what in?" Cassandra asked, totally confused. "I don't even know what I want."

"You don't always ask with words, but the Universe knows your desires down to the tiniest detail. Your thoughts create a grid, a framework that the Universe fills in with specifics. Your job is to trust that what you want is coming to you in the perfect way, at the perfect time. Then just enjoy life, have fun, and be open to new ideas and new people."

New ideas? New people? Cassandra petitioned silently. *How will I know?*

"You'll know."

Her aunt seemed to read her mind, and it caused the tiny hairs on the back of Cassandra's neck to stand up. Something beyond her understanding was at work. She sensed, as she had the day before, that their visit was over. As if an indistinguishable force was directing her, she stood up to leave.

"Thank you for coming, dear," Sophia smiled and embraced her niece. "Let's have tea again, soon. I have some things I want to tell you."

The old woman's words implied that she'd already forgotten what she'd had Cassandra write down moments before. Cassandra didn't know how to respond. *Could she be suffering from dementia? Does she actually have something important to tell me, something worthy of putting in print, or is she just lonely, wanting someone to talk to?* Whatever it was, Cassandra was committed. She was determined to follow it through, sensing somehow that she needed to hear what her aunt had to say. Before she left she made tentative plans to return the following weekend.

JACE COULDN'T believe it. He sat up, rubbed the sleep from his eyes, and ran his hands through his hair. He'd dreamed about her—the rich bitch. Of all the women he would have welcomed into his dreams, she was the last one he thought would have affected him that way.

It left him with a bizarre mix of emotions, as though two opposing substances had been poured together, causing a chemical reaction throughout his entire being. The woman who had just yesterday aroused anger and resentment was now arousing something entirely different.

He tried to recall what she looked like. Given his feelings the day before, she might easily have had warts on her face or hair on her chin. Now, although he had no clear image of her in his mind, he could feel her . . . and she felt amazing.

He longed to step back into his dream and hold her, touch her, talk to her some more. The connection they'd had was exhilarating, deeper and richer than he had ever known. It was more than physical intimacy; the woman in his dream felt like his soul mate.

Soul mate? The absurdity of it struck him. *There's no way in hell a woman like that could be a soul mate. She'd have to have a soul . . . and a conscience. That snobby debutante probably has neither.*

Sweeping the thoughts from his mind as best he could, he got up from the sofa he'd passed out on the night before and looked around Chad's living room, which was littered with beer cans and pizza boxes.

Images of the game, as well as post-game parties, filtered into his mind. They were a welcome replacement for the dream that had awoken him.

They'd begun partying on the train ride back from the city. Once in Port Hayden, they'd gone to two parties, maybe three; he couldn't remember. As for female company, they'd picked up some girls, and he recalled making out with one of them. That caused Jace to question again why he would dream of the stuck-up debutante instead of the cute chick he'd been with the night before. If the decision had been his to make, he'd never choose a rich, haughty bitch over a cute girl he met at a post-game party. He had his standards.

Jace left without waking Chad. He went outside, attempting to ignore the queasiness in his stomach and the vise-grip tightening around his head. He'd been in worse shape but had to admit it had been awhile. As he sat in his car, letting his head clear, he opened his wallet to see what, if anything, remained of the money he'd borrowed. A lone five was all that was left—not even enough for breakfast. He shrugged. *At least I've got groceries at home. I won't starve.*

As he drove, Jace pieced together the fragmented memories of the night before. Though there were blurry patches, what stood out clearly was the euphoric feeling he'd had when the game ended in victory. It had been easy to get caught up in the celebration; he'd given himself over to it entirely, effortlessly shedding the tiresome burden of worry he'd been carrying for months. His mind went there again easily, experiencing the thrill as if he were still in the pulsing arena witnessing the memorable event. It caused him to question how the mind worked. Feelings seemed arbitrary and illusive, governed by circumstance, yet they held the power to transport him to a place he longed to be. *I'd love to feel that way all the time,* he admitted. *No cares, no worries—just blissed out on life.*

His reasoning mind retorted quickly. *What a stupid, unrealistic way to think! Get a grip on yourself. Get real.* It was the conversation with the old woman that had put those thoughts in his head. The problem was, deep down he wanted to believe her. Part of him wanted to hear more. Another part was telling him how dangerous that would be.

Turning onto his street, Jace began looking for a place to park. As he drove by slowly, he noticed an Aston Martin parked in front of his building again. He was quite sure it was the same car, only it looked to be a different color. It was darker, almost bronze in the morning sun. He drove another half block and slipped into a spot that someone had just vacated. As he neared his building on foot, he stared at the expensive vehicle. What he saw now was silver. To be sure his eyes weren't playing tricks on him, he walked past the car and looked again. This time he saw a muted copper color. He walked by once more, his still-foggy brain entranced by the chameleon effect he was observing. He was about to turn and go up the steps of his building, when a female voice addressed him.

"May I help you?"

Jace turned to look straight into the eyes of the woman he'd met the day before. Her eyes were a distinct copper-brown color, not unlike her car when viewed from a certain direction. He noticed her skin as well; it was smoother and softer-looking than any he had ever seen. He wondered what it would feel like to touch.

"Are you okay?" she demanded sharply. "I just asked you a question, and you're standing there staring at me."

"What? Oh sorry, I . . . I . . . ," he stammered. "What did you say?"

"Are you drunk?"

"No, I'm not drunk!" His mind snapped to attention. The question was a direct allegation, and it put him on the defensive, reminding him of his disgust for her.

"Well, I asked you a question, and you didn't answer." She spoke slowly, repeating herself as if talking to someone with a learning disability. "You were staring at my car, and I asked if I could help you."

"Can't a guy look at a car?" he shot back. "You park an expensive car like that on a street in this neighborhood, you're bound to have people take a second look."

"You looked more than twice. I thought you were casing it out," she accused blatantly.

"You assume because I live in this neighborhood that I'd steal your car, that I'm a criminal? What are you doing here, anyway? This is a long way from your part of town."

"It's none of your business why I'm here," she replied haughtily. "I have every right to be in this neighborhood or any other."

"Well, you're not welcome here," Jace growled, suddenly remembering Chad's suggestion that she may be buying the building. He reached for self-control, but it eluded him. "Why don't you take your fancy clothes and your fancy car and go back where you came from?"

He turned and walked up the steps before he could say more. It wasn't like him to get into an argument with a complete stranger on the street, yet this woman infuriated him. *It's not her,* he reminded himself. *It's what she represents.* Nevertheless, he couldn't seem to separate the two. Nor did he see the need. He loathed what she represented, and he didn't mind letting her know.

CASSANDRA HAD NEVER been treated so rudely in her life, and the shock of it left her unsure how to react. She simply watched him walk away. He'd disappeared into the building before she could think of an appropriate comeback.

How dare he tell me I'm not welcome here! she seethed, clenching her fists and stamping her foot. *He acts like he owns the building, the whole damn neighborhood for that matter. Are all the people around here this rude?* She hoped not, for her aunt's sake. When she thought of her sweet, soft-spoken aunt being treated that way, her anger surged.

Needing to cool off, Cassandra got in the car and drove, quickly distancing herself from the unsettling incident. As she regained her composure, she began to think about future visits. *I hope I never run into him again, but there's a chance of it if I continue to meet with Aunt Sophia at her apartment.* She was aware that it could take several visits to document all that her aunt wanted to impart to her. Cassandra was willing to make that commitment despite the possibility of running into her aunt's ill-mannered neighbor. *I'm going to be the bigger person here,* she asserted. *I'm going to treat him like he doesn't exist. I won't let him get me riled up. I won't give him that satisfaction.*

Content with her decision, she headed back to the Town House. The garden party was about to begin, and she was to be the guest of honor. Her mother loved showing her off and bragging about her accomplishments to all her friends. Although Cassandra found social functions like that tedious, it was easier to comply with her mother's wishes than explain why she objected to them.

She would have preferred to spend the afternoon roaming the grounds or relaxing by the pool. Moreover, she still hoped for time alone with her father to discuss the ideas Sophia had brought up and get his take on them. He was wise and levelheaded, and she valued his opinion.

They got the opportunity later that afternoon as he drove her to the airport. Cassandra appreciated the gesture, knowing he could have sent Wallace. She sensed that he wanted to talk to her, too.

"How was your weekend, kitten?"

"Interesting." Though she didn't lie, she chose to omit the unpleasant details. Turning to her father, she asked, "Daddy, has Aunt Sophia ever told you what she believes?"

"I guess she's imparted some of her wisdom," he grinned. "I used to shrug it off, but in recent years it makes more sense. There's truth to it," he remarked pensively. "She's happy. If nothing else, we could learn from that. It's not everybody that finds the secret to happiness in their lifetime."

"She is happy, isn't she? And yet she lives such a simple life.

"Most people believe an accumulation of assets equals happiness," her father remarked. "And yet . . . I've seen plenty of people with material wealth, and I wouldn't describe many of them as truly happy."

"I know what you mean. It seems like we start out happy and then lose it along the way. We spend our whole lives looking for it. You're right, Daddy. Few people find it. I think that's what she wants to tell me!" Cassandra exclaimed, suddenly understanding. "I don't think it's her memoirs at all."

"You may be right, kitten," he glanced at her as he drove. "Her achievements, her possessions—those don't mean much to her anymore. Maybe she knows she's not going to be around much longer and wants to pass on what she's learned."

"I feel honored that she chose me."

"She probably knew you'd receive it better than most." He winked at his daughter as they pulled up to the departure gate. "She can read people. I'd trust her judgement of anyone."

"We'll see," Cassandra laughed. "She seems to think my future husband is close by. When I meet him, I'll have to take him there so she can read him."

Cassandra signaled a porter to carry her luggage and turned to say goodbye to her father.

"See you next weekend, kitten." He embraced her warmly.

"Bye, Daddy. I love you."

Chapter 5

Jace tried not to think about the unpleasant encounter with the woman at his apartment or the dream he'd had of her, though the feeling of it remained etched in his mind. He sincerely hoped she was done with whatever business she'd had in his building and would never show her face again.

He didn't want to think about finances either, yet he was painfully aware that payday was still several days away, and his debt was building quickly. It left him irritable. He'd even blown up at Chad for asking him to go for drinks after work. Jace had been telling himself it was only temporary, that his life would turn around. In the past, he'd been able to hold on to that hope. Lately, doubt had been prevailing.

Luck had never been his ally, and that belief reinforced itself the following day as his car died on the way home from work. He pushed it the final block and a half and laid it to rest down the street from his building. The transmission had been giving him trouble. He'd been meaning to have it looked at but had been putting it off. Now it was gone completely. He might have gotten a thousand bucks for it if he'd sold it in running condition. As it was he'd be lucky to get five hundred, and it would cost a lot more than that to have it repaired.

On top of that, his mom told him that her washing machine had quit working. It was old, too, not worthy of repair, and she didn't have the money to buy herself a newer one. She told him not to worry; she didn't mind going to the laundromat. However, she worked full time, and her employer often asked her to work extra hours if they had a special function. He hated to see them take advantage of her that way. It meant she had little time for herself, and Jace couldn't bear the idea of her lugging clothes to a laundromat on her rare days off. The following day after work he went to a used appliance store, bought the best washer he could afford on credit, and paid to have it delivered to his mom's place. When he got home, he put a for-sale sign in the window of his car. Defeated, he sat down on the front steps of his building and with his chin in his hands let out a solemn breath.

"Does it feel like life is beating you up again?"

He turned to see his elderly neighbor walking toward him. Nodding a reply, he turned away. He wasn't in the mood for her pie-in-the-sky advice.

"I have a proposition for you." She stood at the bottom of the stairs, her face level with his. "I'm not as spry as I used to be, and I don't get around easily anymore. I've been thinking of getting a car, but I don't drive now."

"Are you . . . asking me to drive you?"

"I'd pay you, of course. I don't go out much—two or three times a week."

Jace contemplated her offer. She hadn't mentioned an amount, yet whatever she paid him would be a bonus. He could certainly use the extra cash. Ready to jump at the opportunity, he forced himself to relax. She didn't know how bad his situation was, and he didn't want to appear desperate. "Sure, I guess I could do that for you," he shrugged, trying to act indifferent but knowing deep down that she was doing him a favor.

The old woman started to go past him up the stairs. Before she entered the building, he jumped up and grabbed the door for her. "Um . . . thank you, Mrs. Langdon."

"Call me Sophie."

She smiled her sweet, grandmotherly smile, and Jace noticed for the first time that she looked pleasant for her age. Her white hair was full of tidy curls, and her skin was like silk with soft, delicate wrinkles. Her fingernails were manicured, and her clothes looked as though they'd been bought at a respectable store, not a bargain department or thrift store. Now it seemed she had money to buy a car.

In his apartment, Jace pondered the situation. Something about the old woman didn't add up. The furniture and china spoke of wealth, but that could be from the past. *If she has money, why does she live in a place like this?* he continued to speculate. *Why would she buy a car just to have someone drive her a couple of times a week? It would be much cheaper to take a cab.* Try as he might, he couldn't sort it out.

CASSANDRA REMAINED unsettled after returning from Port Hayden. She was sure it had to do with her aunt's prediction. She'd had a mild yearning, a faint desire to do more with her life than she was doing. Something bigger was definitely calling her. The unsettling part was not knowing what it was.

"That's all she told you?" Tanisha asked after listening to the voice recording. "What does it mean, anyway?"

"I'm not sure; it's all new to me," Cassandra answered. "I mean, I understand what she's saying about energy, but this connectedness and the order and perfection she talks about . . . "

"Is she talking about God?"

"She's not the religious type, and this isn't the kind of message you'd hear in church. It's deeper than that. It's like a puzzle, I guess. I'll know more once I have all the pieces."

"What does she want you to do with it?" Tanisha inquired. "Besides write it down, I mean?"

"I don't know; she didn't say." Cassandra shook her head. "She's mysterious. Sometimes she seems like a sweet, little old lady who forgets, and I have to remind her what day it is. Other times she looks right through me like I'm not even there and tells me stuff no one else could possibly know. I really think she's psychic."

"Why? Because she told you you're going to meet a guy?" Tanisha laughed. "You meet guys all the time. You *do* realize you could have any guy you wanted, right?"

"I don't want just any guy," Cassandra contended.

"So what do you want?"

"I want a guy who's everything that Nick wasn't."

"Okay, you want a poor, dumb, unsophisticated slob who won't cheat on you," Tanisha teased. "Maybe the guy at your aunt's apartment would qualify after all."

"Definitely not!" Cassandra shuddered at the outrageous suggestion. Having recounted the incident to her best friend, they'd laughed about it. She wasn't as angry as she had been. Still, she hoped she'd never see him again. "I think I'm giving myself tangible examples of what I *don't* want in a relationship, so I'll know more clearly what I *do* want and be able to recognize it when it comes along."

"Or maybe it's one of those situations where the guy is the exact opposite of what you *think* you want, and he turns out to be your dream come true," Tanisha suggested.

"You watch too many movies."

"I wonder what he'd be like under different circumstances," her friend mused. "What if you met him at a bar or nightclub? Is he good looking? How tall is he?"

"For starters, we'd never go to the same clubs." Cassandra was getting annoyed with the teasing. She didn't know why the guy irritated her so much. It was unusual for someone to affect her in such a negative way, especially someone she'd only met twice. "And good looking? I really don't know. His personality was unattractive; I guess I assumed his physical appearance was too." She tried to recall what he looked like, wanting evidence to support her assumption. She found none. The image that came to mind was a pleasant-looking man about her age, and that annoyed her even further. "It doesn't matter, anyway," she added defensively. "I'll be happy never to see him again."

"You're going to Port Hayden again this weekend. You'll be visiting your aunt," Tanisha continued teasing. "Maybe the fates are setting you two up."

"I don't believe in fate," Cassandra replied curtly, putting a stop to the conversation by signaling their server to bring the check. She needed to put the experience behind her, lock it away somewhere. The very thought of him perturbed her. It bothered her much more than she'd expected. She felt violated in a way she didn't understand. Whether it was him or merely people like him that put her on the defensive, she wasn't sure. Whether she saw him as a threat to herself or to her aunt, she couldn't tell. It was a big, indiscernible knot of emotion, and it didn't feel good.

In the days to follow she tried to erase him from her mind, but his image remained. The image was connected not only to thoughts of her aunt but to the inexplicable knowing that something big was about to happen in her life.

AS JACE RETURNED home from work, he noticed a car parked in front of his building. Shiny black and gleaming in the sun, it looked as though it had just been driven off the showroom floor. He admired it as he walked past. It was the exact vehicle he'd buy if he had the money.

Not lingering to dream, he went up to his apartment and began making dinner. He turned on the TV and was enjoying his meal when he heard a knock on his door. He opened it to find Sophie with her coat on, her purse on one arm and a grin on her face.

"I wonder if you'd mind driving me to the market. I need to pick up a few items."

"I... um..." Jace hesitated as questions filled his mind. *Is she expecting me to take her in my car?* He hadn't told her it wasn't running. Moreover, he was surprised she would make that assumption. *Does she expect me to be available whenever she needs me?* He wondered if he'd made a mistake agreeing to be her driver.

His thoughts came to a halt as she pulled a set of keys from her purse and handed them to him. Staring at the distinctive "H" on the key, he responded awkwardly. "That new Accord... it's yours? I mean... you got a car already?"

"I bought it today. I asked Peter to get me one that wasn't too big," she smiled in her sweet way. "It seems like a nice, practical vehicle, don't you think?"

"Peter?" Jace asked, suddenly curious about his elderly neighbor. "Is he your son?"

"No dear," she shook her head. "Peter looks after my affairs—has for over twenty years."

Jace forgot about the remainder of his meal and followed the old woman down to the street. She was becoming more of a mystery every day. Not only did she have the money to buy a new car, it seemed she paid someone to look after her financial dealings. *I guess, if she doesn't have family,* he reasoned, *it makes sense that she'd hire someone to look after her finances.* He couldn't help but wonder what it must be like to be that old and have no family to call on.

As he neared the vehicle, the car unlocked automatically. Smiling at the new technology, he stepped ahead of Sophie to open the door for her.

"Thank you, dear," she said, settling into the passenger seat of the two-door coupe.

He tingled with anticipation as he rounded the car to the driver's side. Being a chauffeur to an old woman wasn't something he'd brag about to his friends. But being behind the wheel of the very car he'd been dreaming of, was.

The car didn't disappoint. Loaded, it had a six-speed manual transmission, leather interior, and power everything. It even had a push-button start and a large LCD display. Jace was in heaven. He longed to take it on the highway and see what it could do. Instead, he drove with extreme care. He was eager to play with the interactive touch screen but resisted the urge, hoping he could remain with the car while Sophie did her shopping.

"I'll be at least half an hour," she informed him as they pulled up to a small grocery store Jace wasn't familiar with. "Peter mentioned that a new engine could use some highway miles to break it in. Why don't you take it for a drive? No sense you sitting here waiting for me."

Jace couldn't believe it. His pulse quickened as his mind soared with anticipation. Yet thinking practically, he jumped out to open the door for her. It wasn't like him to be such a gentleman, but he wanted to make a good impression, wanted to prove he was worthy of her respect.

The Dunsmuir bypass was only a few blocks away, so he headed to the nearest on-ramp and drank in the feeling of power as he shifted gears to get up to speed. Once outside the city limits, he turned on to a paved side road and pushed the pedal down. *I could get used to this,* Jace breathed, opening the driver's window to enjoy the breeze on his face as he sped down the deserted road. With the audio controls on the steering wheel he was able to access internet radio, and soon his favorite music blasted through the premium sound system.

The time flew by too quickly, and he regretted having to go back. He was grateful for the experience, however. It wasn't likely she'd let him take the car on his own each time. As he returned to the market, Jace reflected on the events that had led up to his being behind the wheel of his dream car. Sophie was a kind and generous woman, that was obvious. She reminded him of his grandmother, who had lived with his family the last few years of her life. Jace was an only child, and she'd enjoyed spoiling him. But it was more than that. While there was something endearing about Sophie, there was a quality that confused and intrigued him at the same time. She lived simply, yet she was a complex woman. Her words, while sometimes confusing, held wisdom that Jace couldn't deny. She seemed to understand more about life than most people—at least her beliefs served her well. And she was happy. He felt good when he was around her. *I like the old bird,* he admitted. *Driving her around won't be that bad.*

CASSANDRA LOOKED forward to the weekend with an enthusiasm that surprised her. With her parents leaving for the summer house, Sunday, she would only have a day to spend with them, yet she hoped she and her father might continue the conversation they'd begun the week before. It was spending time with Sophia, however, that had her keyed up with excitement. She'd given much thought to her aunt's predictions and was still pondering her fascinating views. Having done some research, she'd learned that her aunt's beliefs were far from crazy. The internet was abuzz with the very subject matter they'd talked about. The wisdom her dear old aunt had acquired in her lifetime was a topic of widespread interest.

When Cassandra arrived at the Town House, Saturday morning, her mother was busy preparing for the move to their summer home. She had the new housekeeper, Sarah, running nonstop. They kept a minimal staff in town for the summer. Sarah would be staying on, along with the grounds keeper. Wallace and Mrs. Harper, the cook, always accompanied the family to the beach. The couple had been with them since Cassandra was a little girl. They'd met and married while working for the family and now lived in the servant's quarters behind the house.

Watching her mother, she realized that managing a household was in some ways like overseeing a company, and she had to admire the way everything ran smoothly. A friend of Cassandra's, who was married and had a child already, constantly complained that it was a full-time job running a household and managing staff. Cassandra wasn't sure she wanted that kind of life. She liked her independence, and although she hoped to marry and have children one day, she didn't see it as a full-time role. She wanted to do more with her life—so much more.

Her aunt's predictions came to mind, followed by the unwelcome image of her aunt's rude neighbor. Her thoughts must have been visible on her face, causing her father to question her.

"Everything okay, kitten?"

"Oh, yes," she fibbed. "I was just . . . um . . . thinking about my visit with Aunt Sophia."

"Is something about it bothering you?" He searched her face. "The look you had a minute ago—it seemed like you were upset."

Her father could read her well. She didn't like lying to him, so she offered a toned-down version of what had happened the weekend before. "It was weird running into him twice like that. And both times, getting into an argument over something trivial. It's no big deal, though. I don't know why I'm letting it bother me," she shrugged, hoping to convince him the matter was irrelevant.

"You say he's a neighbor of Sophia's?"

"He lives in the same building; I saw him go in and out a couple of times."

"I wonder . . . ," her father frowned and then shook his head. "No, it can't be."

"What?"

"Well, I talked to Sophia this week. She's bought herself a car if you can believe it."

"She shouldn't be driving at her age!"

"No, she's not planning to drive, thank goodness." He nodded his approval of the fact. "She's hired someone to drive her whenever she needs to go out. I asked who it was, wanting to be sure she'd gone through an agency and gotten someone with proper credentials. She told me she'd asked a young man in her building."

An icy chill inched its way up Cassandra's spine. A voice inside told her it was the same man she'd met. "She can't! Daddy, you have to do something," Cassandra blurted, surprised by her own fervor. "I mean, we don't know anything about this guy. What if he's just being nice, gaining her trust while he's planning to swindle her? She could be in danger."

"Hold on, kitten." Her father held up his hand. "Let's not jump to conclusions."

"But how can she trust a stranger?"

"He's obviously not a stranger to her," he reasoned. "Besides, you're overlooking two important points here. Remember what I told you about her ability to read people?"

"Yes, but . . . ," Cassandra protested. "What if she's wrong this one time?"

Her father shrugged his shoulders. "The other is that Sophia Langdon is a headstrong woman. Even at eighty-seven, if we try to oppose her she'll likely do it to spite us."

"Surely she could be made to see reason."

"Maybe, but not without proof." He stared at her for a second, a question forming on his lips. "I was thinking . . . "

"You want me to check him out?" Convinced it was the same man, Cassandra was already building a case against him. She was eager to share her findings with her too-trusting old aunt.

"No . . . not exactly," he frowned at her, obviously taken aback by her enthusiasm. "But you'll be spending a bit of time with Sophia over the next while. You could ask her questions, maybe meet this guy. If we knew his name we could learn a lot about him. I'll get Dave Hillson from the police department to run a check on him. He owes me a favor."

"Yeah, I see what you mean. I can do that," she replied, happy to do what her father asked. Still, her mind raced ahead with ideas of her own. *A police check could turn up nothing. This guy might not have a criminal record, but that doesn't mean he's above being dishonest or trying to con Aunt Sophia. If I could plan to run into him again . . . not let him know I'm associated with her . . . maybe flirt a bit.* She felt an immediate distaste, yet knowing it was for a worthy cause, continued with her plan. *He knows I have money; I can't pretend otherwise. But if he's the lowlife I think he is, he'll jump at the chance to get to know me. And maybe, just maybe, he'll let down his guard so I can get the evidence we need.*

JACE HAD PLANS of his own on Saturday, but given his new arrangement with Sophie, he decided to see if she needed him to drive her anywhere. She had a hair appointment at one, and again she urged him to take the vehicle rather than wait on her. Reveling in the freedom, he stopped by Chad's place and decided to have some fun. As he pulled into the driveway of the semidetached rental that Chad shared with his younger brother, Jace saw his friend under the hood of his car. Chad looked up to see who was pulling in the driveway and did a double take at seeing Jace behind the wheel.

"Whose car?" he asked, wiping his hands on a rag as he walked toward him.

"Mine," Jace smirked. "Just bought'er."

"Really?" Chad frowned. "Whad'ya do, win the lottery?"

Jace continued smiling, saying nothing.

Chad opened the passenger door and looked inside, sizing up the vehicle. "Six-speed manual, leather, sunroof . . . whoa, nice sound system!" He looked at Jace. "Seriously? You bought this?"

Jace couldn't keep a straight face. "Okay, not exactly," he laughed.

"It's not hot, is it?"

"No! Are you kidding?"

"So whered'ya get it then?"

As Jace told the story, he braced himself for the inevitable smart-ass comeback about driving Miss Daisy. Chad's response surprised him.

"You're a lucky son of a bitch," he shook his head. "I can't believe she lets you drive it around like this."

"She's the one who suggested it," Jace shrugged. "I couldn't believe it, either."

"The old broad must have plenty of dough to spare if she buys a brand new car and hires a dipshit like you to drive it," Chad teased.

"I'm not sure; she's hard to figure out." Jace ignored his friend's jab.

"Could be like my great-grandma," Chad suggested. "She went kind of crazy before they put her in a nursing home. Started spending her money on all kinds of stuff she didn't need. My grandpa became power of attorney and took away her bankbook and rights to her own money. I always felt kind of sorry for her, ya know? I think old people should be allowed to spend their money on whatever they want. They worked hard for it. She only lasted a year after that and was never the same, either."

The idea of someone taking away Sophie's rights and shutting her away in a nursing home was deplorable. Jace hoped that would never happen. "Maybe you're right." He pondered his friend's suggestion. "Maybe she's spending whatever money she has left. Can't take it with her; she may as well enjoy it."

"Looks like you're getting to enjoy it, too, my friend," Chad remarked, gazing enviously at the new car. "Plus she pays you for this? Better hope she sticks around for a while."

"I don't think she's ready to croak yet." Jace laughed, feeling a little guilty talking about Sophie that way. He'd never admit it to Chad, but she was more than just a source of extra cash. He had a soft spot for the kind old woman.

Chapter 6

Jace had a few errands to run before he picked Sophie up, but he was back with time to spare. He didn't want to keep her waiting. She might reconsider letting him use her car in the future if he inconvenienced her in that way.

She had another stop to make before he took her home. Since she'd only be five minutes, Jace waited in the car, familiarizing himself with the multi-information display. The touch screen provided hands-free access to phone calls, text messages, and even e-mails. He was flipping through the manual to learn how to program his cell phone into the interactive system when she returned.

Looking at him with a smile, and in a pretentious voice so unlike her own, she instructed, "Home, Jace."

He laughed at the old woman's humor. *It must make her feel important, like she's got money again,* he decided, *to pretend that I'm her chauffeur and the car's a Rolls Royce instead of a mid-class import.* He was even more convinced that there was truth to Chad's suggestion. She'd obviously had money at one time in her life. For whatever reason, she'd been reduced to living a simple life and had learned how to scrimp and save. Now, as she neared the end of her life, she wanted to experience some of the luxuries she'd once known. He couldn't blame her. In fact, he admired her. If she wanted to pretend he was her chauffeur, he'd play the part.

Jace saw her up to her apartment, and as usual she invited him in for tea. He had time to kill, so he accepted. As she busied herself in the kitchen, he took off his jacket, put the car key on the small table by the door, and perched on a stool by the kitchen counter. He was comfortable around Sophie now, and though they hadn't talked much more about her strange beliefs, the questions had been building. "Sophie, I've been meaning to ask you something."

"Of course, Jace." She turned to him. "You can ask me anything."

"When we first met, you talked about focus, getting what I expect out of life, and being in control. I don't know . . . it's weird," Jace hesitated. "Part of me wants to argue that that's not true. In fact, it really pissed me off . . . sorry," he apologized for his language. "It made me mad at first, but the more I think about it, the more it seems stuff like that *should* be true, like that's the way it's supposed to be."

"It is the way it's supposed to be," Sophie smiled. "It's the way it *is*."

"But how does it work? I don't understand."

Sophie poured him some tea. "Have you ever heard people in the financial world talk about leverage?"

"Yeah, sure," Jace looked at her strangely. "It's using other people's money to make money." He wasn't sure whether she was answering his question or whether she'd moved on to another topic. She was kind of odd that way.

"Well, what you can do with focus, compared to what you can accomplish with your own efforts," Sophie explained, "is the same idea."

"You're going to have to expand on that," he frowned.

"I'll give you an example," Sophie replied. "Let's say you want a new car. You know how much it costs. You know how much you make every month. If you're relying on your own efforts, you sit down and make a plan to put a certain amount away every month, or maybe you go to the bank and apply for a loan, hoping your credit rating is good enough. You can calculate how long it will take to get the car you want. And it will probably happen eventually," she paused, "if all goes as planned."

"But that's the thing," Jace interrupted. "We don't have control over the unknown."

"Exactly. That's why that way doesn't work." The old woman sipped her tea. "People struggle and struggle and barely get ahead by those kinds of efforts."

"So what's the alternative—to borrow other people's money?" Jace was thoroughly confused.

"The alternative is to change your focus. Change the story you're so valiantly telling. Expand your expectations. You can learn from the rich, you know."

Jace noticed a twinkle in Sophie's eye before she turned away to set her cup on the counter. "What are the rich going to teach me?" he asked, his frustration evident. "How to take advantage of the little guy?"

"They're not all like that, Jace," she replied, maintaining her sweet, even tone.

"Maybe not," he conceded respectfully. "But I don't see what I could possibly learn from them."

"Listen to the stories they tell; notice what their focus is on; see how they expect wealth to come to them," she replied. "If you want to be like them, you'll have to start thinking like them."

Jace's frustration increased. "That's where you're wrong," he declared. "I do want to be rich one day, but I'll never be like they are—taking advantage of those who don't have as much."

"Then just don't focus on that aspect of them," she said simply.

"Yeah, I guess you're right." Jace regretted giving in, but he was done. *I'm not spending my Saturday afternoon arguing with an old lady,* he grumbled silently. "I should go. I'm meeting my friends later."

"It was nice talking with you, Jace."

"Do you need me to drive you anywhere tomorrow?"

"I don't think so," she replied. "I'm expecting company. But thank you for asking."

Jace left her apartment, relieved yet still full of questions. Sophie's words made sense, yet they stirred him up and left him confused. *Is it possible to become rich by thinking like they do?* he wondered. *Can I learn from them even though they're arrogant assholes?* The questions continued to pull at him for the remainder of the afternoon.

Maybe Sophie knows what she's talking about, he speculated later as he walked to Chad's place. *If she was rich once, that is. But why isn't she rich now if she knows the secret? Does she live this way by choice or is there something screwy in what she believes?* He preferred to think that it was by choice and not the fault of the belief itself. Like it or not, he was invested in what she was telling him. More than ever, he wanted it to be true.

WITH A CLEAR PLAN in mind, Cassandra left the Town House, Sunday morning. She was dressed more casually than she had been on previous visits with her aunt, and though her father had left the keys to her mother's Bentley, she took a cab instead.

After instructing the driver to park across the street from her aunt's building, Cassandra remained in the back seat, donned her dark glasses, and waited. She'd brought along the latest copy of her company's magazine but didn't open it, not wanting to take her eyes off the front door in case she missed him.

She was filled with nervous excitement. It wasn't the first time she'd played the spy. After hearing a rumor that Nick was cheating, she and Tanisha had followed him one night. Driving a borrowed car and wearing ridiculous disguises, they'd giggled like children as they maintained what they'd deemed to be an appropriate distance behind Nick's vehicle. At first it seemed like a game, but it quickly turned into a painful reality as they discovered the rumor was true. Shaking off the unpleasant memories, Cassandra checked her watch. It had been twenty-five minutes. She didn't know how much longer she was willing to wait or whether she'd see him, but she had a plan in mind if she did.

After another forty minutes, she'd begun to think her plan was foolish when the front door of the building opened and he emerged. Scrutinizing his appearance this time, she was somewhat annoyed to find him good looking. He had on the same leather jacket, this time with a light blue polo shirt underneath. He wore jeans and running shoes. His hair looked like it might have been blond when he was a child. Now it was light brown with highlights she suspected were natural.

She watched him walk around to the driver's side of a shiny, black Honda parked in front. Recalling the older vehicle she'd seen him driving previously, Cassandra was surprised. *Hmm,* she mused. *Did he get a new car?* Her mind had barely formed the question when the answer became apparent. *Oh my God!*

I wonder if that's Aunt Sophia's new car? It seemed like a logical explanation, and it evoked more questions. *Why is he driving it without her? Does she let him keep the keys? Does she trust him that much?* Although Cassandra had no solid evidence, she was sure he was the same young man her aunt had hired—sure, too, that he was taking advantage of her trusting old aunt by driving her car for his own use.

She had the cab driver follow him without being obvious. After several turns, he pulled into the parking lot of a grocery store. Cassandra waited until he entered the store, then she got out of the cab, instructing the driver to wait. As she walked by the black car, she jotted down the license number. *So far, so good,* she congratulated herself. *Now I need to make it look like a coincidence, running into him here.*

Having been awake half the night rehearsing, she'd thought she was prepared. Yet her nervousness heightened as she picked up a grocery basket, tossed a few items into it, and began to look for him. She found him in the frozen dessert section, took a deep breath, and began walking toward him, pretending to shop.

JACE STOOD looking at the selection of frozen berries. Sophie had been specific about the kind she wanted, but he couldn't seem to find them.

She had stopped by his place that morning, asking if he'd mind picking up a couple of items from the grocery store. He'd jumped at the chance to drive the new car. However, he wondered whether the novelty would wear off, whether running errands for her would become a drag. He hoped not. They hadn't talked about his pay, but he was quite sure she'd compensate him fairly. If not, he'd tell her he was too busy to continue and chalk it up to experience.

This is the brand she mentioned, he recalled as he examined a package. *But this one has strawberries and blueberries, and this one . . .* Jace picked up another package. *This one says bumbleberries.* He frowned. *What the hell are bumbleberries? I wish I had Sophie's phone number.* He made a mental note to ask her for it when he got back.

His thoughts were disrupted when someone opened the freezer next to him. A woman smiled politely and reached for a frozen cake from the shelf. Jace nearly gasped. It was the same woman he'd met at his apartment the previous weekend, the one he'd dreamed about. She had the same flawless complexion, the same golden blond hair. Only this time she wasn't dressed to the nines; she had on jeans and a sweater. *Maybe the rich bitch has a look-alike,* Jace thought, truly hoping it was a different woman. He didn't want a repeat of their last meeting.

She turned back to him, smiling again as she shook her head. "Excuse me. You look familiar; do we know each other?"

"Not really," Jace replied, "but we kind of met at my apartment building last weekend—twice actually."

"Oh my God!" she exclaimed. "You're the guy I blew up at. I feel awful about that. I was having such a bad day. I was supposed to deliver a package to an address in your building. It was a favor for a friend of mine in the city, only she'd given me the wrong apartment number. When I finally got in touch with her later that day, she gave me the correct one. I tried again the next morning, only to discover that the person had moved. I had a difficult time finding the building in the first place and then to have it turn out the way it did . . ." She paused, looking truly penitent. "Anyway, I *am* sorry. I was wrong to take it out on you."

Jace didn't know what to do, except to offer an apology, too, for what he'd said. She readily accepted it, and he found himself having a civil conversation with the woman he'd hated for the past week.

CASSANDRA HAD him exactly where she wanted him. He'd taken the bait, and all she had to do was reel him in. "Look, I still feel bad." She offered a smile that she knew could sway a man. "Would you let me buy you a cup of coffee, a latte maybe? Or am I keeping you from something?"

"Um . . . not really," Jace replied awkwardly. "I was just . . . picking up some things." Glancing down at the package of fruit that was starting to melt in his hand, he added, "For this woman in my building. She's old, and I . . . um . . . help her out sometimes."

"That's nice of you." Smiling sweetly at him, she processed the information. *So he is the one that Aunt Sophia hired. Good.* That meant her earlier assumption was wrong, however. He wasn't using the car for his own purpose; he was on an errand for her aunt. Nevertheless, determined to uncover his true character, she proceeded with her plan. "Well, I won't keep you then . . . if you're busy."

"We could go for coffee . . . if you like," he offered, still sounding uneasy. "I just have to drop these off. We could meet somewhere."

"I noticed a Starbucks about a block from here. Do you know the one I mean?"

"Yeah sure," he shrugged. "Why don't I meet you there in, say, twenty minutes?"

"Perfect," she replied. Realizing she had items in her basket that she might have to justify, including a frozen cake, she laughed. "I can do without this." She returned the cake to the freezer. "Way too many calories, anyway."

"I'll see you in a bit, then."

Their eyes met, and Cassandra noticed something stir inside. For a moment he seemed like a regular guy, a decent guy, and she felt an attraction.

Oh God, Cass, she scolded, *don't let his looks sway you.* Watching him walk away, she reminded herself he was the same jerk that had treated her rudely, not to mention the guy who was very likely planning to swindle her aunt. *The only reason he's being nice to me is because he thinks I'm offering something.* The negative emotion quickly returned, and Cassandra strengthened her resolve to get the information needed and have nothing more to do with him.

WHAT THE HELL just happened? Jace laughed as he got into the driver's seat of Sophie's car. *The rich bitch I met last weekend is now a good-looking chick I met in a grocery store, and suddenly we have a date?* Despite her hot looks and penitent attitude, he still had reservations. She belonged to what he considered the snobby upper class, and that was a definite mark against her. He'd also seen a side of her he didn't like and hoped never to see again. On the other hand, he'd been a bit of a jerk, too.

As he drove the short distance to his apartment building, he assessed what he'd learned about her. *She obviously has money to drive a car like that.* He pictured the sleek, sporty Aston Martin. *She was doing a favor for a friend in the city. Does that mean she lives in the city, too? Why would she be here two weekends in a row? She must live here. But if she lives here and drives a car like that, why would she be shopping in this part of town?* He shook his head. *Something doesn't add up.*

When he'd delivered the items, Sophie thanked him and addressed the questions that had been mounting.

"Jace, I've been thinking about what to pay you for all you're doing for me. We could agree on a monthly salary, or you could keep track of your time, and I could pay you by the hour." She paused. "However, I noticed your car isn't working. I wondered if you'd like to have the use of my car as part of your payment."

"Wow." He looked at her in amazement. "That would be great. My car's not worth fixing, and I don't have enough to get another one right now. I'd really appreciate being able to use yours once in a while."

"You can use it any time you like, Jace. We'll talk about a salary as well. But I can see you're in a hurry, so I won't keep you. Go ahead and take the car. I don't want you to feel you have to ask every time you need it. And keep the keys; they're of no use to me."

Jace left Sophie's apartment feeling charged. *Maybe things are starting to turn around after all. I have the use of a really great car, and she says she's willing to pay me something as well.* On his way to the coffee shop, the irony struck him. Had Sophie not offered the use of her car, he would have been walking. He was meeting a gorgeous, rich chick for coffee, and he was so broke he had to rely on the charity of an old woman to get him there.

He wasn't going to delude himself. *The chick just wants to buy me coffee to soothe her conscience. It'll be the last I see of her, no doubt.* He was glad to learn that she wasn't a real-estate tycoon buying his building. He laughed at how quickly he'd jumped to that conclusion. *Maybe Sophie's right,* he decided. *Maybe the rich aren't all as bad as I judged them to be.*

SHE FOUND A TABLE near the front of the coffee shop. From that vantage point, Cassandra could see the entrance as well as the parking lot. Nearly twenty-five minutes after their meeting in the grocery store, the shiny new Accord pulled up in front. She still had no proof that it was her aunt's car, but she was determined to learn the truth.

He entered the cafe, and she watched him walk toward her. Being tall, he appeared slim at first glance, yet he filled out his six-foot frame well. He had a sincere smile and blue eyes that made her want to trust him despite her decision to the contrary. His slightly disheveled hairstyle suited his youthful good looks, and his not-yet-shaven face added a sexy quality. She'd guessed him to be around her age, but looking at him now she wondered whether he might be younger.

After inquiring about his preference of drink, she went to place their order. She returned to her seat with a smile. "I guess we should introduce ourselves. My name's Tanisha." Not willing to reveal her true identity, she used her friend's name instead.

"I'm Jace," he replied.

"Is that short for Jason?" She wanted accurate information to do a search on him.

"No, it's a name my mom read in a book once. She liked it because it was different. I don't mind it, but I'm constantly having to answer that question."

"It's unique, I like it," she replied truthfully. Then, hoping for more, she added, "It sounds distinguished, like it might belong to a news correspondent." Holding an invisible microphone to her mouth, she mimicked reporters she'd heard on CNN. "This is Jace Reynolds, reporting live from Afghanistan."

"Close," he laughed. "It's Rutherford, but I'm not a news reporter."

The barista called out their drinks. Cassandra was about to get up when Jace offered. She sat back, pleased with what she'd uncovered. *Thank you, Jace Rutherford,* she smiled to herself. *Now let's see what you do for a living.* When he returned, she took a sip of her latte, beamed a smile his way, and asked, "So what do you do, Jace, with such a distinguished name, if you're not a news reporter?" She realized she was laying it on a bit thick, but he seemed to be buying it.

"I work at a manufacturing plant—assembly line stuff, not very exciting."

Port Hayden had three manufacturing plants. She knew the families that owned them. It would be easy enough to check up on him and see what his work record was like. "I guess it depends what you assemble," she shrugged, trying to act indifferent but hoping for more details. "Some things would be more interesting than others."

"It's a job," he replied. "It's not what I'd like to be doing, but it's okay for now."

"What would you rather be doing?" Although the information was irrelevant to her quest, Cassandra was curious. Jace was different from what she'd expected, and she was beginning to wonder whether she'd misjudged him. What she saw before her was an average guy who worked for a living, someone trying to find his way in life like everyone else. He seemed open and honest, and though that should have been good news for her aunt's sake, it left Cassandra feeling odd.

JACE WAS ACTUALLY enjoying himself. It was easy to forget his previous encounters with the haughty bitch and simply see her as a good-looking woman he'd met less than an hour ago. However, he couldn't stop thinking of his dream. It had left him with a longing to meet the kind of woman that could make him feel complete. It was preposterous to think she could be that person, yet here she was listening, talking, laughing—appearing to be truly interested in him. He didn't know what to make of it.

"I used to want to be an airline pilot," he responded to her query. "Now I'm not sure. I'd like to stay in Port Hayden, probably keep working where I am. I'm thinking about taking night classes. Maybe get my business degree." It was a notion he'd been considering. He'd had a taste of the program during the partial semester he'd attended college. At the time, he'd found the assignments easy and the subject matter interesting.

The conversation was becoming one-sided. Jace wanted to learn more about Tanisha, so he asked what she did for a living. As soon as he'd said it, he wished he had worded it differently. If she came from a wealthy family, she wouldn't have to work for a living. Her answer surprised him.

"I'm an editorial assistant for a fashion magazine," she replied easily. "I liaison with freelance writers, do proofing and copy editing, and review the magazine's layout."

She smiled and Jace could hear enthusiasm in her voice. The woman was becoming more intriguing by the minute, and he felt an attraction.

"I love to write," she added. "I studied journalism at Berkeley and got hired by one of the most prestigious magazines in the country, but I'm starting to think I could be doing more with my life. I'm just not sure what it is yet."

CASSANDRA HEARD herself telling Jace what she'd only told her closest confidants, and suddenly she was annoyed that she'd lost focus. *He's smooth; I'll give him that. He knows how to act charming and innocent at the same time. That's probably how he wormed his way into Aunt Sophia's good graces.*

"So you live in the city?"

"Yes, I . . . ," Cassandra paused. She didn't want to chance revealing too much. *I have plenty of information. I need to find a way to wrap this up.* She glanced at her watch. "Wow, I didn't realize we'd been here this long. I really should go; I have some more errands this afternoon before I go back to the city."

"Well, thanks for the latte," he smiled politely.

Jace stood up as she did, and they walked outside together. As much as Cassandra was eager to be done with the pretense, part of her didn't want their time together to end yet. She hesitated, pretending to check something on her phone.

"You're not driving the same car?" he asked when she didn't leave right away.

"Oh . . . the Martin? No, I borrowed a friend's car last weekend. I had to pledge my soul before he'd let me drive it," she laughed, hoping to sound convincing. "Some guys are so obsessive about their vehicles."

The moment that followed was awkward. He seemed to be waiting for her to head to whatever car she was driving. Thinking quickly, she came up with a way to get more information. "I was going to call a cab." She offered an entreating smile. "But maybe I could bother you for a ride . . . unless you need to be somewhere."

"Yeah . . . sure, no problem. I'm parked right here."

"Nice car," Cassandra remarked as she clicked her seatbelt in place. "It looks new." Inhaling, she added, "It even smells new." Then she held her breath, waiting to catch him in a lie, sure he wouldn't admit it belonged to an old woman.

"Yeah, it is," he said simply.

She tried again. "You must make decent money where you work. That's great."

He looked as though he was about to respond, but instead put the car in reverse and started backing up.

"So," he asked. "Where to?"

"Macmillan Tower on Emerald Street." The high-rise where her brother had once lived was about fifteen blocks away. It was the only place she could think of in short notice.

The trip was short, and the conversation centered on their taste in music, which was surprisingly similar. He pulled up in front of the building, put the car in neutral, and pulled the hand brake. Then he turned to her. There was nothing suggestive in his behavior, yet she found herself wondering what it would be like to kiss him. She fought the impulse for a moment and then decided, given the character she was playing, it wouldn't be inappropriate or even unexpected to give him a quick kiss. She opted for the cheek and thanked him for the ride.

"That's all I get?" he responded with a smile and a suggestive tone.

"I didn't realize this ride was going to cost me," she teased. "Maybe I should have taken a cab after all."

"Sorry, I should have my fares posted," he joked. "Anything over ten blocks is a kiss on the mouth. You still owe me."

Cassandra couldn't suppress her laughter. She didn't think he was serious, yet she was tempted to kiss him anyway. "That's a very interesting fee schedule. May I assume, then, that you only give rides to desirable young women?"

He looked slightly embarrassed by her question, and she realized he was probably thinking of her aunt. She instantly regretted asking. "Jace . . ." She turned her body to face him and moved slightly closer. "I *am* truly sorry for my behavior last weekend, and I *do* appreciate your kindness." She leaned in and smiled. He met her lips with his own, and they shared an extraordinary kiss. Then she moved away to open her door. "Thanks again, Jace. Take care."

SHE WAS GONE before he could think of an appropriate response. He was completely taken aback by the kiss. It wasn't simply that he had dared her, and she'd taken him up on it. It was the kiss itself—he felt that soul connection again, like in his dream. He'd never felt that with a woman before, and he'd been with quite a few. He'd dated a girl for three years and even considered marrying her, yet her kiss had never made him feel that way.

What's going on here? he asked as he pulled away from the building Tanisha had disappeared into. *What kind of weird spell does she have on me?* He decided to go to Chad's place. He needed to hang out with a friend, drink some beers, and put a stop to thoughts that were beginning to mess with his head.

ENTERING THE high-rise, Cassandra breathed easier as the smoked glass door closed behind her. She didn't think Jace could see her, but just in case, she walked to the reception desk and pretended to inquire about a resident. Within minutes, the full implication of her actions hit her. Never in her life had she done anything that outrageously impulsive. Never in her life had she told as many lies as she had in the past hour. She had convinced herself it was for a good cause, but now she felt wretched and deceitful.

Her opinion of Jace had changed dramatically, too. He was no longer a would-be con artist trying to take advantage of a trusting old woman. Far from it. She began to wonder how she could have been so convinced that he was.

She shouldn't have kissed him—she was acutely aware of that. Unfortunately, that was only one item in a long list of things she shouldn't have done.

Chapter 7

As expected, his friend was at home on a Sunday afternoon. Jace walked in, helped himself to a beer from Chad's refrigerator, and slumped back on the sofa. The sports channel was blaring on the mammoth flat screen TV, and Jace relaxed a little as he integrated into the familiar surroundings.

The room didn't have much furniture. The sofa was one that Jace had helped Chad and his brother pull from a dumpster. Chad's favorite chair was a piece of patio furniture, also reclaimed from the trash during a midnight raid in a more affluent neighborhood. The large television was the focal point in the small room and was Chad's true love. He'd borrowed the money when he found the entertainment system of his dreams at a pawnshop. He and his brother lived on macaroni and cheese for the next year to pay it off.

Jace had to admit he was comfortable in that environment. His place wasn't any different—secondhand furniture and the best TV and stereo he could afford from the pawnshop. It certainly wasn't the kind of place he could bring a woman like Tanisha to. She lived in the city, worked at a fancy job, and had friends who lived in high-rise condos and drove ultra-expensive sports cars.

So why did she come on to me? The question had been burning in his mind since he'd left her. *She knows where I live. She accused me of trying to steal her car last weekend. And today she flirts with me as if I'm actually in her league.* He longed to understand.

She did seem impressed by the car, he maintained, grasping for answers, . . . *which belongs to an eighty-year-old woman!* He groaned inwardly as reality slapped him in the face.

But that kiss . . . Jace couldn't erase it from his memory. He could still feel her full, soft lips and taste the deliciousness of her mouth. The scent of her perfume was in his nostrils, and the warmth of her hand remained where she'd touched his face.

"Jace!" Chad yelled.

He turned to his friend, startled. "What?"

"I asked if you wanted another beer. Are you deaf?"

"Uh . . . yeah, sure," Jace responded, embarrassed that his friend had caught him daydreaming.

"What's the matter with you, anyway?" Chad inquired roughly. "You haven't said a word since you walked in."

It wasn't unusual for them to watch TV without saying much. However, that was usually preceded by some type of communication—acknowledging recent sports scores or talking about parties they'd been to. Jace was eager to talk about his date with Tanisha, but he didn't think it would provide him with more clarity than he had now. "I went out with the rich bitch," he stated bluntly, referring to her as he had for the past week, although he no longer thought of her in that way.

"Out…seriously? Like on a date?"

"Sort of," Jace replied. "We went out for coffee."

"Howd'ya manage that?"

"She asked me."

"Okay, shit head," Chad scowled. "Is this like the brand new Accord you supposedly own?"

"No, that was…" Jace tried to explain. "That was a joke. This really happened; I swear."

Chad scrutinized him, obviously trying to decide whether he was telling the truth. Finally he frowned. "She asked *you* out?"

"Mmm hmm."

"I'm gonna need details, buddy." Chad opened another beer and sat back on his patio lounger. "How'd it happen?"

"I ran into her in the grocery store this morning," Jace began. "She didn't recognize me at first." He recounted all the details except the last, the most important.

"That's just strange," Chad scratched his head. "Maybe she's schizo."

"Maybe," Jace acknowledged. The thought had crossed his mind, too.

"So that's it? She asks you to go for coffee, you drive her to a friend's place . . . now what?" Chad looked puzzled. "Are you gonna see her again?"

"Doubt it," Jace shrugged. "I don't have her number. Don't even know her last name. Besides, I'm not sure I want to; we're too different."

"The Rich Bitch and the Pauper," Chad grinned. "Sounds like a Disney blockbuster to me."

"Thanks."

"Oh well, it's not the first time you struck out on a first date," Chad laughed, downing the rest of his beer.

"I didn't exactly strike out." Jace couldn't resist letting his friend know that more had taken place.

"So . . . what? You made out?"

"We kissed," Jace replied nonchalantly. "I dared her to, and she took me up on it. I could tell she wanted to."

"And then what? She gets out of the car and walks away?" Chad's furrowed brow indicated he was trying to figure it out, too.

"Pretty much."

THE CAB DROPPED HER OFF at the Town House just after one o'clock. Cassandra ran up the steps, seeking the comfort her childhood home offered, hoping that being there could wash away the shame she was experiencing. It was all too clear now. Jace wasn't the person she'd judged him to be. Sophia had been right after all, and it left Cassandra in a predicament.

Confident that she could uncover his true nature, she'd intended to present her aunt with evidence that afternoon. She was supposed to be at her aunt's place in less than an hour, yet she couldn't go near the building for fear of running into Jace. "God, what have I done?"

Though she'd directed her query heavenward, the dogs came rushing to her side. Letting them in the house was against the rules when her mother was home, but Cassandra didn't care; she wanted the company. She breathed evenly as she paced the marble foyer, dogs at her heels, trying to come up with a solution.

"I could call and tell her I'm not well," she suggested to Delilah. The old dog gazed up at her with an inquisitive look. *No, that might worry her,* she concluded, forgetting her aunt's view about worry. *I could tell her I have to go back to the city early, a work emergency maybe. God! More lies. I have to stop this!*

I could invite her here. The idea was by far the best she'd come up with—she truly wanted to see her aunt—however, the idea wasn't free of complications. *Mother said she rarely comes here anymore.* Knowing that the reason was the tension between her mother and her great aunt, Cassandra was still willing to ask. *But if she does come, what if she gets Jace to drive her? I wonder if she calls him any time she needs a ride or if she has to arrange it in advance?*

The clock ticked on, and she needed to make a decision fast. She opted to invite her aunt to the Town House, praying that she'd be willing to come, and praying that

Jace wouldn't drive her. Her anxiety increased as she heard the sweet, old voice answer the phone.

"Aunt Sophia, this is Cassandra. I wondered . . . I know I said I'd stop by this afternoon . . . but I thought, maybe . . . "

"Are you all right, dear?" Sophia asked calmly.

"Yes, yes. I'm fine," she assured her. "I just thought we might have more time together if you were to come out to the house. Mother and Daddy left for the summer house this morning, so we'd have the place to ourselves. It's lovely in the garden this time of day," Cassandra offered enticingly.

Sophia was quiet on the other end.

In a final effort, Cassandra added, "Daddy said you have a chauffeur now. Don't feel obligated, though; it was just an idea."

"I'd be happy to come out to the house, dear," Sophia replied cordially. "I can't remember the last time I've been there."

"Will your driver be available on such short notice?" Cassandra closed her eyes and crossed her fingers, hoping the answer would be no.

"I'll see if Jace is home," Sophia replied. "If not, don't worry; I'm quite comfortable taking a cab."

Her answer did little to relieve Cassandra's jitters, and hearing his name intensified her guilt. "All right," she said, trying to sound enthusiastic. "I'll see you in a little while."

Calculating that her aunt could be half an hour if she waited for a cab and sooner if Jace were to drive her, Cassandra went up to her bedroom and sat on her window seat where she had a view of the long driveway. As she waited, she replayed the morning's events in her head, going over the information she'd underhandedly acquired. *His name is Jace Rutherford. He's approximately twenty-five years old. He works on an assembly line in one of the factories here in town. He drives a Honda Accord—although it belongs to my aunt. No, wait...that's still an assumption.* She found herself arguing for his defense.

Jace... She smiled, remembering their conversation as he dropped her off at the high-rise. *It was so cute the way he told me I owed him a kiss for cab fare. And that kiss...* It had been more than she'd bargained for. She hadn't expected him to respond the way he did, hadn't expected to feel the instant heat. Truthfully, it was one of the most exceptional kisses she'd ever experienced. *I wonder if he felt it too.*

Her thoughts were suspended as she heard the dogs barking. She'd put them outside before going upstairs, and they were letting her know that a car was approaching. She moved back from the window and peered from behind the heavy drape. The sight of a blue car made her rapid pulse begin to slow. She watched until she had no doubt that it was a cab, then ran down to welcome her aunt.

Chapter 8

Cassandra was relieved when her plane touched down. It was comforting to be back in the city. The distance helped ease her mind. She'd come to realize that future trips to Port Hayden would be devoid of pleasure because of the anxiety she possessed. Port Hayden was associated with Jace Rutherford and having to be constantly on guard for fear of running into him. If he discovered that she was Cassandra Van Broden, that she'd lied to him and led him on to get information for a background check, that she'd suspected him of taking advantage of an old woman with money, he would hate her—plain and simple.

The whole matter upset her for many reasons. Her aunt would surely learn that she'd acted in an underhanded way, and that pained her because she valued her aunt's good opinion of her. Furthermore, acting that way was out of character. She didn't like the way it felt or how easy it had been for her to step into that role. She'd acted impulsively, immorally. Finally, it weighed on her because she cared what Jace thought of her. Though they barely knew each other, they were connected by their association to Sophia Langdon.

But it was more than that. She'd been trying unsuccessfully to wipe him from her mind. She'd been smitten by his good looks, his openness, his sense of humor. Although they were an unlikely match, had they met under different circumstances, something might have developed. Now that wasn't even a possibility.

JACE APPRECIATED the use of Sophie's car and did his best not to take advantage of her kindness. She'd had him drive her several times and always invited him in for tea afterward. He obliged at first, wanting to be polite. After a time or two, he began to enjoy her company. He still had reservations about her unconventional beliefs yet found himself with more and more questions as the days went by. After driving her to get groceries one evening, Jace sat down at his usual spot by the kitchen counter and watched her put the items away.

"You know, Jace, people aren't always what they appear to be at first glance."

Her comment came from nowhere, yet it seemed to address what was on his mind—he'd been thinking of Tanisha. He stared at her for a moment, not knowing how to respond.

"You can feel what's right for you, though."

"I'm not sure I know what you're talking about," he replied uneasily.

"You seem to have a lot of hostility toward rich people," she explained, referencing their prior discussion. "Why is that?"

"I've seen the way some of them operate."

She didn't respond, so he went on. "My mom works for a rich family. After my dad died, she didn't have much choice. I hated seeing her reduced to a servant, but it was either that or factory work." He sighed audibly. "And factory work sucks. I know what kind of profits the owners make on the products we assemble, yet we get paid peanuts."

"Remember what I said about leverage, Jace?"

Jace had to think a minute. He recalled what she'd told him, yet he wasn't sure how it applied to the current topic. "You said that focus works the same way. I'm still not sure what you meant by that," he admitted.

"What are you focusing on?"

"You mean, what am I thinking about?" He gave her a confused look. "Right now?"

"In general," she clarified, "when you think about money. Your job, your mother's employers, other wealthy people. What kinds of thoughts do you think?"

Jace frowned. He'd never paid much attention to the content of his thoughts. He couldn't see the relevance.

Sophie smiled sweetly and set a plate of cookies on the counter in front of him. "I know you think I'm a crazy old lady sometimes," she began, "but I've learned a few things in my lifetime, things I wished I'd known at your age. Your thoughts are making you miserable, Jace. It's your thoughts that determine how you feel, and how you feel is everything."

"And you're saying I can do something about that?"

"That's the power of focus." She studied him for a moment. "You've experienced it—something happens to change your focus, and suddenly you feel good."

Jace remembered his experience at the hockey game and relayed it to Sophie. "I'd love to feel like that more often, but it doesn't seem possible."

"It is with focus."

A light went on in his mind. "So you're saying I should purposely think about what feels good and choose not to think about what makes me miserable?"

"Yes!"

Her enthusiasm caught him off guard, and he had to laugh. "Okay... positive thinking. I can see the benefit in that."

"Oh, it's much bigger than that, Jace," she went on, passion still evident in her voice. "That's where the leverage comes in. Focus means that you're directing your thoughts on purpose. Your thoughts are like magnets, and when you learn to choose them deliberately, you have a powerful tool."

More light seeped in. "Are you saying I can think about something and make it happen?"

"You're already doing it."

"I am?"

"I want you to do something, Jace," she instructed. "Pay attention to your thoughts this week. Notice what you think about, especially how your thoughts make you feel—that's important."

"All right," Jace complied. Curious now, he was willing to try Sophie's little exercise. The woman was persuasive, her words compelling. He felt better than he had in a while. Hope began to surge as his understanding increased. *The high I had at the hockey game was short-lived and out of my control,* he realized. *But what Sophie's talking about is different, it's powerful.* It was the power he'd been craving. Suddenly hope turned to excitement as he caught a glimpse of what could be. "That's what you meant by thinking like the rich do," Jace exclaimed. "They're attracting money and stuff by their thoughts, their focus. I get it!"

Sophie laughed. "I knew you would."

Jace took the last of the cookies on the plate in front of him. They were the kind his grandma used to buy, gingery with a swirl of icing on top. He thanked Sophie and headed down to his apartment, his mind racing with the possibilities before him. He'd just received an important piece of the puzzle, and that one piece suddenly made the whole picture much clearer.

SHE'D BEEN BACK several days, and Cassandra still hadn't told anyone about her weekend. She was trying to sort through emotions that ranged from guilt and regret when she thought of how foolishly she'd acted, to pleasure and longing as she remembered the kiss.

Other thoughts had been vying for her attention, too. Sophia's words were affecting her in a profound way. Cassandra had done more research and found plenty to support what her aunt believed. She kept coming across the term *Law of Attraction*, a teaching that was in line with the laws of the universe Sophia talked about.

Sophia held that the universe was governed by five principles, and had explained two of them in detail so far. The first stated that all things are one. The second described thought as creative. Her aunt had explained that all matter exists in thought form before it manifests into physical. As Cassandra searched the internet, she found another term that caught her interest. *Vibration* was used to describe not only the energy itself, but people's relationship to their desires. She learned that people, being essentially energy, vibrate at different frequencies depending on what their thoughts are focused on. Like a radio dial, thoughts could be tuned to match the frequency of a desire, therefore attracting it into their experience.

Her aunt had talked about the power of focus. She'd claimed that a person could have whatever they wanted in life if they could focus on it in a positive way. Cassandra clearly recalled her powerful words: You get what you expect from life, but what most people don't know is that they can raise their expectations.

She stopped to ponder the statement. *I have high expectations already. Is that why I'm living such a wonderful, satisfying life?* She'd never questioned why she had all the affluence and luxury a person could want when so many others didn't.

All of a sudden, she was struck by the reality of it. *Some people live on the street and don't know where their next meal is coming from, yet I've come to expect a never-ending supply of lattes and caviar, designer clothes and holidays in Europe.* The acute awareness left her sad. Logic told her that even with her family's considerable wealth, it would be impossible to help all the poor in the world. Not only that but if what she was learning was true, the poor were that way because they expected it. They were attracting it vibrationally. At an unconscious level, they expected struggle and hardship, and they got it.

Why did Aunt Sophia tell me this? she wondered. *Does she want me to raise my expectations?* Her first thoughts were of material goods, and wanting more made her feel greedy. Then she examined other areas of her life. *Relationships,* Cassandra affirmed silently. *That's one area I definitely want more than what I've experienced in the past.*

Jace came to mind as he had often in the past few days, and she allowed herself to think about him. He had many of the qualities she wanted in a man. What had stood out the most to Cassandra was that he was real, down to earth, and not at all pretentious. He'd shown her his true self, even though he was aware of the difference in their circumstances. He'd told her about his dreams and the story behind his unusual name. She'd found it easy to be open with him, too, acknowledging her desire to do more with her life, knowing that he could relate.

Maybe I met Jace so that I could raise my expectations. Cassandra could never settle for anyone like Nick again. He was too shallow and self-serving. She wanted someone like Jace. *Someone like him,* she sighed regretfully. *But not him.* Her actions the previous weekend had forever ruined the possibility of a relationship with Jace Rutherford.

JACE LOOKED through the brochures he'd picked up for night classes at the local college. He'd been thinking a lot about it since he'd mentioned it to Tanisha, and he was ready to pursue it. He wasn't sure whether it was simply him wanting to improve himself so that he could justify attracting someone like her, or whether he was truly following his dreams. If the latter were true, his dreams had changed. Nevertheless, the idea of a business degree was appealing. He decided not to question his reasoning.

He figured he could afford it now. Sophie had offered to pay him three hundred a month plus unlimited use of her vehicle, and Jace was more than happy with the arrangement. The five hundred dollars he'd received for his old car had helped ease his debt load somewhat, and that was a relief. He tried to be aware of his thoughts, as Sophie had suggested, particularly how they felt. *Thinking about getting a business degree feels good,* he confirmed. *The thought of paying down my credit card does, too.*

Congratulating himself on his efforts, he continued with his mission. He called the college administration office and asked to talk to someone about night classes. The woman was extremely helpful and gave him a plethora of information on the business programs they offered as evening courses. When he asked about prices, he was shocked at what she quoted him. She was obviously used to hearing silence after she informed people of the cost of programs, because she went on to tell him about his payment options.

Jace thanked the woman and hung up the phone. *It doesn't matter how they break it down,* he sighed. *There's no way I can afford to take classes right now.* Their programs were set up to allow working people to get their degrees quickly, so it would mean classes three to four nights a week. When he'd inquired about taking the same courses at a slower pace, she informed him that if he wanted to do it that way he would be considered a non-degree applicant and would be put on a waiting list. Priority was given to those serious about the program. Moreover, the courses were more expensive if he took them individually; he'd pay considerably more in the long run.

As the all-too-familiar discouragement settled over him, he was reminded again of Sophie's advice. "Well, Sophie," he addressed her aloud. "That thought felt like crap."

Change your focus.

Jace frowned as he heard the typical response his wise old neighbor would give him. He had no idea how he could possibly change the way he felt about it when he couldn't change the college's policies or prices. He wanted to understand, however, so he went up and knocked on Sophie's door.

"Hello, Jace." She opened the door to invite him in. "Are you having a hard time with your thoughts?"

"How do you always know what I'm thinking?" Jace asked, slightly exasperated.

"I don't know what you're thinking," she replied calmly, "but I can sense your energy, and given what we talked about the other night . . . "

"Okay, I'm sorry."

"You haven't offended me, Jace. I don't offend easily," she informed him. "Now, what are you having trouble with?"

"I've been trying to notice how my thoughts feel, like you said." He summed up his recent efforts and then added, "How do you *not* feel bad about something when it just plain sucks?"

"If you could hear the message you're sending out to the Universe right now, it would sound something like: This isn't working. Nothing ever works for me.

Everybody else gets the breaks, but I never get a break. It's not fair!"

Though he laughed at her imitation of him, he had to object. "That's not what I said."

"It's what your words implied." She looked at him intently. "It's what you feel, isn't it?"

Jace couldn't deny it. She'd perfectly summed up how he had been feeling for a long time. "Yeah," he conceded, releasing a long, slow breath. "It is."

Chapter 9

"I can't believe you did that!" Tanisha exclaimed. "That's so unlike you."

"Tell me something I don't know," Cassandra replied miserably. "I feel terrible."

"So you told a few lies to get some information," her friend shrugged. "You were concerned about your aunt's welfare. And given how rude the guy was the first couple of times you met, you had good reason to assume he was a creep."

"I may have given him reason to be rude," Cassandra admitted. Having reflected on their first two meetings, she'd concluded that she had been at fault. "I got mad at him for opening the door in my face when I was the one who opened the wrong door to begin with. And the next day I practically accused him of stealing my dad's car."

"Really?" Tanisha sounded surprised and a little annoyed. "You didn't tell me any of that."

"I guess I was so focused on his initial lack of decorum, I didn't consider how offensive I must have seemed to him."

"Still, what's the big deal?" Tanisha asked. "You'll probably never see him again."

"I could easily run into him if I were to visit Aunt Sophia, and I can't very well pretend to be you if my aunt is standing right there. Besides, I lied about my reason for being in the building in the first place."

"Oh what a tangled web we weave . . . ," Tanisha quoted piously.

"I know, I know," Cassandra moaned. "I've created a real mess, and I don't know what to do."

"Don't worry; I'm going to help you," Tanisha assured her. "We'll figure something out."

"I don't see how," Cassandra shook her head. "I've been over this a hundred times." She appreciated her friend's support, yet she remained skeptical.

"Let's look at your options."

"Well, first of all, I can't set foot in my aunt's apartment building unless I know for certain Jace isn't going to be there. I can't keep inviting her to the Town House; she's bound to get suspicious. Plus, if Jace were to drive her, he might walk her to the door. And I can't invite her here; she'd never come into the city." Cassandra was sure she'd exhausted all possibilities.

"What about the summer house?" Tanisha suggested. "If she were to spend a week or two there, you'd have plenty of time to visit."

Cassandra shook her head. "She and Mother don't get along. It's why she never visits them in town."

"It's not like they fight and scratch each other's eyes out. She could stay in the guest cottage, take her meals on the terrace. They'd never have to see each other."

"That could work." Cassandra chewed her lower lip as she pondered the idea. "I'm spending the first two weeks in July there, anyway. Maybe if I asked her, she'd come."

"I know," Tanisha submitted. "Use the excuse that you're busy for the next couple of weekends so you won't be able to visit her in Port Hayden. Tell her you're on holidays after that but you *really, really* want to see her, and invite her to the beach. Pour on the charm," she added. "The old dear won't be able to resist."

"We're not exactly untangling the web here, are we?" Cassandra grimaced, hating the idea of more lies. "And there's still the risk of Jace driving her to the summer house, or picking her up. I can't stay in hiding all the time, and I don't want to chance running into him."

"Maybe you need to face the music," Tanisha advised.

"What do you mean?" Cassandra looked at her oddly. "Tell Jace the truth?"

"No," Tanisha shook her head, scowling. "Tell your *aunt* the truth." Staring at Cassandra for a moment, a sudden knowing lit up her face. "This is about Jace, isn't it? You care what he thinks about you. When did that happen?"

"Ohhhh," Cassandra groaned, burying her face in her hands. Then looking up at her friend, she smiled weakly. "Sometime between interrogating him and kissing him."

"You kissed him?"

"Yes."

"Oh God, that complicates the situation," Tanisha laughed. "Wait a minute! It's like I predicted. He's the exact opposite of what you thought he was, and you've fallen for him."

Her smug look annoyed Cassandra. "Wipe that grin off your face," she ordered. "You did *not* predict this. I had no intention of it turning out this way. Besides, I'm not crazy. I know it could never work between us. I just don't want him to hate me, that's all."

"SO HOW DO I change the way I feel?" Jace asked Sophie.

"By changing your focus," she replied, giving him a sympathetic smile. "I'm not suggesting that you look at what upsets you and magically feel good about it. But you can choose to look at something else, or you can look at a different aspect of it and feel better," she explained. "For example, you want to get your business degree. That's wonderful. Only, instead of saying, 'It won't work; life sucks,' try saying, 'I don't know how this is going to work, but it could somehow. Things have worked in the past. I'm going to stay open to ideas.'" She looked at him expectantly. "Could you feel the difference?"

"Yeah," Jace answered earnestly. "I see what you mean. By saying things won't work out, I'm actually creating them not to work. I'm creating a life that sucks," he smiled wryly.

"Start paying more attention to what *is* working in your life," Sophie suggested. "You must have some good friends, maybe a girlfriend..."

"Sophie, you're the only girl in my life right now," Jace teased.

"Oh my," she laughed, blushing slightly. "Surely you can find someone a few years younger than me. I have a grandniece about your age."

"Really?" Jace was surprised to hear her talk about family. "Do your relatives live nearby?"

"My nephew and his wife are here in town. Their daughter lives in the city. She's a lovely girl. A journalist. Here," she offered, "let me show you her graduation picture." Sophie went into the living room and came back with a silver-framed photograph, which she handed to Jace.

He nearly dropped it when he looked into Tanisha's smiling face. "This is your niece?" He looked at Sophie in disbelief.

"Yes," she replied. "Why? Do you know Cassandra?"

"Cassandra?" He looked at the picture again. The hair was a different style and a different color, but the face was the same. He was sure of it.

"She's a lovely girl," Sophie repeated, smiling at the picture as Jace handed it back to her.

"Yes," Jace agreed, reluctant to say more. "She is. She... um... looks like someone I know. Probably just a coincidence."

He made an excuse to leave, said good night to Sophie, and headed back to his apartment, his mind deep in thought. *The girl I went out with said her name was Tanisha, not Cassandra. There's no way two people could look that much alike and not be twins,* he argued. *And Sophie would have told me if her niece was a twin.*

She was in this building two days in a row. He continued sifting through the evidence. *She said she was delivering a package for a friend. Could she have been visiting her aunt instead? Could she have been lying to me? Why on earth would she do that? And why would she ask me out, pretending to be someone else?* The questions bombarded him.

He remembered the feelings he'd had, both in his dream and after their amazing kiss. He'd experienced a connection he didn't understand. *How is that possible?* His frustration flared. *How could I feel a connection to someone who comes across as a rich snob one weekend, then turns into a flirty little minx and feeds me a pack of lies the next?*

Jace was disillusioned. He was indignant. Painfully aware of his thoughts, he had no idea how he could find a positive aspect to focus on. He didn't even want to try. He was back to hating her. He couldn't ask Sophie's advice, either, because the woman who was messing with his emotions was now her 'lovely' niece.

IT HAD BEEN over a week since Cassandra had seen her aunt. She'd stayed in the city the past weekend with a legitimate excuse, a friend's birthday. She planned to leave for the summer house in ten days and truly wanted to spend more time with Sophia, wanted to hear more of her intriguing wisdom. But scheming to find a way to see her while avoiding Jace, was unacceptable.

She'd made her decision. Tired of the lies, she was ready to face the music as Tanisha had suggested. Nevertheless, she stared at the phone for nearly five minutes before working up the nerve to call her aunt.

"Hi, Aunt Sophia. It's Cassandra."

"How nice to hear from you, dear."

"Aunt Sophia, I need to tell you something," Cassandra blurted.

"What is it, dear? Is something the matter?"

"I've done something," she confessed. "And I'm not very proud of it."

"Well, well," Sophia laughed. "Haven't we all?"

Encouraged by her aunt's lighthearted attitude, Cassandra continued, "It's about your neighbor, Jace."

"Go on."

"Daddy told me you'd hired your neighbor to drive you around and . . . no wait," Cassandra faltered. "Let me begin before that. When I came to visit you the first time, several weeks ago, I ran into a young man in your building. Actually," she laughed uneasily, "he ran into me. I was leaving and he was coming in . . ." She described the incident to her aunt. "I know I was in the wrong, but I had this image of him knocking you over. I got mad at him, and of course he got defensive because I'd been the one going out the wrong door. Anyway, that was our first meeting.

"The next morning, as I left your building, I noticed him staring at Daddy's car. I was still mad at him for being rude the day before, and he obviously didn't think much of me and . . . well, let's just say we had words."

"So you've met Jace." Sophia sounded delighted, as if she hadn't heard what Cassandra just said. "He's such a nice young man."

Cassandra hesitated, wondering how to continue. Her aunt could be so odd. She still questioned the old woman's sanity at times. "That's not all, Aunt Sophia. The following weekend, Daddy told me you'd hired someone from your building to drive your new car, and somehow I knew it was the same guy I'd met. We were worried about you because we didn't know anything about him, and . . . well . . . my dealings with him had been . . . unpleasant.

"I jumped to conclusions. I know I was wrong, but I assumed he was the type that might take advantage of an elderly woman with money."

"Jace would never do that, dear."

"I know that now," Cassandra sighed.

"How did you find out?" Sophia's voice was still patient and loving, but there was a note of curiosity.

"Daddy suggested we get his name . . . to learn more about him. He wanted me to ask you a few questions so he could check into it further." She took a deep breath. "Only . . . I decided to handle the situation my own way." She told her aunt what had taken place between them at the grocery store and the coffee shop but omitted telling her how they'd parted. "I realized he wasn't at all like I'd judged him to be," Cassandra acknowledged. "And that's why I invited you out to the Town House. I couldn't go to your place in case I ran into him.

"Now I feel terrible. I hated telling all those lies." She paused, relieved to have finally admitted her wrongdoing but still wanting absolution. "Aunt Sophia, I'm so sorry. Can you ever forgive me?"

"Of course, my dear. You were only doing what you thought was best. Don't you worry another minute about this; everything's fine now."

"But Jace still thinks I'm Tanisha," Cassandra objected. "It would be incredibly awkward running into him. Plus he'd hate me if he learned the truth. I've given him more than enough reason to."

Sophia remained quiet on the other end, so Cassandra continued. "I'd really like to see you again, Aunt Sophia." She left the statement free of suggestions, wanting to see what her aunt might propose.

"Of course, and I'd love to see you too, dear. We're not done with our little project. We'll work something out. Don't you worry."

Cassandra was filled with immense love for the dear old woman in that moment and didn't hesitate to tell her. She felt lighter, having shed the burden of guilt. What would happen with Jace, she didn't know. She hoped for a chance to ask his forgiveness one day. For now she was relieved to know that her aunt still loved her.

A PASSING WEEK helped Jace to get some perspective. He wasn't as angry as he had been. Nevertheless, it was strange knowing the woman he'd kissed was Sophie's niece. He doubted he'd ever see her again. She wouldn't likely show her face near his building, and being from the city, not to mention a different social class, he doubted he'd run into her anywhere else.

That in itself brought up several questions. *Cassandra's obviously well off. But does she come from a wealthy family? Or does she have a high-paying job, rich friends, and a taste for the extravagant? Who knows, maybe there's a rich boyfriend in the picture.* Jace wasn't ruling anything out.

It doesn't make sense that her family has money, he reasoned. *If so, why would they allow their aunt to fend for herself and live in this old apartment building?* Not that Sophie was suffering in any way. She seemed to enjoy her way of life. And she was definitely happy.

Sophie said she'd had all that once, Jace recalled. Her furniture and china seemed to support her claim, and she spoke of the way rich people think as if it were knowledge she'd gained firsthand. *Maybe they are one of the wealthy families of Port Hayden and for whatever reason don't associate with their old aunt.* The thought amplified his distaste for Port Hayden's upper class.

People aren't always what they appear to be at first glance, Jace. Sophie's remark echoed in his mind. Her words had a way of returning to him at just the right moment and sounding as if she were somehow inside his head. He grinned. *The old gal is getting to me.*

It made him realize that he was judging her family when in truth he had only assumptions to go on. He was judging Cassandra, too, although in her case he had plenty of reason. The trouble was, as much as he wanted to despise her, he kept remembering his dream and the incredible kiss.

That kiss. As he lost himself in the memory of it, more of Sophie's advice came to mind: You can feel what's right for you. Jace had been confused about his feelings toward the girl he'd known as Tanisha. His mind was telling him one thing, his heart another. He'd been shocked when Sophie's comment seemed to address his plight.

How can I feel what's right, when what I feel is so mixed up? Thoughts of Cassandra caused desire to mingle with disappointment and anger, and if Jace was completely honest, somewhere in the mix was a little bit of hope.

CASSANDRA HAD arranged to pick Sophia up at her apartment, Friday afternoon. They would be traveling to the beach house together. She was pleased that her aunt had agreed to go with her to their summer home. It would be a change of scenery for Sophia, and Cassandra looked forward to spending a week with her favorite aunt.

Arriving at the Town House in a car she'd rented from the airport, she greeted the two old Great Danes and spent a few minutes with them. "How are my favorite dogs?" she crooned affectionately. Their response and subsequent tail wagging told her they were perfectly fine. The grounds keeper, Jerry, took great care of them. She looked up to see Jerry trimming shrubs near the front of the house. She called out a greeting, and he smiled and waved in response.

Her parents had taken the pup with them to the beach, and she was eager to spend time with him as well. Everything about the next two weeks excited her. She loved going to their summer home. It brought back cherished memories of her childhood.

As she walked into the house, she was greeted by Sarah who was dusting in the front entry. Smiling at the woman, Cassandra noticed an unexpected familiarity about her. She'd met the new housekeeper twice. This time, however, Cassandra was sure she'd seen her elsewhere. *I wonder why she looks familiar? Maybe she used to work for another family, and I've seen her serving at a party or something.*

"Your mother called to say that you'd be here today, Miss Cassandra, and since Mrs. Harper isn't here, I wondered if you'd like me to prepare lunch for you."

Sarah had addressed her formally, the way the older servants did, and for some reason it made her uncomfortable. "Oh, thank you, Sarah," she replied. "But you don't need to go to any trouble. I can pick up something in town."

"It's no trouble, miss."

Cassandra agreed to lunch on the terrace and went outside to enjoy the lovely weather. When the housekeeper came out carrying a tray of food, Cassandra had to inquire. "Sarah, you look familiar. I'm sure I've seen you somewhere before."

"I worked for the Linnells for four years before I started here," Sarah offered.

Cassandra knew of the Linnells, although she'd never been to their home. An older couple, they'd recently moved to be closer to their children. "Are you from Port Hayden?" she probed.

"Yes, I am," Sarah replied. "My husband was principal at Hillcrest Elementary School."

She seemed talkative, and Cassandra enjoyed the company. Since Sarah had referred to his position in the past tense, she asked, "Is he retired?"

"No, he passed away several years ago."

"I'm so sorry." Cassandra instantly regretted having touched on what was probably still a painful subject. Not wanting to leave the conversation hanging awkwardly, she decided to inquire further. "Do you have family here?"

"I have a son," Sarah stated proudly. "Jace is twenty-five. He lives here in town. Works at Stanton's. It's nice to have him close by. He's been a real help."

Cassandra's heart skipped a beat. *Jace isn't a common name; what are the chances of two people with the same name, same age, working at a factory in town?* She needed to know more. "Jace . . . " She kept her eyes down and her voice even. "That's an unusual name."

"Yes," Sarah smiled pleasantly. "I read it in a book once when I was young. I always knew if I had a son I'd name him that."

Cassandra swallowed hard. It was obvious now why the woman seemed familiar. Sarah was Jace's mother; they had the same eyes, the same smile.

JACE BEGAN TO think about the weekend ahead as he sat down for his lunch break. Sophie had called the night before to tell him she was going away for a week. She hadn't elaborated, and he hadn't asked for details. All he could think of was that the car was his to enjoy for a whole week. Not that he wasn't free to use it whenever he wanted and not that driving Sophie places was an inconvenience, but when she lived so close, he was constantly aware that he was in her employ and was careful not to take advantage of her generosity.

Chad joined him, pulling a large sandwich from his lunch box. He took an oversized bite and immediately asked, "Did you hear? Morry's throwing a big party this weekend."

Jace ignored his friend's lack of manners, all too aware that his mother would have strung him up for talking with his mouth full like that. She was nowhere near, yet he could hear her voice in his head when he deviated from the acceptable rules of behavior she'd instilled in him. "Yeah," he replied. "You going?"

"Mmm hmm," Chad nodded, mouth still full. He chewed for a moment and then continued. "Morry's sister's gonna be there... bringing a bunch of her friends from college. Dirty Laundry is playing at The Brink, Saturday night, too. Maybe we could go there first and hit the party later."

"Sounds like a plan," Jace declared, liking his options. He was freer to enjoy himself now that he had the extra income from Sophie. He wasn't as uptight about finances. He'd set aside his plan to take night courses. Even though it left him somewhat discouraged about his future, it was the right decision, at least for the time being.

He'd concluded that meeting Cassandra had been the main reason for his discontent. His sudden desire to better himself had been a subconscious attempt to be in her league, to date someone like her. It was absurd. He was not, nor would he ever be in her league. And given her behavior and lies, he was probably better off for it, anyway. It did, however, make him aware that he'd like to be in a relationship again. He'd grown tired of it and for a while had been content with parties and one-night stands, but that lifestyle just wasn't satisfying him.

Cassandra may have left him wanting more, but he was okay with that. He realized that it wasn't her, rather someone like her that he was looking for—someone more mature, more confident, more independent than the girls he met at the parties he and Chad frequented.

Chapter 10

Cassandra and her aunt left for the summer house by mid afternoon. It was a two-hour drive, and the views along the coastal highway ranged from scenic to breathtaking. After twenty years, she hadn't tired of them. It wasn't hard to fill the time with pleasant conversation, yet she had a burning desire to talk about Jace. She questioned her motives, knowing she should forget him. The problem was, he was constantly in her thoughts.

"Remember, my dear, sometimes what you're looking for is right in front of you."

She knew she should be used to her aunt's peculiar ways by now, but the woman's comments were so random and unexpected, and they often addressed exactly what Cassandra was thinking. It was unnerving. "Aunt Sophia, you mentioned that once before, but I still don't know what I'm looking for."

Sophia didn't respond. As Cassandra glanced at her, she noticed a smile on her face.

Did she know I was thinking of Jace? How is that possible? Her desire to talk about him suddenly escalated. "Did you know that Jace's mom works for Mother and Daddy?" she began. "Mother just hired her as their new housekeeper."

"No dear," Sophia replied, not sounding surprised. "I wasn't aware of that." She paused and added," Jace is such a nice young man."

"There's something else I didn't tell you." Cassandra was willing to be totally honest with her aunt, hoping the perceptive woman could help her. " . . . about my meeting with Jace."

"What is it, dear?"

"It started as a way to get information, to prove he wasn't the best person to be driving you around. But as we talked, I could notice my feelings changing. By the time he dropped me off . . . well . . . we kissed."

"My, my," Sophia smiled.

"It was all very innocent. It didn't mean anything. At least I didn't think it did," she added.

"How do you feel about it now?"

"I don't know," Cassandra admitted. "I'm really confused. I mean, it could never work. We're too different. Besides, he'd hate me if he ever found out who I really am."

"Would he?"

"You don't think so?"

"You meant no harm. You had my interest in mind," Sophia soothed. "I'm sure he could see that."

"I'd like to tell him the truth," Cassandra acknowledged. "I'd like to ask his forgiveness. Even if nothing more happens between us, I'd like to clear the air."

"I think that's a good idea."

"But when? How?"

"I could ask him to drive out and pick me up next weekend," Sophia offered.

The thought of seeing Jace again made her stomach knot up, yet the yearning was hard to ignore. "I guess," Cassandra responded hesitantly. "It would be so awkward, though. He thinks I'm a girl from the city named Tanisha. He doesn't know I'm your niece."

"Actually, he does, dear," Sophia informed her. "He saw a picture of you in my apartment."

"Oh no," Cassandra groaned. "Did he say anything?"

"No, not really."

"Aunt Sophia . . . " She had to ask. "Do you think anything could happen between us? I mean, do you think he could be the one?"

"It doesn't matter what I think, dear," her aunt replied lovingly. "How do you feel about it? That's what is important."

"I like Jace," Cassandra admitted. "But I don't know if it's him, necessarily. He has a lot of the qualities I want in a man."

Her aunt remained quiet, so Cassandra continued pondering aloud, finding her aunt's listening ear beneficial. "He's easy to talk to," she smiled, remembering their conversation. "He's funny and down to earth. He doesn't pretend to be someone he's not. But I'm wondering if that's part of the problem. I don't know if we could each be who we are and still find common interests. Maybe we're too different."

Her last statement triggered a question that had been on Cassandra's mind for a long time. "Aunt Sophia, may I ask you something?"

"Of course, dear."

"I've often wondered why, when you have money, you choose not to enjoy all the wonderful things your money could buy you."

"I have all I want, dear," the old woman assured her. "I've lived a long life. I've known all the comforts, had every worldly possession I ever desired. I've traveled extensively, had wonderful relationships . . . "

Sophia appeared to be lost in thought, and Cassandra wondered whether she was thinking of her husband, who had passed away so many years ago, or whether there'd been someone else since. Suddenly she was curious to learn more about her aunt.

"Some of those appealed to me and some didn't," Sophia continued. "With all that I had, the one thing I lacked was simplicity. The desire grew as I got older, so I began to shed material possessions that, wonderful as they are, can start to weigh a person down after a while. I've probably gone to a bit of an extreme with my decision. I know people think I'm crazy. They don't understand why I live the way I do. But doing without isn't a bad thing if it's by choice. I can honestly say that I have all I want, and I'm happy."

Cassandra longed to stop the vehicle and give her a hug. She was filled with immense adoration and deep respect for the woman. Her aunt didn't seem crazy at all. She was strong, making her own choices in life, doing what she wanted instead of following what others said was right or acceptable. Cassandra longed to emulate that in her own life. Maybe not the simplicity—she enjoyed what money could buy. It was her aunt's strength of character and positive outlook on life that appealed to her in a powerful way.

Moreover, Sophia Langdon seemed as comfortable with people like Jace as she was with those of her own social standing—maybe more so. Having met Jace, Cassandra could understand why. She had to admit that many of the society people she knew were arrogant. *Do I come across like that?* she questioned silently. *Does Jace see me that way?* It was a definite possibility considering their first two meetings.

As she thought about the lies and the fact that he knew her true identity, her heart sank. *I've given him so many reasons to hate me,* she sighed, longing for a way to change his opinion of her. *If he could see me for who I really am, maybe there'd be a chance for us.*

JACE HAD ENJOYED himself at the parties he went to that weekend. He'd been able to relax and let loose and felt better than he had in months. He'd even met a girl he wanted to see again. Elise was a friend of Morry's sister and a second-year journalism student. She had other similarities to Cassandra as well, but Jace tried not to read into it. *There's nothing wrong with that,* he maintained. *It just proves I'm over this twisted infatuation. I'm ready to move on.*

With Sophie away all week, he let himself imagine that the Honda was his, and he took great pleasure from the sense of freedom the illusion evoked. He'd begun to think about the weekend ahead and the date he had planned with Elise, when he got a call from Sophie asking whether he'd mind picking her up on Saturday. He agreed without hesitation.

"I've spent the week at the beach with my nephew and his wife," she remarked casually. "Their daughter Cassandra is here, too."

At the mention of her name, Jace's stomach tightened. Seeing her again certainly wasn't on his agenda, but he couldn't tell Sophie that. *Maybe with luck I'll avoid her,* he inserted silently. *Besides, after what she's done, she should be the one avoiding me.*

He got the address, and they agreed on a time. He didn't need directions; he knew the area well. It was a popular resort town with a public beach and great camping. Jace had been there with his parents over the years. He and his friends had partied there as well. It was a pleasant drive up the coast, and Jace looked forward to being on the open road with the new car.

His date Friday night went better than expected, and he found himself cooking breakfast for Elise next morning before driving her home. He wasn't totally honest with her. When she admired his car, he led her to believe it was his. He felt guilty, but it sounded lame telling her it belonged to the old lady in the apartment upstairs. He'd been looking for ways to impress. With a second date planned for that evening, he began to think about the best way to tell her.

As he drove to the beach resort, Jace considered the possibility of a future with Elise. Even though they partied in the same circles, even though she was willing to go out with him, he couldn't help noting the differences in their circumstances. She owned a car, and he was borrowing one; she was going to school to pursue a career, and he worked in a factory. Her family certainly wasn't rich, but from what she'd said, they were better off than some. *It's acceptable to be broke when you're a student,* he brooded. *It's expected. But if you're broke and working in a dead-end job, you're a loser.*

He was beating up on himself, and it didn't feel good. Sophie's words came quickly to mind: Your thoughts are making you miserable, Jace. It's your thoughts that determine how you feel, and how you feel is everything. He wanted to feel good, wanted to begin thinking about his desires in a more positive way, wanted to stop comparing himself to the rich and instead begin thinking like they did. Suddenly determination swept in to replace self-judgement. Focusing in a more deliberate way was a practical approach to his dilemma, a course of action. And Jace wanted to act; he wanted to do something to change his situation.

Jace contemplated his new plan as he pulled into the resort. Passing the public beach and camping area, he recalled with fondness the good times he'd had with his parents. His father had been a serious man, a studious type who spent his down time reading. At the beach, however, he'd taken time to play with his son. Jace was filled with appreciation as he thought about it. More than ever he cherished those memories of his father.

He looked around as he drove through town. The snug cottages that lined the streets offered enticing getaways for long weekends and summer holidays. He added owning one to his growing list of desires. Focusing on it in a positive way wouldn't be difficult. He'd simply envision the shady street with its white-washed homes and picket fences. He could see himself relaxing on a hammock in the front, listening to children playing happily in the distance.

Glancing at the address Sophie had given him, he saw that it was on the main drive. However, the numbers he was passing were not even close to the address he had written down, so he continued driving and was soon in new territory. The homes in this area were larger than the cottages in town, but still ones that middle income families could afford if they managed their money wisely.

Before long the scenery began to change again. Gated entrances heralded tree-lined drives curving up to large houses on expansive properties. *This can't be where Sophie's relatives live.* Jace was sure that he was in the wrong neighborhood—either that, or the road continued on to a less affluent area. He slowed the car as he caught sight of an address on one of the ornate wrought-iron gates. It was the number Sophie had given him. Tentatively, he turned into the driveway, and the gate opened before him. The ample property at the end of the drive boasted several buildings. Two houses were joined by a covered walkway. One was a large two-story, its shingled siding adding warmth to the stone turrets and marble pillars flanking the grand entrance. The other house was smaller in stature, yet similar in design.

Staring at the impressive spread, Jace still questioned whether he was in the right place. To be honest, he hoped he had the wrong address, the wrong neighborhood altogether. If Sophie was part of a family that could afford a summer home like that, then he'd misjudged her completely. His answer came as Cassandra walked out of the main house and headed straight toward the car. He didn't move from the driver's seat as he scrambled to think of what to say to the woman who by all rights should have been in hiding if she knew he was coming. His time was brief, and all that he could think to say as she walked up was, "Hi, Cassandra."

Wearing short shorts and a bikini top, she looked sensational. The sun had turned her skin a rich, deep bronze. Her long hair was pulled back in a loose, casual style with tiny strands drifting down around her cheeks and forehead. She looked more beautiful than he'd remembered.

"Hi," she said softly and then took a deep breath. "I guess I have some explaining to do."

Jace nodded, but didn't move. He sat back and crossed his arms.

"Do you want to go for a walk?" she asked.

He did. And yet he didn't. Part of him wanted to put the car in reverse and get the hell out of there. Another part—the part that didn't listen to logic—caused him to shrug his shoulders and mumble, "I . . . guess I could. I mean, if Sophie doesn't mind waiting a bit."

He followed her on a path that led between the two houses and down a wooden staircase. They descended to a private beach, which Jace was glad to see was deserted. He was uncomfortable enough being around Cassandra, let alone having her family see them together. They walked for several minutes before Cassandra turned to him.

"Jace . . . I'm sorry. I know what I did was wrong, but please let me explain."

SHE'D REHEARSED it a hundred times and knew exactly what she wanted to say, yet words failed her. She stared at him helplessly, her mind desperately searching for the polished speech that she'd prepared.

Before she could gather her thoughts, he turned to her. "Which part do you want to explain," he asked sharply. "The part where you acted like an arrogant bitch? Or maybe you want to explain the reason you happened to be in the same grocery store as me on a Sunday morning in a part of town you obviously don't frequent. Or maybe," he continued, his frustration evident, "you'd like to explain who Tanisha is." He paused. "But you know what I'd really like to know? I'd like to know what that kiss was all about."

She deserved his wrath and took it in stride. "Jace," she began, "I judged you. I jumped to conclusions, and I'm sorry. I was a bitch... you're right. I was arrogant. I treated you like dirt simply because of where you live."

"Why did you have to lie?"

She told him everything—her Sunday morning surveillance in front of his apartment, her reasons for the interrogation in the coffee shop, and the convenient excuse to check out what she had rightly assumed was her aunt's car.

"So why did you come on to me?" he asked again. "You had the information you wanted. You could have left it at that."

Keenly knowing the reason but not how to tell him, she declined to answer right away.

"What did you learn about me, anyway?" he continued in a sarcastic tone. "Do you want me to tell you? Let's see . . . I have an outstanding parking ticket. I was a month late paying my last phone bill. Oh, and here's a biggie: when I was sixteen, some friends and I got caught smoking up. Lucky for me, the cops let us off with a warning."

"Jace," she interrupted. "What I learned is that you're a really nice guy and that I should have trusted you. My aunt does."

He looked at her curiously, but she continued. "And I kissed you because . . . well . . . because you dared me to." She wanted to say more, yet she wasn't sure how much to say or how to say it.

"Do you kiss all the low-life, would-be felons that you interrogate?" This time, something close to a smile appeared on his face.

"No," she smiled back. "Only the really cute ones."

He laughed, and she breathed easier. At least he wasn't as angry. He still hadn't forgiven her, and there may be no hope for a relationship, but she felt better having confessed.

JACE WAS TEMPTED to pinch himself to see if what was happening was real. Here he was on a private beach with a gorgeous rich chick, and she was flirting with him again. He didn't understand why, when she most likely had men falling at her feet, she would pay him any attention. Nevertheless, he couldn't deny what was taking place. Since he had nothing to lose, he decided to test it. "I keep thinking about that kiss, you know. It was really . . . great."

"I thought so, too."

He searched her face, trying to read her. She smiled and he saw sincerity in her eyes. His icy determination to remain unaffected by her charm began to melt.

She reached for his hand and murmured softly, almost apologetically, "I like you, Jace."

He wasn't sure which one of them made the first move, but suddenly their lips met, and they reenacted the kiss that had been on his mind for the past couple of weeks. The kiss deepened and she melted into his embrace, her lithe body pressing against his. His hands explored her smooth, sexy back, while hers moved up to his neck and the back of his head, drawing him closer as her tongue searched the recesses of his mouth.

The passion mounted rapidly, and Jace was increasingly aware that they needed to stop before the situation got out of control. He pulled away first, explaining, "Cassandra, I . . . like you too . . . but I'm not sure this is a good idea."

"Why?" Her sexy eyes were inviting; her crimson lips, irresistible.

Suddenly he couldn't remember the reason. Cassandra kissed him again and stood gazing into his eyes, a playful grin on her face. He grasped at one fleeting moment of clarity to inquire, "What about your parents, your aunt?"

"My parents are at a neighbor's party, and Aunt Sophia is resting."

It was enough for Jace. He might question it later, but for now, the beautiful temptress in his arms was all that he could think of. He found her mouth and tasted, again, the deliciousness it had to offer. After a few minutes, she took him by the hand and led him to a clump of bushes that offered privacy should anyone be walking on the terrace above. Cassandra knelt down on the soft sand, took off her bikini top, and looked up at him with a smile. Jace quickly joined her and no more words were needed as they let their desire have its way.

"Leverage your time . . .
Spend more time imagining and less time doing
. . . until most of what's happening is in the cool,
calm, anticipatory state. Imagine yourself into the
successes, and watch what happens."
---Abraham-Hicks

Chapter 11

She waved to Jace and her aunt as they drove away. Her father's Aston Martin pulled in the yard moments later. Realizing she had some explaining to do, Cassandra approached him as he opened the car door. "Where's Mother?" she asked casually.

"You know your mother," he shrugged. "She has to catch up on every last bit of gossip before she can leave."

Cassandra smiled knowingly. Her parents were very different, and she had become a blend of both. Her father was a quiet unassuming type who liked his hobbies and intimate family time. Her mother was a social butterfly, not complete without people around her at all times. Nevertheless, they seemed happy together. As different as they were, they complimented each other.

"Whose black car was that?"

"It was Aunt Sophia's. Jace just picked her up."

He gave his daughter a questioning look. "So it's Jace, is it? What have you learned about him?"

She wasn't sure where to begin. She'd learned plenty, including that he was an exceptional lover, but that wasn't a detail she was willing to reveal to her father. "I've met him a few times now. I was wrong, Daddy." She tucked her arm in his as they walked to the house. "He's a nice guy. Aunt Sophia really *can* read people. I should have trusted her judgement."

"A nice guy," her father repeated, a hint of suspicion clouding his voice. "Well, that's good to hear."

Cassandra decided that her new policy on honesty was serving her well, so she told her father about her little fact-finding mission.

"Whatever possessed you to do a thing like that?" he demanded, sounding alarmed. "What if your suspicions had been correct? You might have put yourself in danger."

"Daddy," she rubbed his arm with a soothing caress. "I trusted my instincts, and I think deep down I wanted to trust Aunt Sophia's opinion of him as well. He's really nice."

"Yes," he responded warily. "You mentioned that."

"Daddy . . . " She decided not to hold back. If she knew her father, he'd support her. "I think I'm falling in love with him."

"What?" He pulled his arm free and turned to look her in the eye.

"I've never met anyone like him."

Her father took a deep breath and sat down on the porch swing, inviting his daughter to join him. "I've always trusted your judgement in these matters, kitten. But I'm having trouble here," he admitted. "Tell me more about him."

Cassandra curled up beside her father and began to tell him about Jace's admirable qualities. When she finished, he let out an uneasy sigh, but remained quiet.

"How can you be sure he isn't after *your* money?" he asked after a few minutes.

"The same way I knew he wasn't after Aunt Sophia's. He isn't like that, Daddy," she implored. "Just wait till you meet him."

"And when might that be?"

"Well," she hesitated. "It's complicated. "There's one other little detail I didn't mention."

"What's that?"

"Your new housekeeper, Sarah… She's Jace's mom."

LOST IN A daydream, Jace tapped his fingers to the tune on the radio as he drove. He draped the other arm out the window, enjoying the breeze.

"You seem to be in a good mood," Sophie noted. "I assume you talked with Cassandra."

"Yeah, we talked," he affirmed, not liking the direction of the conversation. Sophie had a way of knowing things, and he hoped she didn't suspect what had gone on between them.

"She's a lovely girl," Sophie smiled.

"Yes, she is." Jace was still frowning at the old woman's words when a light went on in his mind. "You knew what she was going to say to me, didn't you?"

"More or less," she replied.

"Were you talking about Cassandra when you told me that people aren't always what they appear to be?"

"That statement can apply to everyone, Jace."

"Yeah," he persisted, "but you knew something would happen between us, didn't you?"

"It seemed like a nice idea." She smiled again.

Jace pondered the "nice idea" for a moment. "It is," he admitted reluctantly. "But it's complicated. I'm not sure it can work."

"Do you like her?"

"Of course," he shrugged. "But it takes more than that. Our lives are so different. I can't imagine what we'd have in common."

"The differences you talk about are out there." She waved her arm. "What you both have in here . . . ," she said, tapping her finger on her chest, "it's the same."

Jace didn't know what Sophie meant. *How are we the same inside?* he questioned. *And is she suggesting that the outward differences don't matter?* As pumped as he was over what had taken place between Cassandra and him, doubts were growing at an accelerating rate. Elise was in his life now, too, and Jace felt more than a little guilty that he hadn't given her a single thought all day. After all, he had a date with her that evening. He wasn't the type to date two girls at once; he had to make a decision. At the moment he had no idea what that decision would be.

"MAYBE WE SHOULD keep this to ourselves for now, kitten," her father advised. "Your mother might not be as open minded about it."

Cassandra hadn't stopped to consider what her mother might think of Jace. It would no doubt be a touchy issue. Helen Van Broden had high expectations of her children, especially when it came to marriage. Cassandra's older brother, Trevor, had given in to the expectations and married the daughter of a wealthy family in Port Hayden. The marriage had only lasted a year, and now he lived abroad enjoying his freedom. Tension still lingered between Trevor and their parents, especially their mother, and he didn't come home as often as he used to. It had been a year since Cassandra had seen him.

They'd been close—though not in age; he was six years older—and she missed her big brother. She'd always looked up to him. Over the years he'd been her best friend and confident, her advisor, her protector. Cassandra smiled, recalling the good times they'd had, especially in the summers. Endless walks on the beach, rainy nights in front of the fireplace playing board games, and his obsession with home movies. He was always filming, and she was, more often than not, the subject of his films. He adored her, too, calling her *doodlebug* as he picked her up off her feet, swinging her around.

She remembered their long talks, how she appreciated a listening ear when she was going through her formative teenage years. She remembered his advice to her, as well, when his failed marriage became known: You've got to live your own life, doodlebug. You've got to do what's right for you.

Her father had gone inside, but Cassandra remained on the porch swing, daydreaming. She closed her eyes and thought back to lovemaking with Jace on the beach. It had been beyond what she'd imagined. Her body still quivered at the memory of his touch. They hadn't talked much. Neither had they made plans to see each other. But she couldn't wait to see him again, so she decided to leave for Port Hayden, Saturday morning. *I could surprise him, and maybe we could spend the day together before I go back to the city.* She wasn't deluding herself; there were no guarantees. Making a relationship work would be tricky, but she wanted to try. She truly hoped Jace felt the same.

JACE PREFERRED not to talk about Cassandra, at least not with Sophie. He'd have to resolve that issue himself. He had something else on his mind. Having begun to formulate a plan earlier that day, he wanted to discuss it with her. "Sophie, you said I need to change my focus; I need to think like the rich. I want to learn how to do that."

"Well," Sophie began. "The subject of money is really two subjects. You can think of the presence of money or you can think of the absence of it. Most people focus on the absence. But those who focus on the presence—they're the ones who have it. Do you see how this works?"

"The rich are focused on the presence of money." Jace repeated the statement, contemplating it. It almost seemed too simple.

"Yes. They talk about money and investments. They talk about making more money. They think about their padded bank accounts and the trips they're planning to take, the renovations they're planning to make, or the parties they're planning to throw . . . "

"It's easy for them to talk about it when they already have all that."

"Maybe so," Sophie insisted. "But you can do it, too. You just have to want it badly enough, and be determined to keep focusing in a way that feels good when you think about money."

"I've been focusing on the absence of money for so long; it's no wonder I'm always broke," Jace grinned. "But I still don't understand. How do I focus on the presence of something I don't have?"

"You can visualize it, even if you don't have it yet. But start small," she advised. "If you try to envision mansions and yachts and exorbitant bank accounts from where you are now, you'll run into trouble. Instead, imagine your bank account in the black each month. Imagine having money for the activities you like to do with your friends. Imagine being able to buy something special for yourself every month."

Her advice didn't seem very exciting. Jace was eager to dive in the deep end, and what Sophie suggested was like sticking his little toe in the water.

"The process has to happen in your mind first. You need to be able to think about your situation in a way that feels good before anything can change. A coin is a good reminder." She took a quarter from her purse and held it up. "This coin represents money. One side is lack." She turned it over. "The other is abundance. You can only focus on one side at a time. Whenever you're thinking about money or talking about it, you can tell which side you're focused on by how you feel. If you're discouraged or frustrated or impatient when you think of money, you're focused on lack. If you're hopeful or excited about the idea of having money one day, then that day isn't far away."

"I guess." He couldn't argue with her, but he wanted something more substantial, something that would help him know he was moving toward his dreams.

"I know this doesn't feel like much of a plan," she responded, somehow reading his mind. "But your thoughts create your reality. They're like building materials. If you construct them carefully, if you follow a blueprint, before long you'll have a framework that will fill in with all the good you want."

Jace liked the analogy. He could picture his thoughts coming together like the frame of a house. It wasn't hard to see what the completed structure would look like, even though all the finishes weren't in place. He understood the need to follow a plan and build with care to get good results. He'd been building with shoddy materials and not paying attention to the quality of his construction. *No wonder I keep building hovels that fall down around me,* he surmised. "Okay, I want to think better thoughts. I want to be more aware of what I'm creating."

"That's good," Sophie encouraged. "The best thoughts to begin with are usually the most basic. Statements like: I'm doing okay. This situation is temporary. I don't have to figure it all out right now. I'm on a journey, and I'm doing just fine."

Jace was about to object when he realized that her statements, though general in nature, felt good. They soothed him in a way he hadn't anticipated. He was beginning to understand Sophie's reasoning.

"Those thoughts have the power to neutralize your deeply rooted negative beliefs," she explained. "From there, you can start to construct your framework. You construct it with words like *ease, comfort, harmony satisfaction, anticipation.* When you meditate on those words, you'll be reminded of times in your life when you've felt that way, and you'll feel good. The more time you spend feeling good, the stronger your framework."

"I get it. That's the leverage!" Jace responded enthusiastically, smiling as his wise old friend nodded with satisfaction. "I can do that. Thanks, Sophie." The excitement was building again. He had a solid plan. Sophie was right. He needed to take smaller steps. Any steps that would take him in the direction of his dreams were worth the effort.

CASSANDRA WOKE from her daydream as a car entered the yard. She looked up expecting to see her mother returning from the party. Instead she saw a car she didn't recognize. Leaning forward, she squinted to see through the sun's glare on the windshield and shrieked as she saw her brother's face. She quickly ran to meet him.

He picked her up in an affectionate bear hug, swinging her around like a child. "Hey, doodlebug," he smiled, "it's good to see you."

"Oh my God, Trevor," she cried. "I'm so glad you're here! Do Mother and Daddy know you're coming?"

"No," he replied tentatively. "So I'm not sure how welcome I'll be. I was hoping the guest house would be free."

"It is," Cassandra affirmed. "Aunt Sophia just left an hour ago."

"Sophia's still alive?" he laughed. "God, she must be nearly a hundred."

"Eighty-seven and still going strong."

"How's everything with you?" he inquired. "You look good. Are you still with Nick?"

"No," she responded easily. "We're done."

"Good."

"You never liked him, did you?" Cassandra slipped her arm around Trevor's waist. "I guess I should have listened to my big brother."

"I've learned a few things." He squeezed her shoulder lovingly.

"I met somebody else."

"Yeah? Who is he?"

"You wouldn't know him."

"I take it he's not from the approved breeding stock of Port Hayden," he remarked cynically.

"Oh, he's from Port Hayden," she laughed. "I wouldn't exactly call him approved breeding stock, though."

"Good for you, doodlebug," he exclaimed. "Has he faced the judge and jury yet?"

"No," she shook her head. "I've told Daddy about him, but Mother doesn't know." Cassandra's qualms increased as she considered the possible ramifications of a relationship with Jace. Given her brother's experience, and her father's apprehension earlier, she was suddenly aware that the road ahead might be a bumpy one.

"YOUR FAMILY seems to be pretty well off." Jace was curious about Sophie's relationship with them. He wondered how close she was to them or whether they assisted her financially.

"Yes," she replied. "They are."

"Do they help you out at all?" He couldn't resist asking.

"I'm not lacking for anything, Jace."

"Yeah, but wouldn't you rather live in a big house and have servants?"

"Would you?"

Jace had to think. Her question had caught him off guard. Since his mom worked as a servant, he'd come to think badly of her employers because of it—not because they treated her poorly, but because they presented themselves as better than working-class people. Lately he was starting to think differently. Cassandra's family was well off, and she didn't act that way with him. She had at first, however. "I don't know," he answered honestly.

The remainder of the trip passed without much communication. Jace's mind was full with all that had transpired that afternoon, both unspoken and spoken, on the beach with Cassandra and in the ensuing conversation with Sophie. When they arrived at their building, he carried Sophie's luggage to her door and then sought refuge in his own apartment. He opened a can of beer and went to sit in the living room to sort through his thoughts.

"Knock, knock."

Jace recognized his mom's voice and her familiar way of announcing her arrival. "Hey," he acknowledged, not moving from his chair.

She went into the kitchen, set a bag of groceries on the counter, and began to put the items in his fridge.

"What's all that?"

"The Van Broden's are away for the summer, and there's so much food in the house, plus fresh produce from the garden every day. I just have myself and Jerry, the gardener, to cook for, so there's always plenty left over. Her highness said I was welcome to use it up. I've been taking some to my neighbors. I thought you might like some, too."

"Sure, thanks." Jace had heard his mother refer to her new employer as 'her highness' before and had laughed with her over several interesting and not-so-pleasant experiences working there. This time, something about her comment left him uneasy. "Where do they go for the summer?" he asked hesitantly.

"Oh, up the coast," she replied. "They have a summer home not far from Walden Beach. Do you remember going there when Dad was alive?"

"Of course," he replied, trying to ignore the rising panic in his chest. He turned away, pretending to look at sports scores in the newspaper. His gut told him that what he suspected was true, but he needed to know for sure. "So, the Van Brodens . . . " he asked as dispassionately as he could. "Do they have kids? I've never heard you mention any."

"They have two grown children," she replied as she finished putting the groceries away. "Do you mind if I have a soda?"

"No, help yourself."

His mom joined him in the living room, sat back on the sofa with a relaxing sigh, and took a drink before she continued answering his question. "Their son lives in Europe. I've never met him. He's thirty-one or thirty-two, I think. Divorced. Apparently, that didn't go over well with her highness," Sarah laughed, "so he doesn't show his face around there much.

"I've met the daughter a couple of times," she continued. "She's a bit younger—probably closer to your age. A real pretty girl. She lives in the city and works for some fashion magazine."

Jace's mind attempted to absorb the full shock of what he'd just heard. Cassandra was a Van Broden. She was a member of one of the wealthiest families in Port Hayden. As if that wasn't enough, his mother worked for her parents.

God, this is messed, he groaned inwardly. The searing heat in the pit of his stomach was hard to ignore, yet he maintained an outward calm as he assessed the situation. *Then it's the Van Brodens that Sophie's related to as well.* He wasn't about to tell his mom that he knew Cassandra, and he doubted she'd ever discover it—especially now that he had no intention of ever seeing her again. However, he decided it would be wise to inform his mom about Sophie's connection to the family she worked for. "Did you know that Sophie is related to the Van Brodens?" he remarked, working hard at keeping his voice from cracking.

"Sophie?" she asked, frowning in disbelief. "The Sophie that lives upstairs? The Sophie you work for?"

"She just spent a week at the Van Broden's summer house. I picked her up there this afternoon."

"You can't be serious!"

"Trust me, I am." The events of the afternoon were still fresh in his mind.

"Oh my God, Jace!" Sarah looked at her son in dismay. "Sophie . . . I wonder if she's Sophia Langdon? Lady Sophia Langdon?"

"Yeah, her last name is Langdon, but why 'Lady'?"

"It's a title," his mom explained. "She was married to Lord Phillip Langdon. I heard he was directly related to the monarchy in England. Jace, I've heard all kinds of stories about that woman! Some say she went crazy after he died. Lost all her money or gave it away or something. Some say she hides it in her apartment because she doesn't trust the banks." Sarah paused. "Just be careful . . . okay, son?"

Her warning struck him as preposterous, not to mention hilarious. "You think I'm being taken advantage of by an eighty-year old crazy lady?" he laughed. "Remember, she's paying me a salary and letting me use her car. Besides . . . " He had to add a word in Sophie's defense. "She's not crazy."

"No, I don't mean that," Sarah continued, still looking concerned. "It's her connection to the Van Brodens. They're a powerful family. Just watch yourself."

Jace had no idea what she meant. *How could I possibly be in danger because of my connection to Sophie or because of her connection to the Van Brodens? If I'm in any danger at all,* he acknowledged painfully, *it's my lack of resistance when it comes to Cassandra's charm.*

Chapter 12

The dog barking brought her father outside to see what the commotion was about. Cassandra watched her father's face as he noticed Trevor on the veranda. She saw pleasure mixed with pain and something else she couldn't decipher.

Regardless of what he felt, Richard Van Broden smiled and opened his arms without hesitation. "Welcome home, son."

"Thanks, Dad," Trevor replied. "I wasn't sure if I'd be welcome or not."

"The past is past," Richard offered amicably. "Let's put it behind us and move on. It's good to have you back."

"Does Mother feel the same?"

Before he could answer, a car pulled in the yard, and Helen Van Broden emerged from the passenger seat. She said goodbye to her friend and stood waving before turning to notice her family on the veranda.

"Trevor." She smiled outwardly, but her eyes revealed her true feelings. Her voice was strained as she continued. "What a surprise. We weren't expecting you."

As Trevor acknowledged his mother's words, Cassandra could feel his discomfort. She didn't understand what had gone on between mother and son that could cause such lasting discord. She hoped to be able to talk to her brother while he was there, hoped to understand and maybe help—be a mediator, if possible, to heal the rift.

"I wish you'd given us some warning, dear," Helen said, her reproach lightly coated with sweetness. "The guest house isn't made up, and the maid is off today. I suppose you could stay in the main house. . . ."

"Look," Trevor replied tersely. "I don't want to inconvenience you. I can go to the motel in town. I'm not staying long, anyway."

"Don't be silly," Cassandra interrupted. "I'll make up the bed in the guest house." She gave Trevor a pleading look. "Please stay. I want to catch up. It's been so long." Glancing around, she saw her father nod, yet the reservation on his face was hard to miss.

Her mother, yielding to the consensus, addressed Cassandra. "Very well, then. The linens are in the storage room beside the laundry. I'll let Mrs. Harper know we'll be having a guest for dinner." She turned without looking at Trevor and walked into the house.

Cassandra knew perfectly well where the linens were kept. She'd played in the basement as a child and remembered with fondness the smell of freshly washed laundry. She and her friends had often taken sheets or blankets from the storage room to facilitate their imaginative adventures. Smiling at her brother, she left to get the needed items.

When she arrived at the guesthouse she found Trevor standing in the middle of the room, suitcase in hand. He set down the luggage as she walked in.

"I'm not sure this is a good idea, doodlebug."

She went over, put her hand on his arm, and looked up at him. He was a handsome man, tall and good looking, yet he had a softness about him. He was sensitive and caring, and that made Cassandra love him all the more. Why he was such a disappointment to their mother, she couldn't understand. "What's it all about, Trev?" she implored. "Why the tension between you and Mother after all this time?"

He let out a deep breath and took her hands in his. "Cass, there's something you should know."

"What is it?" Her heart began to pound at the seriousness of his tone.

"I'm gay," he stated, searching her eyes.

"Oh." Her barely audible response contained no shock or dismay. The revelation caused everything to make sense, and she realized that at some level she'd known all along. "And Mother knows." It was a statement rather than a question.

"Yeah," he nodded. "About a year and a half ago, one of her cronies saw me and Brad, my partner at the time, in a little bistro in Dijon. The next time I came home, Mother confronted me. I was tired of living a lie, so I didn't deny it. She freaked out and threatened to disinherit me. Then she tried to bribe me to change my lifestyle. When that didn't work, she made me promise to keep it a secret so that I wouldn't tarnish our family name."

"Oh, Trevor." Cassandra could feel his pain. She wrapped her arms around him. "I'm so sorry."

"Hey," he smiled, caressing her hair lovingly. "It's okay. I'm happy. I've been in a great relationship for almost a year now. And I've been learning some amazing stuff that's helped me to see life differently."

"Really?" She looked at him. "What kind of stuff?"

"I was searching for meaning in life," he began. "I went through a few rough years. Even thought about packing it in, if you know what I mean."

Cassandra gasped. Her eyes filled with tears.

Before she could speak, he put his finger on her lips. "Shhh," he soothed. "That's in the past. I don't dwell there. I'd rather focus on what is working and how wonderful my life is now."

She smiled through her tears. "I'd like to hear about that."

WHEN HIS MOM left, Jace remained glued to his chair as he struggled to absorb what he'd learned about Cassandra. *She's a Van Broden. There's no way*

I could ever go out with her. He hadn't decided to, but an hour earlier he'd been entertaining the idea. *It would never work. Besides, I'm probably just the flavor of the month.*

What's wrong with that? he argued, vividly recalling their escapade on the beach earlier. *What's wrong with taking what she has to offer? So what if there's no future in it.* Something about the reasoning left him feeling empty. He wanted more than that, but he knew he couldn't have it with Cassandra.

Sophie had advised him to pay attention to how his thoughts made him feel. It wasn't hard to do. The revelation had left him discouraged. He was disillusioned and confused.

What's to be confused about? he challenged. *I know what I have to do. I have to stop thinking about her. And seeing her . . . that's out of the question.* He lacked the will power to resist her enchanting ways.

Continuing to apply Sophie's advice, Jace reached for some general thoughts to diffuse the hotbed of emotion. *I know this seems messed, but I don't have to figure it out right now.* He was surprised at the tangible relief the simple statement brought him. Repeating it several times, he honed in on the relief each time, liking the control that deliberate thinking afforded him. In his improved emotional state, he revisited the plan he'd formulated earlier—the plan to change his thinking, to create a framework that would allow him to realize his financial dreams. As he deliberately focused on what he and Sophie had talked about, his clarity returned and with it a sense of hope. That, he realized, felt good, so he poured himself into it with determination.

CASSANDRA LISTENED as Trevor told her about his new relationship and the career he was pursuing. He made reference again to what he'd been learning.

"Tell me more about that," she encouraged. "I'd like to know what you believe."

"Do you feel like walking?"

It was late afternoon, and a refreshing breeze blew off the Atlantic. The two of them headed down to the beach. The tide was out, allowing them to walk on the ocean floor along the craggy cliffs bordering the properties above.

"I've been studying the Tao," Trevor began.

"I've heard of that." Cassandra was thrilled with the direction of the conversation. "What is it, exactly?"

"That gets tricky," he laughed. "The Tao is fundamentally indefinable. But let me try. It's a metaphysical concept. It's everything that is, yet it existed before anything else. In it, nothing exists except by comparison. For example, there's no such thing as *high* unless it's being compared to *low*; no *small* unless compared to *large*.

"Tao is often referred to as 'the way.' It's an unseen force, and yet it's characterized by its lack of force. It says, 'The softest thing in the world overcomes the hardest.'

"Basically, that means slight, simple, continuous movements accomplish the greatest results. By letting go and trusting that movement, we can see miracles happen in our lives."

"That's beautiful," Cassandra exclaimed. "Tell me more."

"The teaching stresses non-action—living in harmony with the Universe and letting circumstances develop naturally. It teaches how to overcome by yielding, to be full by emptying ourselves, and to gain by wanting little. It says that all we need will come to us when we find harmony and balance with All That Is."

"Wow." Cassandra was amazed at how the teaching compared to what Sophia had been telling her. "I can't believe you know all this. I've been learning stuff, too, and it sounds similar." She highlighted the first two principles that Sophia had given her. "And this past week she talked about a Source of wellbeing. She compared it to a stream that's always flowing to us. It's good and positive and loving, and it contains all that we could ever want. We have the choice to let it in or to resist it. She said that most people, by their very thoughts, are resisting the good that they desire.

"I had doubts at first," Cassandra admitted, "about the things she was telling me. So I did some research on my own. I found endless references to it on the internet. It's called the Law of Attraction. People are really into this kind of teaching."

"People used to say Sophia Langdon was crazy." Trevor smiled and shook his head. "Turns out she's a wise old owl after all. I wouldn't mind seeing her while I'm here."

"I'm sure she'd like that," Cassandra replied. "I'm going back next weekend. Why don't you come with me? We could visit her together."

"Maybe," he laughed. "If I can last a week here."

Cassandra tucked her arm in Trevor's to show support. "I'm here for you, Trev."

"Thanks, doodlebug, I appreciate that."

They continued walking and sharing what they'd been learning. Cassandra was fascinated by her brother's spiritual understanding. Trevor had heard of the term *Law of Attraction* and wanted to hear more of what Cassandra had to say.

"Does your boyfriend believe this stuff, too?" he asked as they turned to walk back.

"He's not exactly my boyfriend." She had to laugh at the confused look Trevor gave her. "We're not dating—at least not yet. It's complicated."

Cassandra spent the next few minutes telling her brother how she and Jace had met. She included the fact that he was Sophia's neighbor and that his mom worked for their parents.

"And you really like this guy?" Trevor probed. Cassandra didn't hear judgement in his voice, simply brotherly concern.

"Yeah," she nodded. "I do."

"I'm assuming he feels the same."

Cassandra couldn't answer. She had no idea how Jace felt about her. Her brother's words caused her to question what existed between them, and doubt began to creep in. She longed to talk to Jace, to discuss the status of their relationship, among other things. There was so much they didn't know about each other. She truly hoped they could spend time together on the weekend.

"ELISE!" THE THOUGHT was like a blow to the side of the head. Jace had a date with her in an hour, and he'd forgotten all about it. Suddenly he wasn't sure he wanted to go. Being with Cassandra earlier and then dealing with the realization that he could never see her again had left him in a strange place. It was like breaking up with someone and wanting downtime before seeing someone new.

But that's not the case here, he argued. *I haven't actually broken up with Cassandra, because we're not dating. And I'm already going out with Elise. God!* He groaned at how screwed up the situation had become. *I've had sex with them both today!*

He wasn't proud of his actions. He certainly hadn't planned it that way. He wasn't even sure how it had happened with Cassandra. One minute they were walking on the beach—he remembered feeling angry and wanting answers—and the next, they were making out.

Jace longed to understand why she had such a spell over him. *What is it about the woman that makes me lose all common sense?* Away from her, he could think rationally and knew what he needed to do. He could feel the resolve, yet it left him with a decision. Whether he ever saw Cassandra again or not, he needed to decide whether he wanted to continue seeing Elise.

He weighed the pros and cons. *She's pretty and fun to be with. We have things in common. She's mature and knows what she wants in life. We're in pretty much the same social class.* He had no trouble listing her positive assets, yet the negative left him stumped. He couldn't think of anything specific. Nevertheless, something was amiss.

He sat for a moment before it dawned on him. *The only thing wrong with her,* Jace sighed, *is that she's not Cassandra.*

CASSANDRA SILENTLY observed her family's interactions as the week unfolded. Her mother was distant and uncommunicative, and Trevor was clearly ill at ease. Her father was quieter than usual, as well, and she could see signs of stress showing on his face. She found him alone in the den one afternoon and went to sit next to him.

"It's been an interesting week, hasn't it?" he remarked ruefully.

She was considering how to respond when he added, "I'm glad that you and Trevor are close."

"Me, too," she replied. "It's so good to see him again."

"Your mother is having a hard time."

"Mmm," Cassandra nodded. "The tension around here is pretty thick." She laid her hand on his arm. "Daddy, what about you? How are you doing with all this?"

"I'm caught in the middle, kitten."

"How do you feel, though?" she persisted.

"You're starting to sound like your old aunt," he laughed softly.

"Maybe that's a good thing."

"It *is* a good thing," he granted. "Don't get me wrong; we could all learn from her. It's just...I'm feeling like an old dog these days. I don't know if I can change my ways of thinking that easily. I want to, but..."

Cassandra wasn't sure whether he was referring to his views on homosexuality or his willingness to embrace Sophia's unconventional beliefs. Though she wanted to discuss Trevor's situation, she had to allow that it might be the latter. "Daddy, you're not old," she comforted. "Besides, much of what Aunt Sophia believes is just common sense."

"It's not that, kitten," he replied. "It's changing my views about life and the ways of society—what's deemed acceptable and what isn't. When you've been taught to think a certain way for nearly sixty years, it's not easy to change direction. And even if I could..." he shrugged helplessly. "Your mother...she's not likely to change her thinking."

"So what then?" Cassandra started to get frustrated. "If no one is willing to change their thinking, where does that leave Trevor?" She couldn't say it aloud, but her thoughts naturally led to her own situation. *Where would that leave me, if I chose to marry someone like Jace?*

Her father sighed heavily, and Cassandra noticed for the first time that he looked older than his years. His eyes were troubled, reflecting the pain caused by issues he wrestled with. She regretted her outburst. "Daddy, I'm sorry. I can see how hard this is on you."

"I love my son..." His voice was choked as he turned away. "But I'm having trouble understanding, and certainly relating to, the lifestyle he's chosen."

Cassandra reached for his hand and held it while she waited for him to continue.

"It's being caught in the middle that's the hardest, though. If I were to speak up..." He had to stop again. "If I were to show my support for the choices Trevor is making, your mother would think I was opposing her. And yet my silence is sending a message, too. I'm sure Trevor takes it to mean that I'm siding with your mother. He's been here five days, and we've hardly said a dozen words to each other." He shook his head. "I feel like I can't win, kitten."

Cassandra felt his pain and wanted more than anything to help. "You know, maybe what Aunt Sophia believes could apply here," she offered. "She says that our thoughts create our reality, that what we focus on expands to become what we experience in our lives."

"I've heard her say something similar, but how do you think it applies in this situation?"

She was glad her father was willing to listen. Sophia's advice had come to her for a reason, and maybe that reason was to share it with others who needed it. Her newfound wisdom could help her family; Cassandra was convinced of it, and she was eager to put it to the test. It might be what they all needed.

SOPHIE SEEMED especially cheerful as Jace drove her to the market. He had to admire her spunk. She was well into her eighties and showed no signs of slowing down. Her mind was relatively sound, and she was happy. He felt honored to know her, to have the opportunity to learn from her. She brought out the best in him, and he decided to tell her how he felt. "I really appreciate all that you've been telling me, you know."

"I know," she nodded. "I can see the change in you."

"Really?" Jace knew he felt different but didn't realize others could see the change. "In what way?"

"You're more confident. You know more clearly what you want, and you know what steps to take to get there. Remember what was missing in your life when we first talked?"

So much was missing in his life then, and for the most part much of it still was. He had to ask what she was referring to.

"Control," she replied. "You wanted to feel like you were in control."

"You're right," he exclaimed. "I'd forgotten about that."

"And don't you feel like you have more control over aspects of your life now than you did back then?"

"Yeah, I do," he smiled.

"Feels good, doesn't it?" She sounded pleased, and her expression oozed with satisfaction. "A good feeling always means you're heading in the right direction."

Jace *was* heading in the right direction; he could feel it. Not much had changed in respect to his financial situation, yet he was on the right path. If he kept going he'd make it. "Sophie," he grinned, "what would I do without you?"

"You'll do fine, dear." She patted his arm. "You needed someone to remind you of what you'd forgotten, that's all. You'll be just fine."

He frowned at her response. It sounded as though she wasn't planning to be around much longer, and it left him with a strange sensation in the pit of his stomach. When he glanced at her again, her eyes were closed, and she looked content. She nodded as if agreeing with her own thoughts and then murmured, "She's found what she's looking for, too."

She? Jace didn't know who Sophie was talking about. She was acting peculiar again, but he let it go, smiling as he thought about the gossip that circulated about this once-wealthy socialite. She wasn't crazy; he knew that for a fact. She was his friend, and given his fondness for her, it wasn't hard to overlook her occasional odd behavior.

Chapter 13

"What if we could imagine Mother being more open minded about this?" Cassandra began to express the thoughts that were bubbling up within her. "What if we could imagine the four of us together, laughing and talking? Everyone getting along and looking for the best in one another, accepting one another?

"Daddy," she continued excitedly, "if we could focus on that instead of what's wrong, maybe the situation could change."

Her father caressed her cheek. "I believe it could, kitten. It's a pretty big *if*, though."

"Aunt Sophia talks about focus." Cassandra ignored her father's last comment. "She says it's like the hub of a wheel. Our thoughts, our feelings, even our experiences are dependent on our focus. I think I get it now!" The exhilaration increased as the insight unfolded in her mind. "We get to choose. We don't have to let whatever's in front of us dominate our thoughts or determine how we feel. We don't have to let society's views shape our beliefs. You know..." She paused as another idea called for her attention. "I think that's why Aunt Sophia is happy. I think that may be the key to what she's discovered, the secret to happiness!"

Trevor walked by the doorway to the study and stopped to give his sister a puzzled grin. "You've found the secret to happiness?"

"I think so," she laughed.

As Trevor walked into what was deemed his father's private space, Cassandra could see how unnerving it was for him. She looked at her father and saw the lines in his jaw tighten. *How can I not see this in a negative way?* She longed for her aunt's wisdom.

"Trevor . . . " She decided to draw him into the conversation. "You and I have talked about this a little. Do you think it's possible to control your focus, thereby controlling your experience?"

"I think that's part of it," he replied, relaxing slightly. "I believe it's beneficial to change our thoughts—to look at any situation in a more positive way—but the real power comes when we align our thoughts with the Universe and trust that everything will work out for the best."

"Aren't they the same, though?" she argued. "If we align our thoughts with the Universe, it makes sense they'd be positive, uplifting thoughts. And if we're doing it deliberately, then we *are* controlling our focus."

"I'll give you that, doodlebug," he smiled, enjoying the interaction. "But one is active and one is passive. One is working at changing our thoughts in order to change the situation; the other is allowing things to happen and trusting they'll be in our best interest."

"Okay, I can feel the difference," Cassandra nodded. "I'm just trying to understand what exactly Aunt Sophia has found. It sure doesn't seem like she works at it. She believes that everything will turn out fine and it does."

"So it's our belief system, then," Richard interjected. "Our belief system determines our experience."

"I'm sure of it," Cassandra stressed. "And we have the power to change that. Whether we're aligning with the Universe in an attitude of trust or deliberately focusing in a more positive manner, we have to come to a state of believing that all can be well before anything can change."

"I think you're right." Both men said the words in unison, and Cassandra glanced from one to the other in surprise. No one spoke.

"Maybe I'm not too old to change," Richard admitted.

Cassandra watched her father. He was gazing at Trevor with love in his eyes and an air of determination on his face.

"I'm proud of you kids." He looked at them and stressed, "Both of you. I know things haven't been very pleasant around here, but there's got to be a way for that to change. Cassandra's got the right idea, wanting us to be a real family again. I want you to know that I love you both, and I'm going to do whatever I can to make that change possible."

Cassandra brushed away the tears streaming down her cheeks. She was bursting with pride for her father, knowing how difficult the speech had been for him. Trevor's eyes were misty as well. She could feel her brother's joy. As she thought about the change her father spoke of, an image came to mind. She saw her family together, laughing as they had in the past. Suddenly she had an idea. "Daddy, do we still have those old home movies?"

"Sure, kitten," he replied. "I believe they're in the basement somewhere. Why?"

"We used to watch them every summer. It might be fun to dig them out and watch them as a family tonight."

JACE STOPPED by Sophie's, Saturday morning, to see whether she needed to go out.

"The harbor festival is on this weekend," she informed him. "I'd like to go down to the waterfront."

"I made an appointment to get your car serviced this morning. Why don't I drop you off first? They said it should take less than an hour. I can pick you up when it's done."

"That sounds fine, Jace."

He couldn't help but notice that she was dressed up more than usual. She had on a pale pink skirt with delicate white flowers all over the pleated fabric, and a white blouse with a lace collar. Her hat was pale pink as well, and the fabric on the band matched her skirt. What really caught his attention was her jewelry. She had on a glittering pendant necklace and matching earrings. They looked old. She had several rings on her fingers as well. He questioned whether the jewels were real. *I doubt it,* he surmised. *They'd be worth a fortune if they were. She probably got rid of the real stuff long ago.*

"You look nice this morning, Sophie," he grinned as he held the car door for her.

"I never wear these anymore." She held out her hands and studied the rings. "I'd forgotten I had some of them."

She reminded Jace of a child playing dress-up. On such a petite woman who was always modestly dressed, the jewels stood out and looked somewhat garish when he was used to seeing her unadorned in that way. He decided it was just another way of trying to recapture her youth or pay tribute to what once was—a sincere act that made her even more adorable.

As they arrived at the festivities, they could hear a band playing. People were beginning to gather on the street corners. "Hey, a parade!" Jace almost wished he could stay. Something about a parade brought out the kid in him. Instead, he pulled into a loading zone and got out to open the door for Sophie.

"Thank you, Jace."

As she smiled up at him, he noticed how radiant she looked. He was tempted to take her picture with his cell phone, but he didn't want to embarrass her. "I'll be back in about an hour," he reminded her. "Do you want to meet here?"

"Yes, that will be fine."

The dealership was on the outskirts of town in a new auto mall that had been built the year before. Jace parked the car, left the keys with the service technician, and went into the main building. With nothing to do but wait, he got himself a coffee and picked up the morning paper.

When he'd finished his coffee and looked over the entire newspaper, he got up and wandered around the new vehicle showroom. He sat in the driver's seat of a shiny new Accord, this one metallic gray, and imagined that he was there to buy it. He pictured himself talking to the salesperson, bartering for the best deal, and even getting some extras thrown in. They shook hands after signing the paperwork, and he saw himself pulling away in the new car. Though the feeling was conjured, pride of ownership swelled within him. He'd begun to practice similar scenarios, and being in the showroom added detail to his visualizations. It gave him a real rush.

He glanced at his watch and realized he'd been at the dealership forty-five minutes. The car would likely be done. It would be tight, but if he left right away, he could get back within the hour to pick up Sophie.

"Sorry," the girl at the desk shrugged, "they're really busy back there. One of the guys is sick today. They just started on your car; it'll be twenty minutes or so."

Jace frowned. He hated making Sophie wait. *I wish she had a cell phone.* He'd suggested it on more than one occasion, but she'd laughed at the idea, insisting it was unnecessary.

The time dragged as Jace checked his watch every few minutes. He wished he had arranged to meet Sophie at one of the venues rather than on a street corner. The idea of her waiting in the hot sun distressed him. He got up to check again. "I've been here over an hour, and now I'm late for a meeting," he explained politely, hoping they might be willing to rush if they saw him as a busy young professional. "Can you check to see if my car is ready?"

"It's almost done, sir," the young girl replied. "I'll get the paperwork for you." She typed something into her computer. "How would you like to pay for that today?"

"Pay?" Jace felt the familiar panic that often accompanied an unexpected bill or expense. "I thought it was covered under warranty."

"Let me check." After typing some more, she apologized. "You're right; it's covered. I'll just need your signature." She handed him the paperwork.

After ten minutes he was on the road, but it was nearly forty minutes past the time he'd agreed to pick Sophie up, and he felt really bad. With nothing to do but get there as quickly as the speed limit would allow, he tried to downplay the guilt he was feeling. *Hopefully she got tired of waiting and went to find shade or a place to sit down. I'm sure she won't be upset. She knows I can go and look for her.*

He'd become accustomed to analyzing his feelings, so he questioned the panic that had arisen when asked to pay for the work done on Sophie's car. *What was that all about? Why the panic? It wasn't a big deal. I have room on my credit card, and Sophie would have reimbursed me right away.* Having believed he'd made progress in that area, Jace felt discouragement creep in. *Obviously I've still got some work to do.*

What he longed for was solid evidence to show that his change in thinking was paying off. *How long does this process take?* he wondered. *How long will it be until I see proof?* He decided to ask Sophie about it when he picked her up. He decided, too, that he'd offer to take her somewhere for lunch to make up for being late; it was the least he could do.

When Jace arrived at the spot he'd dropped her off, Sophie was nowhere in sight. He was relieved, hoping it meant she'd gone back to one of the venues. He found a place to park and walked toward the tents set up near the waterfront. After checking several, he found her sitting inside the opening of a security tent. He immediately offered an apology.

"It's all right, Jace." She responded in her familiar, sweet voice, but her face looked pale. "These things happen. I'm fine."

"But I feel bad for making you wait," he insisted. "Can I take you out for lunch or something?"

"Oh, that would be lovely, Jace," she said. "Maybe another time, though. I'm feeling a little tired now. I'd like to go home and have a rest."

"Okay." He could see how tired she was and didn't try to convince her otherwise. The advice he sought would have to wait as well. As he drove her home, she lay back against the headrest, her eyes closed. By the time they arrived at the apartment her color had returned, and she looked a little better. He walked her to her door. "Are you sure you're all right?" he asked. "I could pick you up some lunch, or make you something. Have you eaten?"

"Jace." She put her hand on his arm and gripped it firmly. "I want you to stop worrying. I'm fine. I had a corn dog down at the fair." She shook her head as a far-off look appeared in her eyes. "I haven't had one of those in years. Phillip used to say that I'd live to be a hundred if I'd just stop eating those wretched things." She laughed at the memory, then turned to go into her apartment.

Jace knew he should leave so that she could rest, but he couldn't resist the impulse. "Just a minute." He pulled his cell phone from his pocket. "Don't move; I want a picture of you."

She smiled lovingly at him, not at all daunted by his impulsiveness.

As he turned to leave, she said his name. "You're doing fine. Don't take stock too soon. Just keep focusing on what you want. You'll know you're on the right track by how you feel. Remember, every coin has two sides."

Deciding to acknowledge rather than ignore the odd timing of her advice, he gave her a kiss on the cheek and a promise. "I will, Sophie. Thanks."

Jace had plans with Chad that afternoon, but his gut told him he should stay home. He was concerned about Sophie. She'd probably be all right after a rest, but he wanted to be close by if she did need anything.

IT WAS EASY to persuade Trevor to travel back to Port Hayden with her. He was returning to Europe in a couple of days, and Cassandra wanted to spend as much time with him as she could. She was truly glad he'd made the effort to visit. Not much had changed in their mother's attitude or behavior. However, Cassandra had noticed Trevor and their father sitting down together on several occasions. She was thrilled to see that a change in focus was already producing positive results. "I saw you and Daddy talking," she acknowledged. "That's progress."

"Yeah," he laughed. "It was awkward, but he took the initiative, and I appreciated that. He can't seem to bring himself to ask about my relationship with Maurice, though. I decided not to make him more uncomfortable by offering details."

"That's probably best. This is going to take some time, Trev," Cassandra advised. "What else did you talk about?"

"I told him about the screenplay Maurice wrote, told him I'm planning to produce it. He offered to put up the financing."

"Really? That's wonderful."

"I may have to use a false name, though," he added.

"Did Daddy say that?"

"No, not at all. It's just . . . you know what Mother said about not bringing shame to the family."

"Trevor, I'd be proud to see your name on a film! And I'd tell all my friends about it, too."

"It's just that the subject matter is . . . well . . . it portrays a gay man. It's really well written, though, doodlebug. Not like recent films and TV shows that stereotype homosexuals. This depicts the main character as human with struggles and issues that anybody could relate to."

"I can't wait to see it."

"You don't know how much that means to me . . . to hear you say that, to feel your support."

"I know," she smiled.

"And what you're learning," he remarked, turning the attention away from himself. "The stuff Sophia's teaching you. I think that's terrific. This could be bigger than you realize."

The word *bigger* caused the hairs on Cassandra's neck to do their dance. "What do you mean?"

"The teaching is clear, and the way you understand it and apply it . . . maybe you could write a book or teach it or something."

She told Trevor about her undeniable sense that there was something bigger in store for her. "That could be part of it," she concurred. "I don't know . . . it feels like there's more. I'm curious, but I guess I'll have to let it unfold naturally. Aunt Sophia hasn't finished giving me all the principles. She mentioned five, but I've only gotten three. I'm hoping that once I have them all, I'll know what I'm supposed to do with them."

"You will, doodlebug. Don't worry."

The time went by quickly, and they arrived in Port Hayden by lunchtime. After a meal at their favorite restaurant, they stopped by the Town House to drop off their luggage before heading to their aunt's place.

"Let's take the Rolls," Trevor suggested playfully. "I'll be your chauffeur."

Cassandra felt some reluctance when she realized her brother was serious. She hoped to see Jace and felt that arriving in that manner would not only emphasize the difference in their situations, the stately car might remind him of their first two unpleasant encounters. She understood the power of a first impression and would give anything if she could erase those altogether. "I guess," she agreed reluctantly. He'd already opened the overhead door of the garage, and was admiring the vintage car. She didn't want to dampen his enthusiasm.

As Jace came to mind, her tension began to grow. She wished they'd at least made tentative plans to see each other again. Simply showing up at his door could be awkward. She acknowledged her qualms as they drove through town. "I can't believe how nervous I am. It's even worse than last weekend," she laughed uneasily. "And then I had good reason to believe he hated me."

"I guess that means there's more at stake now."

"Yeah... I guess." Cassandra hadn't allowed herself to dwell on it, but her brother was right. *There is a lot more at stake. Last weekend, I would have been disappointed if he'd walked away and never wanted to see me again, but now...* She decided not to go there. She was certain that once they saw each other again and had a chance to talk, everything would be okay. *It'll work out,* she breathed, *somehow.*

They arrived at the apartment building and parked behind the black Honda. "He's here," she told Trevor, not sure whether it was good news or bad as her anxiety increased dramatically. Entering the building, she turned to him. "This is killing me. Do you mind if I stop by Jace's before I go up to Aunt Sophia's? I'm hoping we can make a date for later."

"No problem, doodlebug." He gave her shoulder a squeeze. "I'll go and surprise the old girl, see if she remembers me."

As Trevor went up the stairs, Cassandra stood looking at Jace's door. She took a deep breath and knocked.

"Come in."

It sounded as if he were expecting someone. She hesitated, quite sure that someone wasn't her. Opening the door slowly, she called out his name. It was a few long seconds before he appeared from the kitchen. "Trevor and I..." She paused, wanting to make herself perfectly clear. "My brother, Trevor, and I came by to see Aunt Sophia. I saw your car... the Honda, I mean, and..."

JACE STARED AT the familiar face as Cassandra offered an awkward explanation for being in his apartment. He felt the overwhelming urge to run, just as he did when he first saw her at the beach. With her standing in his doorway, that wasn't possible, yet he had to act quickly. If he kept staring at her, he'd be in danger of losing all power of reason. He steeled himself to say what needed to be said. "Cassandra, I . . . " Before he could continue, a man appeared behind her.

"Hi." The man reached past Cassandra and offered his hand. "I'm Trevor. You must be Jace."

Jace nodded mechanically and shook his hand.

Trevor addressed his sister. "There's no answer at Sophia's. She must be out."

"She's home," Jace countered, suddenly regaining his senses. "I dropped her off about an hour and a half ago. She's probably sleeping. She was pretty tired after going to the Harbor Fair this morning."

Cassandra looked at Jace and then her brother. "Maybe we should come back later."

"Why don't I try phoning her?" Jace replied, recalling how pale she'd looked when he'd picked her up. He dialed her number, and they all stood in silence as it rang repeatedly. "Something's wrong," he declared, aware of the panic rising in his chest. "I think we should check on her."

"Do you have a key?" Cassandra asked, looking concerned for her aunt.

"Yeah." He grabbed it off the table by the door and moved past Cassandra and her brother without another word. He was up the stairs in several long strides, stopping to give a couple of loud knocks before he unlocked the door. He called her name as he entered the apartment with Cassandra and Trevor close behind him. There was no sign of her, so Jace went to the bedroom. The door was slightly ajar and again he knocked, hoping to hear a reply. When there was no response, he entered the room and stopped short. "Sophie?" She was lying on her bed, eyes closed.

"Aunt Sophia?" Cassandra ran to her and quickly diagnosed her condition. "Call an ambulance!" she instructed.

Trevor made the call on his cell phone, and the three of them gathered around Sophia's bed, staring helplessly. "She has a pulse, but it's weak," Cassandra stated, her voice trembling.

"I'll wait outside for the paramedics," Trevor offered.

Jace took in the scene before him. The pale little woman lay motionless, barely alive. He felt sick. He'd suspected something was wrong earlier, and he hadn't listened to his instincts. "I shouldn't have left her," he declared softly, shaking his head.

Cassandra glanced at him, but said nothing. She was rubbing Sophia's arm, repeating her name, trying to get her to respond.

"She was really tired when we got back. I offered to get her something to eat, but she insisted she was okay. She had to wait on me . . . at the fair this morning," he explained clumsily. "I was getting the car serviced, and it took longer than I expected. I had no way of getting in touch with her."

"Jace, don't blame yourself," Cassandra admonished softly, still holding her aunt's hand and rubbing her arm. "You couldn't have known."

"I did; I felt it," he acknowledged bitterly. "I felt it in my gut, and I didn't listen."

Cassandra looked up at him again. This time, with compassion in her eyes. She was about to say something when the paramedics burst through the door. She stepped back to where Jace was standing, and the two looked at each other silently.

"She's strong," Cassandra encouraged. "She'll be all right." The confident-sounding words couldn't hide the fear in her voice.

Jace wanted to believe it, but he was struggling. *I'm so sorry, Sophie,* he breathed as he watched them carry her from the room.

Chapter 14

Cassandra stayed by her aunt's side in the ambulance, while Jace and Trevor both drove to the hospital. She didn't let go of the frail woman's hand, wanting her to know she wasn't alone. A troubled look at the paramedic conveyed the question on her mind.

"She's stable," he informed her, "but extremely weak. The oxygen is helping, but the sooner we can get her to the hospital, the better."

A slight squeeze of her hand made Cassandra turn back to her aunt. The woman's eyes were open, and she looked as though she wanted to speak. The attendant removed the mask from her face. "Cassandra," she smiled weakly. "How lovely to see you."

"Aunt Sophia," Cassandra advised gently, "don't try to talk. You're on the way to the hospital, but you're going to be all right. We can visit later . . . once you're feeling stronger."

"No, dear," she insisted, her voice so low that Cassandra had to put her ear close to Sophia's face. "I have some things I want to tell you."

"Yes, Aunt Sophia, I know," she assured her. "We'll have plenty of time for that."

"You'll know what's right for you by how you feel," Sophia continued, straining to lift her head. "You have an internal guidance system. We all do. Keep following what feels good, and don't give up." She lay back and closed her eyes, exhausted by the effort.

"Don't you give up either, Aunt Sophia," Cassandra implored, willing her to be all right.

The old woman opened her eyes again. This time the struggle was gone, and she had such a look of joy and contentment on her face that Cassandra could only stare at her in wonder. All at once she realized what was happening. "Don't go," she cried. "Please don't go."

"I'll always be with you, dear," Sophia smiled. "We'll have some tea."

With that, she closed her eyes and took her last breath. Sophia was gone. Hot tears streaked Cassandra's face as she continued to hold her aunt's hand.

AS JACE ARRIVED at the hospital, he watched for Cassandra and Trevor. When he didn't see them, he went to the front desk to inquire about Sophie. A nurse directed him to the emergency waiting room and told him to have a seat. He wasn't family, so he couldn't be with her, but he longed to know how she was. With a heavy heart, he attempted to pray. It was a pathetic effort, being his first time. He hadn't even prayed when his own father died. Never before had he felt so responsible for someone's life, and he couldn't stop beating himself up for not listening to his gut.

"Not everything is as it seems, Jace."

He heard Sophie's voice in his head as clearly as if she were with him, and in his distraught state he answered her. *But if I hadn't left you alone . . .*

"I'll be all right. Don't you worry; I'm just fine."

Though the conversation wasn't real, it comforted him. He sat back, closed his eyes, and began to imagine her well. He pictured her in her little kitchen, humming, putting on a pot of tea. But when he tried to see her smiling face, the image of her lying pale and unconscious dominated his mind. Then he had an idea. Pulling his cell phone from his pocket, he found the picture he'd taken of her earlier. She was smiling. He had perfectly captured the sweet old woman he'd come to know. It was exactly how he wanted to remember her, and suddenly he was glad to have that keepsake. Just in case . . .

He looked up to see Cassandra walking toward him. She was crying, and he didn't have to ask why. A chill rifled through his body as the truth hit him. Sophie had died. Cassandra walked straight into his arms, and he held her tightly, needing as much as offering comfort. They stood silently for several minutes.

When Trevor joined them, they both turned to him, still holding each other.

"I called Mother and Dad; they're on their way," he informed them solemnly.

Jace remembered all too well the feeling that followed his father's passing—that helpless, 'what do we do now' feeling. After waiting, worrying, and praying, there was nothing to do but go home. The thought left him deflated. Going back to the apartment building, knowing he'd never see Sophie again, was too weird at the moment. He considered going for a drive, but that too was a distressing thought since the car belonged to her. Instead, he addressed Cassandra and Trevor. "Do you guys want to go for a drink or something?" He didn't feel like being alone, and they were the only ones that could relate to the sorrow he was experiencing.

"Thanks, anyway, but I'm going back to the Town House." Trevor addressed Cassandra. "Why don't you and Jace go? I'll see you at home later."

He kissed her cheek and left them alone, not waiting for a response from his sister.

"Are you okay?" Jace asked.

"I've never seen anyone die before." Her eyes filled with tears again.

Jace kept his arm around Cassandra as they walked to the car. She seemed fragile, and the intimacy helped soothe his sadness as well. Before he opened the door for her, he took her in his arms again. He wasn't thinking, merely responding, doing what felt right.

There would be time for regrets in the following days. For now he didn't care.

CASSANDRA'S TEARS flowed unrestricted. Being in Jace's arms soothed her. He was the only one she wanted to be with. He understood; he could relate. She went with him, not knowing or caring where they were going as long as they were together. He took her to a little bar she wasn't familiar with. It was dark and nearly deserted that time of day, and he led her to a booth in the back. They both released a sigh as they sat down across from each other.

"You said you knew," Cassandra said after wiping her eyes. "How? Did she say anything unusual?"

"Sophie was always saying unusual stuff," he laughed, easing his pain slightly. "A couple days ago, I . . . I just wanted her to know how much I appreciated her. I was joking when I said, 'What would I do without you?' She gave me this serious look and said, 'You'll be fine.' I got a weird feeling then.

"And again, this morning . . . ," Jace continued, picturing Sophie in his mind. "She looked . . . I don't know . . . kinda sweet . . . all dressed up. She had jewelry on," he frowned. "I've never seen her wear any before. And then I was so late picking her up . . . " The painful sting of guilt swept in, nearly overwhelming him.

"What happened after you picked her up?" Cassandra prompted.

"I had to look for her. She wasn't where we agreed to meet. When I found her, she looked really pale. Once we got back to the apartment, she insisted she was fine . . . and she did look a little better. Said she just needed to rest. Still, I had that feeling in my gut again." He shook his head.

"Jace." Cassandra reached across the table and took his hand. "You've got to stop blaming yourself. It's not your fault."

"When did she die?" For some reason he needed to know the details.

"In the ambulance," she replied softly. "She came to, though. She talked to me."

"What did she say?"

"It didn't make much sense." She tried to recall what her aunt had said. "And it took so much of her strength. She closed her eyes, and when she opened them again she had the most amazing smile on her face. She looked absolutely peaceful, and that's when I knew she was going to die. I begged her not to," Cassandra sniffed. "I guess that was selfish of me. She just smiled . . . and told me . . . she'd always be with me." Cassandra could barely finish; she was overcome with emotion. "She said . . . we'll have some . . . tea."

Jace moved to sit with her. His arms were around her and his breath warm on her shoulder. She felt a strange mix of grief and glory. Watching her aunt die had been heart wrenching. Being in Jace's arms was wonderfully soothing. After several minutes, she noticed the drinks in front of them. "Thanks." She took a sip, wanting to gain her composure.

Aware that she must look a mess, she excused herself to go to the washroom. When she returned, Jace had moved to the other side of the booth. She slipped in across from him and smiled. He was looking at something on his cell phone with a sad grin on his face. Handing her the phone, he remarked, "I took this a couple of hours before she died."

"She looks happy," Cassandra noted. "It's hard to believe she's gone." The tears had run their course for the time being, and she felt mellow. "At least I got to say goodbye."

"I was there when my dad died." Jace spoke after a few minutes. "He was in a coma; most of his organs had shut down. We made the decision to take him off life support. Mom and I watched the machines as his heart rate got slower and slower and finally stopped. We said goodbye then, but it felt like he was already gone long before that."

"I met your mom," she inserted, not sure if it was the best time to bring it up, yet wanting to know where they stood. "She's nice."

Cassandra saw him stiffen. His eyes narrowed and his jaw clenched as he shook his head. "It won't work," he said simply. ". . . you and me."

His words were like daggers. Cassandra wanted to argue, yet something made her hesitate. Ultimately, she knew that trying to persuade him wouldn't be the best course of action. He had to want to be with her. He had to believe it could work. Still, she needed to know the truth, needed to see it in his eyes. "Is that what you want, Jace?"

"IT DOESN'T MATTER what I want." As Jace heard himself say it, Sophie's words filled his mind.

"You can have anything you want. You get to choose. It's up to you."

He ignored the advice, ignored the uncanny sense that he was actually hearing the old woman's voice. He was sure that the decision he was making was the only viable one. "We can't see each other. There's no sense fooling ourselves. We'd both end up getting hurt."

She was quiet for several long minutes. After taking a slow sip of her drink, she looked at him. Jace couldn't tell what she was thinking, couldn't tell if the sadness in her eyes was a result of the pronouncement he'd just made or the loss she'd suffered.

"I can live with that, Jace." The steadiness of her voice didn't match the tension on her brow, or the beseeching look in her eyes. "I'll have to live with it. But please tell me the truth. Is that what you really want?"

God, why is she doing this to me? He reached for his drink, downed half, and then did *not* what he wanted but what he needed to do. "Yes, Cassandra." He forced himself to look her in the eye to reinforce his words. "That's what I want."

CASSANDRA TOOK a cab home from the bar, crying most of the way. She'd just lost her beloved aunt, but her tears were for Jace, for what might have been. Her friends would tell her she was better off without him. Her father would tell her not to worry; she'd meet someone new. But she didn't want pat answers; she wanted Jace. Unfortunately, he didn't want her.

Trevor would understand her pain. She was glad to find him alone in the garden. He looked up as she walked toward him. Rather than waiting for an explanation he met her with a hug.

"I take it things didn't go well."

"He doesn't believe it can work; he doesn't even want to try."

"He loves you," Trevor contended.

Cassandra frowned at her brother. "How do you know that?"

"I could see it in his eyes. He cares very deeply."

"But I asked him," Cassandra insisted. "When he said it wouldn't work, I asked him if that's what he really wanted." Emotion welled up again. "Trev . . . he looked at me . . . he looked me in the eye and said yes."

Trevor didn't answer. He held her and let her cry.

The tears were a release; they served her in the moment, yet she needed to pull herself together. It wouldn't be easy; life felt overwhelming. She willed for strength, the kind of strength she'd seen in her aunt. Sophia hadn't let herself be beaten down by life's pain and disappointment. She'd held on to what she believed and had found happiness because of it. Ultimately, Cassandra knew she possessed the same ability, and it seemed that life was giving her an opportunity to prove it.

AFTER CASSANDRA LEFT, Jace called Chad. By the time his friend arrived, Jace was feeling immune to the thoughts that had been tormenting him.

Chad sat down across from him and immediately inquired, "Are you okay, man?"

"A few more of these, and I'll be fine," Jace smiled as he downed the last of his drink.

"I think we should get you home."

"No." Jace shook his head adamantly. "I don't want to go there yet."

"Why?" Chad looked surprised. "What happened?"

"Sophie died."

"Jeez, I'm sorry." Chad sounded sincere as he tried to comfort his friend. "But . . . she was really old, wasn't she? I mean . . . everybody's gotta go sometime."

"It's not just that. Cassandra was there."

"So . . . ?" Chad gave him a questioning shrug. "What happened? I thought you didn't want anything to do with her after you found out she lied."

Jace told him about their little tryst at the beach. Then he told Chad what he'd learned from his mom.

"Man," Chad laughed. "That chick is messing with your head. You've gotta get over her."

"I know."

"You're welcome to hang out at my place for a few days. The couch is yours if you want it."

"Sure," Jace smiled weakly. "Thanks, buddy."

CASSANDRA HAD gained a measure of self-control by the time her parents arrived home, but relaying the details of Sophia's death triggered the tears again. This time, however, they were tears of sorrow for her departed aunt.

"It was so sudden," she sniffed. She and her father had found solace in the living room while her mother went to check on the household affairs.

"She didn't suffer," Richard offered. "We can be thankful for that."

"I know. You're right," Cassandra agreed. "Plus, she'd want us to be happy for her, not sad. I know it's selfish, but I was just getting to know her, and she was telling me all these wonderful truths. It doesn't feel like we were done."

"What do you mean?"

"When I first went to visit her, she said not to worry about her because she still had things to do before she went. Then she started telling me about five principles she lived her life by. She wanted me to write them down, but I only got to hear three of them."

"Are you sure?" her father asked. "Could she have combined some of them?"

"She was quite clear about it and only ever mentioned one at a time. The first was at her apartment," Cassandra reflected. "The second was here at the Town House. And the third was at the beach last week."

She was quiet for a moment, contemplating, when suddenly it became clear. "Wait a minute," she exclaimed. "In the ambulance . . . Sophia said she had more to tell me. I thought she was confused. I told her not to talk, to save her strength, but she insisted."

"What did she say?"

Cassandra had to think. So much had taken place in just a few hours; it seemed like days. "She mentioned a guidance system. Yes," Cassandra nodded. "She said we all have an internal guidance system. She told me to follow what feels good; that's how I can know what's right for me. That must be the fourth principle!"

Though the clarity of the revelation brought her joy, it was quickly followed by dismay. "But now I'll never know what the fifth one is," she sighed. "And without that, how will I know what I'm supposed to do with the information?"

"Maybe she left a clue," Trevor interjected as he walked in on their conversation. "A letter or something."

"Yes," Richard agreed. "We might find something when we go through her belongings."

Her apartment. The thought of going back left Cassandra feeling raw. The memory of her aunt lying on the bed, barely breathing, was one she'd rather forget. And knowing Jace lived in the same building made her cringe inwardly. *Seeing him again would be too painful.* Without sharing her concerns she responded, "It's possible, I guess. She might have left something there."

"Besides, kitten." Her father reached for her hand. "What you've learned from your aunt is invaluable. What you saw in her, the example she set. That makes it all worthwhile, doesn't it?"

He was right. It was more than the words Cassandra had written down. It was seeing firsthand the example of a life well lived. Getting to know her great aunt in the past weeks had already changed her in countless ways. For that, she would always be grateful.

Chapter 15

Jace slept until noon the next day. Waking up in Chad's living room, he was disoriented for a moment, until the events of the previous day sifted back into his consciousness. He heard a noise and turned to see his friend in the kitchen.

"Want something to eat?" Chad offered. "I've got scrambled eggs and bacon happening here."

Jace was hungry, but he'd learned from experience that Chad's cooking wasn't something to look forward to. 'Scrambled' was the only thing Chad knew how to do with an egg, and shells weren't always excluded from the mix. Bacon usually came burnt or so saturated in oil that it was inedible. "No thanks, buddy," he declined politely. "I have to get Sophie's car." He vaguely recalled leaving it at the bar and coming back with Chad.

"It's here," Chad replied. "I walked back and picked it up after you passed out." He tossed the keys to Jace as he spoke. "What are you gonna do with it now?"

"I don't know," Jace frowned, realizing he had a dilemma. There was a chance Sophie's family would collect her belongings, and he wanted to avoid seeing Cassandra. "She mentioned a guy that handles her affairs," he recalled. "He's the one that bought the car for her."

"Do you know how to get in touch with him?"

"No, but Sophie must have written his number somewhere. I'm gonna see if I can find it." Jace left with a plan in mind. He'd call the guy—she'd said his name was Peter—and arrange to give him the keys to the car and the apartment. Then he'd never have to deal with Cassandra or her family again.

Back at his building, his heart pounded as he ascended the flight of stairs to Sophie's apartment. He'd dashed up the same stairs the day before, gripped by the knowing that something was wrong. Sadly, his intuition had been correct. As he fumbled with the key, the foreboding he felt was the result of having watched too many horror movies. Thoughts of disembodied spirits, objects moving of their own accord, and noises coming from empty rooms vied for his attention.

He quickly banned the troublesome thoughts and reminded himself why he was there. He hoped to find an address book or if he was lucky, paperwork with the name of the firm Peter worked for. A small desk sat in the living room. Jace noted the fancy moldings and rich wood finish and thought again about Sophie's interesting past. It was hard to imagine her as anything but the sweet little old lady that lived upstairs. Opening the drawer he found papers, but nothing relevant.

As he moved to the kitchen to check more drawers, a sound in the hallway made him freeze. All of a sudden, Jace felt guilty for being there. *What if someone finds me here? What if someone sees me going through her stuff and thinks I'm helping myself?* He realized his plan had been impulsive, not to mention foolish. Now his fear was justified; he could be in real trouble if someone caught him there.

As the sound in the hallway faded, he took a deep breath and continued searching. Thankfully, Sophie had kept her apartment organized. A drawer directly below the telephone contained a coil-bound address book. Names and numbers were listed neatly. After flipping through a few pages, he found the name *Peter* beside what looked like a law firm. He punched the number into his cell phone, locked the apartment door, and slipped down the stairs unseen.

Back in his own living room, he sat for a moment to let his heart rate slow before he dialed the number. It was Sunday; he wasn't expecting anyone to be there. Nevertheless, he intended to leave a message. He was caught off guard when a man answered.

"Harmon, Corruthers, and Scott," the voice said absently. "Peter Corruthers here."

"Um, Mr. Corruthers . . . ," Jace stumbled, not having planned what he wanted to say. "This is Jace Rutherford. I'm a neighbor of Sophia Langdon. I mean, I was. She . . . um . . . " Jace hoped he wasn't the first to bear the bad news. "She passed away."

"Yes," the man replied, "the family notified me."

Jace breathed easier. "I have some of her things." He paused. "I wasn't sure . . . um . . . who to call. I mean . . . I drove her car for her. But she let me use it . . . "

"Yes, Mr. Rutherford." The man sounded professional, yet had a note of compassion in his voice. "Mrs. Langdon advised me of the details of your agreement."

"Oh, good." Jace released the rest of his angst. "I just wondered what to do with the car now. I have a key to her apartment, as well. I could . . . um . . . drop them off somewhere."

"I'm in the office, today, going over the details of her estate," Peter offered. "Why don't you bring the car here? I'll park it in the underground lot. Do you know where the Oceanview Professional Building is?"

"Sure," Jace replied. "I can be there in about twenty minutes."

THE FUNERAL WAS set for Saturday. Cassandra was amazed at the ease with which the details were coming together. Sophia had prearranged all the particulars. She was to be cremated and her ashes buried alongside her late husband. The woman had even planned the music that was to be played at her memorial service.

The family had yet to go through her belongings, but Cassandra was more comfortable with the idea now. Having taken the week off, she was confident that avoiding Jace was possible. Furthermore, she wanted to help. Not only did she hope to find a clue to the fifth principle, she had a genuine desire to learn more about her aunt.

On Monday morning, she and Trevor went to the apartment while their father met with Sophia's lawyer. Cassandra expected to see the black Honda parked in front and was surprised when it was nowhere in sight. "That's funny," she frowned. "I wonder what Jace did with Aunt Sophia's car?"

"He wouldn't still be driving it, would he?"

"No." She shook her head firmly. Then a fragment of doubt crept in. "At least... I don't think so."

As Cassandra unlocked the door with a spare key her father had given her, she remembered that Jace also had a key.

"We should probably get the key back from Jace," Trevor remarked, reading her mind. "We'll have to give them all back to the landlord." He shook his head. "It still seems hard to believe she rented this little, old apartment all these years."

Cassandra had wondered the same, but now she understood her aunt's reasons. She explained it to Trevor. "I have such respect for her. She lived her life her way, regardless of what others thought. It takes a strong person to do that."

"It does," Trevor agreed, smiling at his sister. "You're like her, you know, Cass. I think that's why she chose to pass her wisdom on to you."

"Maybe." Cassandra appreciated the kind words, but they brought up questions that had been simmering in the back of her mind. "But Trev, I feel like I should do something with it. I mean, more than just using it for my own benefit."

"You can be an example to those around you, just like she was."

"Yeah, I guess."

"Doodlebug," he asserted. "This is where you need to step back and trust the Universe. Let the details present themselves. Don't try so hard to figure it out."

Trevor's advice brought relief. Cassandra had been agonizing over the fact that she hadn't learned the fifth principle, that she didn't know what her aunt wanted her to do with the information. It felt good to let it go, if just for the afternoon.

They spent the next few hours, sorting and organizing. Much of Sophia's furniture was antique; it would probably bring a sizable sum at an auction. Some of her household effects were valuable as well, particularly the china and paintings. Cassandra wasn't sure what her aunt had in mind for her belongings, but she was sure Sophia would have wanted them to go to a worthy cause.

Opening a drawer in her aunt's dresser, she remembered Jace's remark about the jewelry. The comment stood out in Cassandra's mind. As she thought back to recent visits, she couldn't recall her aunt with any type of adornment, not even a ring. "Did Aunt Sophia have any jewelry on when you saw her in the hospital?" she asked Trevor.

"Not that I noticed," he shrugged. "Why?"

"I didn't see any either, but Jace said she was wearing some when he drove her to the fair. She must have taken it off before she lay down."

"It would still be here, then," Trevor concluded. "You know, we should probably have it put in a safe. Some of her old stuff may be worth a lot."

"That's what I was thinking, too."

Curious, she searched her aunt's bedroom. She looked in her closet and under the bed. She even went through Sophia's clothing. Trevor joined her in the search, but after nearly half an hour they'd uncovered nothing. Cassandra's mind was working hard as well, trying to solve the mystery. *If Aunt Sophia was so exhausted that she lay down without eating or changing her clothes, it's unlikely she'd take the time to hide her valuables. If she simply removed them, they'd be on her dresser or bedside table—unless she took them off in the bathroom.* She went to check while Trevor continued to search.

"Here we go," he called from the hallway. "I found a jewelry box!"

Cassandra breathed easier. In an attempt to make sense of it all, her mind brought up the fact that Jace had a key and knew about the jewelry. Scolding herself for entertaining such a thought, she went to see what her brother had found. She was eager to see what old jewelry her aunt would have kept from years past, sure that a wedding ring would be among the treasure. As she saw the expression on Trevor's face, however, she stopped short.

"It's empty," he frowned.

They looked at each other, and Cassandra knew what her brother was thinking.

"You don't suppose . . . "

"Let's not jump to conclusions," she retorted. "Aunt Sophia trusted Jace. I felt that, too. I still feel it," she softened. "He wouldn't do something like this."

"But who else . . . ?"

"Let's keep looking." She cut him off, wanting more than anything to find the jewelry and exonerate Jace. "It's got to be here somewhere; she just wore it two days ago."

The two split up and systematically went through the apartment. After an hour and a half, they were no further ahead. Another small ring box was found, but it too was empty.

"Cass," Trevor said gently. "It's not here. We'd have found it by now. It's a tiny apartment."

"Then where is it?" Cassandra demanded, frustrated and distraught by the possibility that they'd all misjudged Jace. She desperately wished another explanation would present itself, yet no matter how she rearranged the facts in her mind, nothing else made sense. Jace was the only one who'd seen the jewelry recently and the only other one who had access to Sophia's apartment.

JACE WALKED HOME from the bus stop. It was a hot, muggy day, and in his work clothes he was uncomfortably warm. Though his negative mood was exacerbated by his physical condition, it wasn't the source of it. He'd been increasingly discouraged by the reality of Sophie's death. She'd been the reason for his hope. Her generosity had eased his financial burden. Now he was right back where he'd been before he met her.

How can I feel better about this? he asked himself, remembering Sophie's advice. Her way of thinking held merit; he just wished she'd stuck around a little longer to help him really get it.

He continued to walk, deep in thought, staring at the sidewalk in front of him. After a moment, his eye caught sight of something shiny. He bent to pick up a quarter. As he turned it over in his hand, Sophie's voice sounded in his mind.

"This coin represents money. One side is lack, the other abundance. You can tell which side you're focused on by how you feel."

The words were in his head, yet they were clear and audible, as though Sophie were standing next to him. He was convinced, as he had been in the hospital, that he was concocting the dialogue, and the reason wasn't hard to figure out. Their conversations had brought him comfort. Her words made sense; deep down he believed they were the answer to his problems.

"Jace, if you can feel excited about the idea of having money one day, then that day isn't far away."

This time, Jace shook his head in dismay. Her voice had interrupted his thoughts. And the sound was so rich and clear, Jace could almost swear he was hearing it with his ears. He didn't mind hearing her advice. In fact, he was glad it had resonated with him enough that he could recall it and ultimately apply it. But what he'd just experienced was more than that. He'd not only heard her voice, he'd felt her presence. On top of that was the compelling sense that she was the reason the quarter was in his path.

Man, he breathed, *this is affecting me more than I realized.* Despite the paranormal nature of the experience, Jace shrugged it off. Hearing her voice, her wisdom, had left him feeling better, and he welcomed the improvement. He decided not to analyze it.

As he neared his building, Jace quickened his pace. He couldn't wait to shed his sweaty clothes and step into a refreshing shower. Climbing the stairs to his apartment, he looked up the stairwell to the floor above. He smiled as he thought of his wise, old neighbor. *Sophie, wherever you are . . . thank you.*

CASSANDRA EXAMINED her options as they drove back to the Town House. *I could just not say anything. It's unlikely that anyone else would know what, if any, jewelry Sophia owned.* She couldn't justify that choice; it was dishonest. *Trevor's aware of the missing jewelry now, too; I could never ask him to join me in covering up what could be a crime. So what do I say, then? If I mention Jace's name, everyone will assume exactly what I did—that he's guilty.*

As they neared the Town House, Trevor asked, "How do you want to handle this?"

"I don't know," she sighed. "We probably should say something. But if we tell them what we know, Jace will be an obvious suspect. I can't believe he'd do this, Trev."

Trevor pulled into the driveway. "It's your call, Cass. I'll go along with whatever you decide."

Cassandra was glad that he understood the difficult position she was in—wanting to do what was right yet knowing any action she took could have serious ramifications. "I need to talk to Jace first," she concluded. It could be awkward, and if she didn't handle it right he'd think she was accusing him, yet she didn't know what else to do. "I'll casually ask about the jewelry and see what he says. I'm sure I'll be able to read him."

They agreed not to mention the missing jewelry until Cassandra had talked to Jace. She was somewhat relieved at being able to postpone telling her father. He was an honest and fair man. He'd weigh all the evidence before he took legal action, but as it stood, all the evidence pointed to Jace being guilty.

"SO ARE YOU going to the funeral?" Sarah asked as Jace walked into her kitchen that evening. "It's Saturday afternoon, one o'clock, at the Harborside Community Center. Strange place to be having a funeral for someone with her connections," she continued, not waiting for a reply. "I hear she planned everything herself. And the word is, her highness doesn't want to attend."

"Why not?" Jace asked, not really wanting to hear, but knowing his mom would probably volunteer the information anyway.

"She wanted Mr. Van to change the location to a more upscale venue like the Regency Room at the Hilton or the Carthright Center, but he wouldn't budge. Said they were going to respect his aunt's wishes. I have to give it to him, you know. From what I hear, he's a pretty decent guy; he puts up with a lot."

Hearing details about Cassandra's parents made Jace wince. It was more proof that a relationship with her wouldn't have worked, for which he should have been glad, yet thinking about her still evoked a longing he didn't know what to do with.

"So are you going?" she asked again.

"Nah," he shook his head, surprised that what had been a clear-cut no in his mind was sounding less than definite. "I don't think so."

"It's probably just as well. Regardless of the location, high society will be on parade. No one will want to chance insulting Port Hayden's 'royal' family," she scoffed.

Jace's discomfort was increasing, so he looked for a way to change the subject. Knowing that his mom's maternal instincts would take priority over her need to gossip, he opened the fridge. "What do you have to eat?"

"There's casserole left over." She immediately switched roles. "Let me make you some cheese toast to go with it. Are you eating all right? You look like you've lost weight."

"I'm fine, Mom," he assured her, glad for the change in conversation. He appreciated the food, too. His own fare at home had been boring lately, and his mom's cheese toast was the best.

As he ate, he thought of something else he wanted to discuss with his mother. "Mom," he began hesitantly. "Do you think that if Dad hadn't gotten sick, you guys would be doing okay financially? I mean, would you have had a comfortable life?"

Sarah frowned at her son. "Yeah... I guess. I mean, it was always a little tight, but we had plans, dreams. Why do you ask?"

"I want to make something with my life," he admitted. "I want to get ahead." As he stated his desires, suddenly they sounded weak. He needed to let his mom know it was more than frivolous dreaming. "I intend to be well off one day, and I'm going to find a way to make that happen," he declared with determination.

"Wow." She looked at him oddly. "Where did that come from all of a sudden? I've never heard you talk like that before."

"I don't know," he shrugged, not wanting to mention Sophie. "I've been feeling this way for a while, but lately... I feel like I could make it happen if I really put my mind to it."

She shook her head, still frowning. "I knew someone once with an attitude like that." She smiled, and Jace noticed a far-off look in her eyes. "He had big dreams; he was determined. You just knew when you heard him talk that nothing was going to stop him from reaching his goals."

"Who was he?"

"Oh someone I knew when I was younger. We dated for a year or so."

"So what happened?" Jace was curious. He suspected there was plenty she wasn't saying, and suddenly he wanted to learn about his mom's past. They'd never had that kind of conversation before—adult to adult—and it felt good.

"He left Port Hayden. We didn't keep in touch. I heard through the grapevine that he became very successful, married . . . all that." Her expression changed as she put a stop to the reminiscing and got back to their conversation. "It's a good attitude to have, though. Probably the key to success. I've sure seen it in the people I've worked for."

"I'll be successful one day . . . and rich, too," he asserted with a confidence that surprised him.

Sarah smiled. "With a mindset like that, I believe you will, son."

Jace felt love and pride radiating from her, and he had to add, "And when I am, I'll buy you a house and hire a maid to do your work. You'll never have to lift a finger again."

A tear glistened in her eye, and Jace gave her a hug. He was glad that his mom saw the benefit in a positive attitude. It was the cornerstone of what he'd come to believe. He was on a path that most didn't understand, let alone endorse, and her support meant a lot to him. He didn't know what was ahead, didn't have a plan that included action, yet he believed that if he stayed on the path and was open to ideas, life would show him the way to realize his financial dreams.

Chapter 16

She watched him walk into the room. Instead of the pleasure normally associated with seeing her father, talking with him, Cassandra felt the need to avoid conversation. It was because of the information she was withholding, and her guilt increased. *I have to talk to Jace as soon as possible,* she resolved. *I want to get this over with. I hate feeling this way.* She decided to go the following evening, praying she'd find Jace at home.

"Well, Sophia's estate isn't going to be as easy to settle as I'd thought." Her father sat down heavily.

"Why?" Cassandra asked.

"Corruthers wouldn't divulge much." He shook his head. "Apparently another party has started legal proceedings. It could drag things out."

"Who would do a thing like that?" This time Helen asked the question. She'd been sitting in her favorite chaise longue, reading a magazine.

"He wouldn't say."

“How can someone contest the will when we don't even know how much the estate is worth or who all Sophia has left it to?” Helen was indignant.

“They wouldn't be contesting it, not yet. They're probably just trying to hold up proceedings with a caveat or lawsuit,” he replied. “Corruthers knows all those details.

“But who could it be?” Helen persisted.

Trevor had been sitting quietly, too. When he looked at Cassandra, she could read his mind.

“I don't know,” Richard frowned. “Obviously, they think they have something to gain by it. They believe Sophia owes them something. Corruthers wants to meet with all the parties involved next week. I hope we'll learn something then.”

Cassandra's body went rigid as she realized that Jace could be the one they were referring to. Again, part of her argued in his defense, while another reasoned that it simply couldn't be anyone else. The odds were mounting against him, and her opinion of him was starting to slip.

She needed to talk to someone unbiased, someone who could help her make sense of what was happening. Tanisha was the obvious choice. Wanting to make sure she wasn't overheard, she went out to the garden and called her friend on her cell phone. “You have to help me,” Cassandra begged after relaying the news. “This is so messed. I can't believe Jace would do it.”

“I may not be a lawyer yet,” Tanisha advised. “But I do know that one of the basic tenets of the law in this country is that a person is innocent until proved guilty. It sounds to me like you've pronounced the verdict already."

"But all the evidence . . . "

"If you want my advice," Tanisha interrupted, "you'll let the professionals deal with the evidence. Cass," she paused. "You misjudged Jace once before. Isn't it possible that you're doing it again?"

Cassandra stopped to re-examine the situation. Tanisha was right. As much as circumstantial evidence pointed to Jace being a thief and possibly the one interfering with the will, she also had to consider that her aunt had trusted him. Cassandra had come to trust him, too. Not only that, but she'd fallen in love with him. He was, according to a wise old woman, her soul mate.

JACE SPENT as little time at his apartment as he could. He didn't feel good there anymore and was seriously thinking of letting it go. Chad's brother was moving away in the fall to go to school, and Chad had offered Jace the room. The rent would be cheaper, and he could use the extra money to save for a down payment on a car. It seemed like an ideal solution—a small yet positive step in the right direction, proving that his deliberate thinking was starting to pay off.

On Tuesday after work, he went for pizza and drinks with Chad and a few other friends. It was nearly eight o'clock when he finally headed back to his apartment.

Though he had no desire to spend time there, he had to be realistic. It was his home, at least for the next couple of months. Besides, he really needed to do laundry.

As he neared his building, he noticed a woman emerge from a car and walk toward the front steps. *Damn! What is she doing here?* He recognized Cassandra immediately and quickly stepped into a stairwell so she wouldn't see him. Watching her from the shadows, he experienced a bevy of emotions. Gazing at the beautiful body he'd held and caressed and dreamed about, part of him wanted to call out to her, throw caution aside, and risk what he was sure would be eventual heartbreak.

Reason returned once she'd disappeared into the building. As he began walking in the other direction, he congratulated himself. It took willpower to resist such a woman. *I'm doing what's right for me,* he assured himself. With his actions came a new resolve. He not only wanted to be successful, he wanted to find happiness in other areas—a relationship, for one. He had to be realistic. Dating someone like Elise made much more sense. He considered asking her out again.

Emotions swayed and shifted as Jace continued walking. He was moving both physically and emotionally away from Cassandra Van Broden. Though he felt good about taking charge, making a decision, his resolve was shadowed with something new. This time it was the distressing sense that he was walking away from rather than toward his dreams.

AS SHE KNOCKED on Jace's door, Cassandra struggled to keep her nerves under control. Tanisha had advised against it, but she still wanted to talk to him. She justified her actions by telling herself that she was no longer passing judgment; she simply wanted to inform him of the situation and see what came of it.

There was no answer, so she knocked again, louder this time, putting her ear to the door in case he had his music turned up. She lingered a moment longer and was about to leave when a girl, appearing to be in her early twenties, opened the door across the hall. "Excuse me. I'm looking for Jace Rutherford. Do you know him?"

"Yeah, sure," the girl replied.

A second girl appearing in the doorway gave her a friendly shove and laughed. "You wish!"

The first girl blushed as she amended her statement. "Okay, I don't know him very well . . . yet. We just moved in."

The girls giggled at what Cassandra supposed was an inside joke. "Have you seen him lately?" she asked, frustrated by their immaturity. "I need to get ahold of him."

"Why?"

Cassandra was losing patience. "I need to get ahold of him, that's all. If you haven't seen him, I'll ask someone else in the building."

"Hey, chill. I was just curious," the first girl shot back defensively. "I haven't seen him for a few days."

"He must be away or something," the other girl stated. "I haven't seen his car around."

"I could give him a message. I mean… when he gets back," girl-one offered, obviously looking for a reason to connect with her good-looking neighbor.

"No. That's fine," Cassandra replied hastily, glad to be done with the conversation. As she walked away, she heard 'bitch' and 'not his type' in the muted exchange that followed. Although she had no reason to care what two strangers thought of her, it stung just the same. For the first time, Cassandra saw the situation from another's perspective. *Maybe they're right,* she acknowledged. *Maybe I'm not his type.* It occurred to her that possibly everyone else, including Jace, could see what she had failed to see.

JACE WALKED for an hour before heading back to his apartment. He was frustrated—frustrated that he'd had to hide, that he couldn't go to his own apartment for fear of running into Cassandra. Frustrated, too, that he couldn't erase her from his mind. The resolve to call Elise and move on with his life had been short-lived. He couldn't resist comparing the two women, and Elise always came up lacking.

As he searched for answers, Sophie came to mind. *What do you think?* he asked the image in his head.

"She's a lovely girl."

Jace laughed as Sophie's oft-used description of her niece came to mind. *She is,* he agreed. *I'll give you that. But I have to forget about her, and I don't know how.* It was verging on psychotic, yet he enjoyed the conversations he kept having with the old woman in his head. It kept her memory alive and kept her much-needed advice in the forefront of his mind.

"What you both have in here . . . It's the same."

The words brought Jace to a halt. This time he not only heard them; he felt a tap on his chest. *What the hell?*

He stood on the sidewalk spellbound as a tingling sensation, beginning on his scalp, spread throughout his entire body. His senses were suddenly heightened. Everything looked different, sounded different. The atmosphere took on a new feel and a distinctive color. Twilight was settling in, and shadows seemed to come to life. The windows of the buildings glowed amber in the setting sun. The scene around him was bathed in cinematic splendor.

An unusual stillness permeated the air. Through an open window, he heard a couple arguing. A cat meowed in the alley as a garbage can tumbled over. Children were laughing in a playground down the block. In the distance, a siren wailed. Traffic rumbled through a busy intersection several blocks away.

He knew it wasn't possible, yet Jace felt as though he was hearing sounds for the first time and peering out through new eyes. And encompassing it all was a sense of well-being, the likes of which he'd never known. *What's going on?* he managed to ask.

"Not everything is as it seems, Jace."

"Sophie?" he inquired aloud.

A woman sitting on a nearby veranda responded. "It's not Sophie, dear, it's Delores. Can I help you?"

"No . . . no thanks," he replied and began to run. He didn't stop until he'd reached his apartment. Once inside, he locked the door and stood leaning against it, puffing hard.

Am I losing my mind? He took several deep breaths to calm himself, then replayed the bizarre events, trying to make sense of them. *I was remembering,* he insisted. *I was just remembering some of the stuff Sophie told me, that's all.*

So why did it feel like someone poked me in the chest? He'd felt it. He couldn't deny it. Only now, he wasn't sure whether it was a poke from the outside, or whether it had been from within—a quickened heartbeat maybe. *That must be it,* he reasoned. *Just a strange physical response to the memory of her words.*

But what about the weird sensations that followed? It had been surreal—almost like being high. All his senses had been heightened, and he'd experienced the world around him in a whole new way. *And that peaceful feeling . . .*

All of a sudden Jace knew. An undeniable clarity filled his mind as the tingling sensation gripped him again. "Sophie?" he asked, his voice barely a whisper. He heard no response, yet something told him she was there. He could feel her presence. He could smell her—a smell he associated with her apartment. It was an odd mix of dusty old books, furniture polish, and ginger cookies. As the realization settled in, he was lifted to a new high. He wasn't sure what to do with the euphoric feeling, so he closed his eyes, savoring it. "You're here," he stated, still whispering as if speaking louder might break the spell he was under.

"Yes, Jace. I never really left."

Her voice was clear and audible, yet he was aware that it was in his head. "Can other people hear you? Does anyone else know?"

"Anyone who believes can hear me. Anyone who is connected to their Higher Self. We're all one, Jace. We're all connected at a higher level."

"Wow." He shook his head, trying to take it in. "So you're always here? I can talk to you anytime I like? Ask you questions, hear your advice?"

"Whenever, wherever. I'll be there," she assured him. "Time-space limitations don't exist in the nonphysical."

"Wow." He was still reeling with the enormity of what he'd discovered. There was so much to talk about, so much he wanted to ask, but one question stood out in his mind—what to do about Cassandra. "She was here at the apartment building earlier," he stated abruptly.

"I know."

"I guess you would," he grinned, realizing he hadn't specified who 'she' was, yet Sophie seemed to know. "So what am I going to do? I can't keep avoiding her."

"You have to determine what you want. Once you know that, your work is to line up with it. Remember, Jace," Sophie's sweet, kind voice filled his head, "you can be or do or have anything. You get to choose."

They were the words she'd first spoken when he passed her in the stairwell that day. They'd sounded strange then, crazy even, but not anymore. Her words had awoken something in him, reminding him of what he'd known but forgotten. Hearing them again warmed his heart. He was filled with appreciation. He was fortunate enough to have met Sophia Langdon in person, and now she'd be forever with him in spirit. Jace's own spirit soared as he contemplated the possibilities before him. *I really can be or do or have whatever I want. I get to decide.*

"Thank you, Sophie," he smiled. "Thank you so much for reminding me of that."

Chapter 17

Cassandra went over the information she'd inadvertently collected: Jace hadn't been at his apartment lately; his neighbors hadn't seen him; his mailbox was full; the car was gone; the jewelry was missing. She knew what it added up to, and it left her feeling sick. Jace was guilty after all, and he'd disappeared.

But why would he interfere with the will? she argued. *That doesn't make sense. If he was guilty of the other things, he'd be long gone. Yet if he is the one the lawyer was talking about…*

Could I be wrong about him? She could still hear Tanisha's reprimand. *If he's hired a lawyer, if he's trying to get something from Sophia's estate*, she allowed, *then he couldn't possibly have stolen the car or the jewelry. Nobody's that brazen. Jace definitely isn't.*

The new thought gave her hope—the first shred of hope she'd felt since she'd discovered the jewelry was missing. However, as her mind continued to sift, she realized it didn't absolve Jace of wrongdoing. That he would challenge the will of a woman he'd known for a relatively short time, someone he'd been in the employ of for a matter of weeks, seemed incredibly petty. *What could he possibly think he might gain from it?* she wondered. *The car maybe. Or extra compensation for having his employment cut short. Still,* she frowned, *that's nothing compared to what her estate is worth.*

She returned to the Town House more confused than when she left. She was relieved to find her brother alone. Trevor looked at her questioningly as she walked into the living room. "He wasn't there," she said simply. "His neighbor said he hasn't been around."

"Hmm," Trevor frowned. "This isn't looking good. I'm really sorry, doodlebug. I know you cared about him."

"I still do," she sighed.

"So where does this leave us? How do you want to proceed?"

She shared her thoughts about Jace, and then looked at her brother pleadingly. "Can we wait until after the funeral to say anything? Maybe more evidence will turn up. Maybe we've been wrong."

Suddenly the weight of it all came crashing down around her, and she burst into tears. Trevor offered comfort, but she resisted. She wanted to cry, wanted to let it out. With a simple apology, she ran up to her room. Her childhood space offered solace that no other place on earth could replicate. She threw herself on the bed and sobbed into her pillow. Everything seemed so final.

Aunt Sophia was gone, and Jace was nothing more than a memory of what might have been.

JACE WAS ELATED by his newfound secret. After discovering that Sophie was with him, he'd stayed up nearly half the night asking question after question. Since then he couldn't seem to remove the grin from his face. Chad noticed at work and made a comment at lunchtime.

"What's with you? You've been in a good mood all week. What happened? You meet somebody new?"

"Kind of," Jace smiled, thinking of his phantom friend.

"Well, bring her tonight," Chad encouraged. "Let's meet her. Is she hotter than Elise?"

Jace tried not to laugh; there were no appropriate words to reply.

"Speaking of Elise," Chad submitted cautiously. "If you're not interested . . . "

"Go for it." Jace was happy to give him his blessing.

"What was wrong with her, by the way?" Chad asked. "Whyd'ya dump her like that?"

Jace shrugged, not sure he fully understood his reasoning. She was too much like Cassandra in some ways and not enough in others.

Chad didn't seem to notice his lack of response. He began to tell Jace who would be at his party that evening. Elise and her friends were among the ones invited. Jace was a little uncomfortable at the prospect of seeing Elise. *I hope she doesn't have hard feelings. I didn't mean to hurt her. The timing was wrong, that's all. If I'd met her before Cassandra...* He decided not to dwell on it. It was too late.

"So you'll bring . . . What's her name, anyway?" Chad inquired.

"Yeah, I'll ask her," Jace lied. At some point he'd have to admit he wasn't seeing anyone—at least not anyone young and in bodily form. Then again, there was always a chance he'd meet someone else. He kept thinking about Sophie's advice: Decide what you want and line up with it.

She was on his mind all afternoon. Having only talked to her in his apartment, he was eager to get home and talk to her there. Although she had assured him she'd be wherever he was, the thought of talking to her at work seemed strange. Nevertheless, his questions kept mounting. Since the work he was doing was monotonous, he decided to try. *Sophie, are you there?*

"Of course, Jace."

This was new territory. Since he'd become aware of her presence, he'd only addressed her out loud. The realization that she could read his thoughts left him unsettled. *Can you hear all my thoughts?*

"Yes."

Oh . . .

"I'm not judging you, Jace."

I know, but still... it's weird.

"There are no new thoughts. Only new combinations of thoughts. There's no right or wrong, either."

Jace frowned. *We're going to have to discuss that one a bit more, but right now I want to talk about something you said the other night.*

"About lining up with what you want?"

Yeah, he replied, still staggered that she knew his thoughts almost before he did. *You said I have to determine what I want. But I don't know how to do that when there's so much to consider.*

"It's not hard to figure out what you want."

Great, Jace exclaimed, expecting to hear something new and profound. *How do I do it?*

"You can tell by how you feel."

That's it?

"That's all you need, Jace. You have an emotional guidance system that serves you well. You need to practice listening to it."

I've been trying, he argued. *And I'm more confused than ever.*

"What do you want in a relationship?"

It wasn't a difficult question, yet Jace's defenses went up. He started to object, reminding Sophie that his situation was more complicated than most, when he realized he was arguing for his limitations. Moreover, he wasn't being entirely honest with himself. *I guess what I want is . . . someone like Cassandra.*

"What is it that you like about her?"

Everything . . . except that she's rich.

"Don't you want to be rich someday?"

Yeah, he asserted. *Someday... but that doesn't help me right now. And it doesn't change the fact that my mom works for her family.*

"Let's go back to the question," Sophie suggested. "What do you like about her?"

You mean specifically?

"Yes," Sophie replied. "I want you to think of all the qualities you like about her. Write them down. That will be a good place to start."

But why? Jace was arguing again, but he couldn't help it. He felt he deserved to know where the conversation was leading.

"You said you want someone like Cassandra," Sophie explained patiently. "So you'll need to determine what qualities you like in her. Then you can begin to look for them in someone else."

I don't want someone else, Jace blurted, the realization slapping him in the face. *I want her!*

"There you go," Sophie imparted somewhat smugly. "Now you know what you want. That wasn't too hard, was it?"

CASSANDRA HAD CRIED all her tears and was ready to move forward. She'd resolved to set aside the knowledge about the missing jewelry and act on it only if it came up. She wanted to feel good, wanted to apply what she'd learned from her aunt. Accusing Jace, thinking of him in such a defamatory way, didn't feel good at all. Not only that, but knowing how highly her aunt had regarded him, Cassandra was happy to honor her by letting the issue rest.

She spent the remainder of the week going through the boxes she and Trevor had brought back to the Town House. Finding a clue to the fifth principle was still on her mind, but more than anything she was eager to learn what she could about the dear woman through a closer look at her papers and personal items.

Untying a bundle of envelopes, Cassandra found letter after letter from people expressing thanks for Sophia's contribution to their lives. At first, she assumed the contribution they were referring to was monetary, but reading further she discovered that what most of the people were thankful for was friendship and advice. The kind words from strangers, all expressing a similar sentiment, gave Cassandra a candid glimpse of her aunt's life, and an idea began to grow. She shared it with her father that afternoon.

"I want to do something with this information, Daddy. I want to write her story. I think the world would benefit from knowing the real Sophia Langdon. She touched so many lives. She made a difference one person at a time. Maybe…," Cassandra acknowledged, feeling the truth of it as never before. "Maybe this is what I'm meant to do." She could see herself conducting research, interviewing people who had known her aunt—particularly those whose names she'd found on the letters—and compiling the information in a book. But it would be more than just an account of Sophia's life. "I want to find a way to combine her story and her beliefs." She began to think out loud. "Something more captivating than a biography, more personal than a self-help guide."

"Kitten . . . " Her father gazed at her with pride and affection. "Would you like to say a few words at the service tomorrow? It might be fitting to let the community know what kind of woman Sophia was. I know it's last minute, and it's totally up to you, but . . . "

"I'd be honored to, Daddy," Cassandra smiled, already thinking about what she wanted to say. Her aunt had given her a wonderful gift, and she wanted to give something back. "Aunt Sophia may be gone, but I'm going to do what I can to see that her memory lives on."

JACE DIDN'T MIND going to the party alone. Given his revelation earlier, he wasn't into hooking up with another girl anytime soon. As he got ready, he tried to resolve his feelings. It wasn't easy. Knowing what he wanted, or rather *who* he wanted, didn't bring him much satisfaction. He couldn't see when or how it could ever happen.

"It never feels good to try to figure out those details."

Jace could distinguish Sophie's advice from his own thoughts. He was beginning to see that she was a part of him and not some strange metaphysical anomaly. *You're right,* he replied. *So how do I go about it?*

"You know what you want. Your work is to think about your desire in a way that feels good."

But if I can't think about when or how… Jace drew a blank; he didn't know what else to focus on.

"Why do you want to be with her?"

Why? Jace frowned. *Because it feels good.*

"Tell me more," she urged.

I don't have to, he joked. *You already know everything.*

"Do it for you, then."

Okay, Jace shrugged, trusting her enough to do as she asked. *The first time I saw her. I mean really looked at her,* he emphasized, *I'd never seen anyone so beautiful in my life. I couldn't erase her image from my mind. I dreamed about her…* He flushed, knowing Sophie was aware of the contents of his most personal dreams. *I'm not going into details, though.*

"What was the essence of it?"

I felt like she was my soul mate, he admitted. *But I still don't understand that.*

"That's what I meant about you and Cassandra being the same in here."

Hey, he laughed as he felt a poke on his chest again. *How do you do that?*

"I could give you a complicated scientific explanation," she offered, "but basically it's just energy moving."

The subject fascinated him, and Jace intended to ask more about it at some point, but for now he wanted to know how he could be with Cassandra.

"You don't know how," Sophie reminded him. "And asking that question doesn't feel good, does it?"

No, he conceded, realizing how ingrained his old patterns of thinking were.

"Remember, your goal is always to reach for thoughts that feel better. Asking why is a good place to start. Ask yourself why you want to be with her, and then focus on the details that feel good. Or you might try some 'what if' statements."

What if statements?

"Yes," she replied. "Like, what if I'm wrong about her family? What if I'm wrong about what others will think? What if being with her makes up for all the potential wrongs. What if being with Cassandra turns out to be the best thing that ever happened to me?"

"Wow," Jace exclaimed aloud. "That was great!"

"That's your work, Jace. To continue to find thoughts that make you feel that good."

"That didn't feel like work at all." His adrenaline was pumping. "It felt amazing!" *I can do that,* he declared confidently. *I can ask those questions. I thought I had to focus on the situation, as complicated as it is, and try to find a way to feel good about it. But this,* he asserted, *this is something different altogether. This is thinking about what could be instead of what is. It leaves me with endless possibilities!*

Jace's outlook shifted radically. All of a sudden he saw what could be and how to achieve it. A relationship with Cassandra no longer seemed impossible. Succeeding in life—even becoming a pilot—began to feel attainable. He'd caught a glimpse of the bigger picture, and he'd never look at anything the same way again.

Chapter 18

Cassandra spent a quiet evening reading Sophia's letters, reflecting on the time they'd had together, and compiling the information she wanted to include in her tribute. In a way it would be a mini version, a preview of what her book was to be about. While she felt it was important to highlight Sophia's life, her charitable work, and her altruistic spirit, she wanted those attending the funeral to be introduced to what her aunt believed.

She read over the notes she'd taken during their visits. The principles she'd received were life-changing; they were powerful, yet Cassandra still felt disappointment over what seemed like an incomplete teaching. She wished she'd had more time with her aunt. The woman was wise; she'd helped Cassandra see her desires more clearly. She could use that wisdom as thoughts of Jace continued to pull her in opposite directions.

As she got lost in her introspection, she recalled something her aunt had said. Excitement emerged as she realized she'd had the voice recorder with her during that visit; the words she was trying to recall were on tape. Finding it, she replayed the conversation.

"Some things need to be believed to be seen."

Cassandra stopped the device. She remembered correcting her aunt, assuming the old woman was confused. *It was me who was confused. I had it wrong,* she acknowledged. *I was stuck in a mindset that didn't question, didn't challenge the status quo.* She turned the recorder on again, wanting to hear more and enjoying the sound of her beloved aunt's voice.

"Once you believe, you'll start to see all kinds of things differently."

The words sent a shiver down her spine. She'd seen the results that a change in thinking could bring. The relationship between her father and brother was miles from where it had been two weeks earlier. She realized that the same wisdom could be applied to her dilemma with Jace. Her current belief allowed for only one possible outcome, and she wanted to change that, wanted to expand her thinking.

What would happen if I believed differently? I want to, she declared. *I want to believe in Jace. I want to see this whole thing in a new light.*

Cassandra sighed. She didn't know how to do what she wanted to do. Nevertheless, she was determined to remain open minded. She turned the recorder on again, hoping to find something relevant.

"Don't overlook the obvious, my dear. Sometimes what you're looking for is right in front of you."

Again, something told her that her aunt's advice applied to the current situation. *Am I overlooking something obvious here? Something to do with Jace?* She replayed the conversation several times, listening carefully, trying to read between the lines, but the words remained a mystery. Setting the thoughts aside, Cassandra finished working on the eulogy. She went to bed that night satisfied that she'd captured on paper the feelings she held in her heart. The picture she intended to paint of Sophia Langdon would accurately portray the extraordinary human being Cassandra had come to know.

JACE TRIED TO enjoy himself at Chad's party, but his heart wasn't in it. It wasn't where he wanted to be. He stayed until his presence, or lack of it, wouldn't be noticed and then slipped out. All he could think about was talking with Sophie. As he walked home, he addressed his friend. *Sophie, are you there?*

"I'm always here, Jace," she answered lovingly.

I know you said that before, he acknowledged, *but it still blows me away that I can talk to you like this.*

"You didn't seem to enjoy yourself at the party."

No, I didn't. Something's changed. Admitting it to Sophie brought up questions. *Will I ever be the same again? I mean, can I ever go to a party like that and have fun like I used to?*

"You can be or do anything you want, Jace. You get to decide. The difference is that now you can base that decision on whether it feels good or not."

Yeah, but I used to look forward to a party for days, and talk about it for weeks. Tonight, I was bored; I couldn't wait to leave. There was no one there I wanted to talk to. And mindless drinking seems so . . . Jace shook his head. He was having a hard time believing let alone understanding his sudden change of heart.

"It's your focus that's changed, that's all. It doesn't mean you'll never have fun again. You'll find immense joy in life's activities now that you know how. Let your feelings be your guide. You can't get it wrong."

I like that, Jace nodded, feeling uplifted. *I can't get it wrong.*

"It's because we're eternal," she explained. "We never stop having desires, never cease creating. Therefore there's no such thing as a mistake. Everything is just an experience. Sometimes those experiences cause contrast in our lives, but it's the contrast that helps us know more clearly what we want."

Like me not having money has helped me know how much I want it.

"Exactly. We come to this time-space reality to have creative life experiences. What we create is irrelevant. That's why we can't get it wrong. It's the feeling of birthing a desire, lining up with it, and seeing it come to fruition that produces joy. It's not having the stuff—although that can bring pleasure, too."

Is that why they say money doesn't lead to happiness? he inquired.

"Yes," Sophie replied. "But what they don't tell you is that happiness can lead to money."

Jace laughed. He loved what he was hearing. Not only did it ring true to the very core of his being, it made him extremely happy. *It's weird,* he noted. *I feel so good right now, so fulfilled, like I have everything I could ever want. And yet I still don't have the things I've been dreaming of.*

"Once you feel that good through the power of focus, you no longer need manifestations to make you happy. You're already there. It's ironic, but that's when all you desire can start to come to you."

Really! You mean I'm that close to getting what I want?

"As long as you can hold on to that feeling and not stop to notice that what you want isn't here yet, then yes, you're very close."

If that's true, I can't lose! Jace exclaimed, enjoying the high he was on. *I get to feel amazing, while I wait for the stuff I want to come to me. I like how this works.*

"It really is a perfect plan."

"Sophie," Jace proclaimed once he was inside his apartment, "you're amazing! No wonder I'd rather spend time with you than a room full of boring humans." He'd just had more fun talking to Sophie than he'd ever had at a party. It was a different kind of fun. It was deep and fulfilling, and it left him exhilarated and clear minded rather than hung over.

An idea came to mind, and he smiled at the absurdity of it. "Sophie?"

"Yes, Jace."

"I've got some free time tomorrow afternoon. What say you and I go to your funeral?"

"I'm looking forward to it."

AS CASSANDRA awoke to the morning sun streaming through her window, a dream was still holding images and emotions captive in her mind. Though she knew she should get up and prepare for the busy day ahead, she lay there a little longer, attempting to analyze it. *I was looking at a picture of Aunt Sophia . . . and Jace was there.* She'd gazed at the picture with such love and appreciation and then felt but not seen Jace, as though he were standing behind her. *I wonder what that means? Could it be symbolic? Could Jace's presence represent his innocence? But he was behind me,* she contended. *He was out of sight. Is it because he's still here but not meant to be a part of my life . . . or is it because he's gone and is nothing more than a memory to me?*

"Don't overlook the obvious, my dear. Sometimes what you're looking for is right in front of you." Sophia's advice echoed in her head

I don't understand, Cassandra frowned. *What's so obvious here that I'm missing?* Try as she might, she couldn't come up with anything that made sense. She decided to let the thoughts go. They were confusing, and she wanted to be clear minded and focused. It was a day to honor her great aunt, to say her last farewell. Cassandra wiped a tear from her eye, admonishing herself. *Getting weepy is no way to honor anyone.* She determined to stay strong and let her strength and confidence be a tribute to Sophia.

After lunch, the limousine arrived to take them to the community center where the memorial service was being held. The building was in an older part of town, not far from where Sophia had lived. The hall was used for community functions. It also housed a senior's club and once a month provided a hot breakfast for the homeless. Cassandra wondered what part her aunt had played in her community and what significance the place had held for her. *It must have held some,* she concluded. *She must have had good reason for choosing to have her service there.*

As they pulled up in front, Cassandra understood why. People were lined up outside the door. There were people she knew—friends of her parents, and others she'd met at society functions—but the rest she suspected were locals.

"Wow," her mother exclaimed. "Everybody and his dog is showing up today."

"They must have known her," Cassandra objected. "Why else would they be here?"

"A society funeral in this neighborhood?" Helen shook her head. "People probably came out to gawk."

"You may be surprised, Helen," Richard Van Broden addressed his wife. "I think there's a lot about Sophia we don't know."

"I just hope there are no unpleasant surprises," she continued in her negative tone. "I'll be glad when this day is over."

The limousine was directed to a designated parking spot and the family ushered in a side entry away from the crowd. They were shown to a room with several shuffleboard tables and a large wall of tattered books. The four of them looked at one another, and Trevor quickly pulled chairs down from a stack in the corner so they could sit.

Cassandra felt uneasy in the surroundings, though she wasn't sure whether it was her own judgment of the place or whether she was anticipating what her mother might say. She decided to pass the time by going over her speech, hoping it would make waiting less uncomfortable. "Do you mind if I read this?" she asked, holding up the paper in her hand. "I'm a bit nervous. It might help if I go over it."

"Not at all," her father replied. "Go ahead."

She read it through, forcing herself to take her time and make eye contact with her audience as she'd been trained to do in speech class.

"Your aunt would be proud, kitten," Richard beamed.

"Sophia believed all that?" Helen asked skeptically.

"I've had to sum it up here," Cassandra replied. "But yes, she had an amazing outlook. She was happy; she lived life on purpose; she understood what true success really is. The example she set is one we can all aspire to."

Helen stared at her daughter for a moment and then looked away, disapproval creasing her brow.

It was obvious her mother didn't agree, but Cassandra didn't care. She was past needing her mother's approval. She had a new outlook on life and was proud to embrace it. A smile from her father and a wink from Trevor conveyed silent encouragement, which she gladly received.

A man in a dated black suit came in the room and announced it was time for the service to begin. They followed him to a row of folding chairs at the front of the large auditorium. Looking around as she walked in, Cassandra was surprised to see the room completely full. The seats were all occupied, and several dozen people stood at the back. She'd expected a small gathering of friends and neighbors and didn't know what to make of the large crowd. *Could it really be what Mother said?* she wondered. *Have people come just to see a society funeral?*

The pianist began to play. Rather than the depressing music usually associated with funerals, it was a lovely, soothing melody that, Cassandra realized, suited her personable aunt. She'd had a sweet, calm way about her—one that could make anyone comfortable in her presence. And though her aunt's presence no longer graced their lives, Cassandra felt very much at ease as she sat in the auditorium. Flowers adorned the front of the room. A colorful mix of potted plants and artistic bouquets lined a platform draped with velvet. A large stand was adorned with roses. In the center hung a gold-framed picture of Sophia.

She sat smiling at the familiar face, her eyes lovingly fixed on the dear woman, when suddenly she remembered her dream. *I was looking at a picture of Sophia. Could this be what I saw?* She felt a tingle in the back of her neck as she recalled the rest. *Jace was in my dream, too. Does that mean he's here?* She didn't dare turn around, yet something told her he was. *It makes sense that he'd attend the funeral. He was her neighbor, her employee . . .* Cassandra wanted to believe he'd been a friend as well. *If he's here,* she concluded, *that proves he's innocent. He'd never show his face otherwise.* Hope returned, but it was combined with an unsettled eagerness as she waited to deliver her speech. Then she could look out into the faces present and see whether Jace was one of them.

The funeral director led the service, introducing several people who got up to speak about Sophia, particularly her contribution to the community. Cassandra drank in their words. They were there because Sophia Langdon had had an impact on their lives. They were there to honor a great woman, and the tone of the service reflected that. It was in pleasant contrast to the other funerals Cassandra had attended in her lifetime. It was celebratory rather than somber. It was uplifting rather than depressing. It made one thankful for a life rather than sorry for a death. It was, in Cassandra's opinion, the perfect funeral, perfectly befitting a woman who'd truly had it all—a long life full of love, wealth, health, happiness, and joy.

JACE ARRIVED at the community center shortly after the funeral had begun. Being in a particularly good mood, it struck him as funny that he was attending the funeral of a friend with that very friend. As he slipped silently into the back of the auditorium, he was shocked to see the crowd in attendance. *I didn't know you knew so many people.*

"I lived a long time. I've met a few people."

Jace looked around the room. It seemed that all ages, nationalities, and social classes were represented. As he listened to the people who got up to speak, he was surprised to learn what Sophie had been involved in during her lifetime. She'd been active in many causes, raised money for charity, fought for change in the socioeconomic structure, and petitioned governments for amendments to various laws.

"That was my action journey," she informed Jace. "Once I learned about the power of deliberate thought, that's when I really began to accomplish things."

Jace almost laughed out loud; her statement sounded preposterous. *Seriously? You accomplished more than all that?*

"They make it sound like a lot. It was years of hard work with relatively small results. Most of what I consider significant probably won't be mentioned here. But that's all right. I didn't do it for the glory."

Jace was tempted to ask what she meant by that, but his attention was drawn to the front of the room and the succession of people getting up to honor his friend. He was fascinated to learn more about the woman who had become such an important part of his life.

The next speaker introduced herself as head of the local community association and coordinator of the outreach program. She spoke of the great loss the city of Port Hayden and especially the community of Harborside had experienced with the passing of Sophia Langdon. Her voice was tinged with emotion as she conveyed her pleasure in having known such a benevolent soul.

She talked of Sophia's tireless support of the Community Center, her generous contributions both in time and money, and then expressed her pride in being able to rename the facility. It would soon be unveiled as the Sophia Langdon Memorial Outreach Center.

Way to go, Sophie, Jace cheered silently, assuming it was one of the accomplishments she was referring to.

The memorial service continued as more people offered words of praise. After a selection of music, during which several candles were lit in memory of Sophia, the facilitator announced that the eulogy would be delivered. Jace's pulse quickened as Cassandra walked to the podium. After telling Sophie what he liked about Cassandra, after admitting to himself that she was what he truly wanted, his heart filled with love at the sight of her. She was lovely indeed.

TAKING A DEEP breath as she stood before the microphone, Cassandra did a quick scan of the room without finding the object of her search. As much as she wanted to know whether Jace was there, her first objective was delivering her tribute to her dear aunt. So instead of looking out, she looked to her family and found support in their smiling faces. She cleared her throat and began.

"I have had the privilege of knowing Sophia Langdon all my life. But only in recent weeks did I get to know the incredible human being my aunt really was. Many of you were acquainted with Sophia personally, and everyone here today has heard the wonderful things she's done for her city and her community. What I want to share with you now is a picture of the woman who changed my life. And though I wish I could have had more time with her, I'll always be grateful for what she taught me and the example she set.

"I want to talk, not about her accomplishments, not about the charities or the lobbying or the donations, but about the people she touched, the difference she made in the lives of individuals. The following letter from one such person sums up the sentiment that so many expressed.

"Dear Sophie, I wish I had more than mere words to thank you for the difference you've made in my life. You caused the sun to shine again. You helped me to find the joy that I thought was gone forever. You've done more for me than anyone else has ever been able to, because instead of trying to rescue me from the shipwreck I called my life, you simply believed in me. And even more, you showed me how to believe in myself. You taught me that I have the power to create the life I desire. You taught me that happiness is the greatest treasure anyone can possess. For that, I will be forever grateful. I know now that I'm the only one who can create in my experience. Therefore, I no longer see myself as a victim. My life has been transformed in ways that others around me call miraculous, but the biggest change is on the inside. I'm a new person, and I owe it all to you. Thank you, Sophie. You truly are an angel."

Cassandra looked into the faces staring back at her. The letter had obviously touched people. Some were dabbing their eyes; others were sniffling or clearing their throats. Still others responded with looks of cynicism or feigned disinterest.

"This is the Sophia Langdon I had the honor of getting to know," she continued, trusting her words would reach those who were ready to hear. "This is the woman I want to commemorate here today. She taught me many wonderful truths—invaluable truths that will shape my life going forward. I got to hear her words, but I also got to observe her living what she believed. Her life demonstrated the value of happiness, the joy of simplicity, and the incredible freedom that comes from carving out your own path rather than mindlessly following others.

"She taught me the true meaning of success. My life will never be the same for having known this extraordinary woman." Tears threatened to engulf her, but she was determined to finish. "Thank you, Aunt Sophia, for all you've given me . . . and for bringing sunshine and hope to so many lives. Your memory . . . will live on forever in our hearts." Cassandra was overcome with emotion. Rather than search for Jace through tear-filled eyes, she simply returned to sit with her family.

Trevor put his arm around her and kissed her cheek. "That was perfect, doodlebug."

"Thanks," she sniffed.

The pianist began the final song, and the funeral director stood to signal the procession. The family was directed down the center aisle and out through the main doors of the auditorium. Cassandra glanced around as she walked, but still there was no sign of Jace.

They formed a receiving line, and people began to pay their respects. The social elite were followed by government and organization officials, charity representatives, and business acquaintances. The locals gathered into small groups and visited among themselves, a few glancing toward the family yet hesitant to approach.

When the well-wishers had finally passed, Cassandra's mother touched her arm. "Let's go, sweetheart."

"I'd like to stay for a bit," she replied. "I want to talk to some of the people that knew Aunt Sophia."

Helen frowned. "All right, dear. Just don't be too long."

While Richard accompanied his wife to the limousine, Trevor stayed with Cassandra. She told him about the dream and her feeling that Jace was there. As she spoke, she searched the crowd again and noticed a woman staring at her. When Cassandra smiled, the young woman approached her.

"Excuse me, Miss Van Broden," she smiled shyly. "I wanted to thank you for reading that letter."

"You're welcome," Cassandra replied. "Did you know my aunt very well?"

"I did." She looked Cassandra in the eye briefly. "I was the one who wrote it."

"Oh my God," Cassandra exclaimed, "I'm so happy to meet you! Your letter was lovely. Dozens of people wrote her, conveying their thanks, but yours expressed it so beautifully. Do you think . . . " Ideas were bubbling, and she was inspired to act on them. "I wonder if I could meet with you sometime? I mean . . . I'm planning to write a book on Aunt Sophia's life, her beliefs. I'd like to talk to people who knew her . . . in more recent years, that is."

"I'd love to." The woman visibly relaxed and gave Cassandra a genuine smile. "There are others. We used to meet here regularly. If you'd like . . . I could see if they'd be willing to talk to you, too."

"I'd really appreciate that. Thank you." Cassandra took down a phone number and then shook her hand.

As the woman walked away, Trevor leaned toward his sister and whispered, "Nice how the Universe takes care of the details, isn't it? By the way, I just saw Jace. He's over there."

Cassandra turned in the direction that Trevor motioned and saw Jace talking to a couple. He looked up and for a moment held her gaze. She smiled, but didn't move. When he started walking toward her, she exhaled in relief.

"Hi, Jace."

"Hi."

His smile caused her heart to skip a beat. He looked exceptionally good dressed in a suit. His hair had been recently trimmed, and his eyes were even bluer than she'd remembered. She had to remind herself of what she needed to ask him about.

"Your speech . . . ," he hesitated. "It was really good."

"Thank you." She wanted to forget about the stupid jewelry, the car, the will, and tell him she loved him, but she couldn't. She needed to learn the truth, needed to hear it from him. "Jace," she began. "I wanted to ask you something."

"Sure," he shrugged. "What is it?"

"Last Sunday, when we were at the bar . . . after Aunt Sophia passed away. You mentioned something about jewelry she'd been wearing. Are you sure? I mean, you actually saw it on her?"

"Yeah, of course. Why?"

"Well . . . we went through her apartment and found nothing, just an empty jewelry box."

"Really?" He looked genuinely surprised.

"She wasn't wearing any in the ambulance. Trevor says he doesn't remember seeing any, either." She looked at her brother for support, but he said nothing.

"So what are you saying?" Jace asked.

"I . . . we don't know what to make of it, that's all." Cassandra didn't know what more to say without asking Jace directly if he knew of its whereabouts. And she wasn't going to do that. His reaction had been genuine; she was convinced he was innocent. "We . . . Trevor and I . . . haven't told anyone. I wanted to ask you about it first. I thought maybe you might . . . "

"Cassandra," he interrupted, frowning. "Just what are you asking?"

She looked at him helplessly. There was so much she wanted to say, but before she could put thoughts into words he asked the question she didn't want to hear.

"Do you think I took Sophie's jewelry?"

"No, I don't. But I'm concerned that others might. I mean . . . you had a key and you live right there."

Jace's reaction was one of pure disbelief. She saw the muscles in his jaw tighten as he turned away. When he looked at her again, he repeated the question slowly.

"Cassandra, do *you* think I took your aunt's jewelry?"

She'd told him no, but he obviously didn't believe her. What he saw, what he'd accurately discerned, was that she *had* suspected him, and he was right. She felt terrible. "Jace," she sighed. "I did…I mean, the thought crossed my mind. I couldn't see any other reasonable explanation. But I should have known. You'd never do something like that. I'm really sorry."

He stared at her for a long moment, saying nothing, yet the hurt in his eyes twisted the dagger in her heart.

"Goodbye, Cassandra."

"Jace, wait!" As he walked away, she looked pleadingly at Trevor, but he shook his head sadly. Cassandra's heart sank. She'd done it again. She'd passed judgment on Jace because of his social stature. Only this time, she'd driven a wedge so deep she didn't know how it could ever be removed.

Chapter 19

Jace heard Cassandra call out, but he didn't dare turn back. He needed to get as much distance between them as he could. When he was sure she hadn't tried to follow, his mind began to process what had taken place. *How could she think I'd steal from Sophie?*

The truth hit him. It was happening again. Just when he'd let down his guard, she had shown a side of herself that he couldn't accept. *It's no different than when she accused me of casing out her car. She still judges me because of where I live and how much money I make. She's nothing but a rich snob. God! I was crazy to think we could ever be together.*

He walked for several blocks, not caring where he was going as long as it was away from Cassandra Van Broden. When he realized he was heading toward his apartment, he paused. His apartment made him think of Sophie, and he wasn't in the mood to talk to her. Not yet. He decided to go to Chad's.

It was the middle of the afternoon, and Chad was just getting up when he arrived. The television was on, so Jace sat down in front of it. As he began to focus, he quickly realized he wasn't in the mood to talk to Chad either, but it was too late to do anything about it.

"Great party last night, wasn't it?" Chad stood with the fridge door open, looking intently, as if some delicacy might suddenly present itself.

"Yeah," Jace agreed, not wanting to highlight the fact that he'd left early.

"I thought you said you didn't mind if I hooked up with Elise."

"I don't," Jace retorted. "I told you that yesterday."

"Bullshit." Chad looked annoyed. "Morry said he saw you talking to her, said you left together."

"What?" Jace couldn't believe it. He was being accused, for the second time in less than an hour, of something he hadn't done. He shook his head emphatically. "I talked to her. But we didn't leave together."

"Yeah, but Morry said . . ."

"I don't give a shit what Morry said!" The anger erupted from somewhere deep inside. Jace glared at his friend. "I left alone, and if you don't believe me then . . . fuck you!" He grabbed his jacket and turned to leave, having reached his breaking point. It was Cassandra he was angry with, but Chad was in his face, and he needed to let off steam.

Chad wasn't a fighter. It was a good thing because he was a big guy, and Jace always suspected that if someone got him mad enough he could do damage. Knowing he'd overreacted, Jace stopped before he reached the door. "Sorry." He returned to the kitchen where Chad stood with a shocked look on his face. "Look, I need you to believe me. I talked to Elise . . . just to make sure she had no hard feelings. I left after that . . . because I was feeling kind of . . . you know." He shrugged, hoping his feeble excuse wouldn't require further explanation.

"I believe you, buddy," Chad frowned at his friend. "But I don't get what's up with you lately. Ever since that rich bitch screwed with your mind, you haven't been the same."

Jace didn't know where to start. Chad was aware of what had taken place between him and Cassandra in the past weeks. What his friend didn't know was that Jace had a ghost for a shrink, and she'd helped him realize that he was in love with the 'rich bitch' after all. He decided to leave out those details and tell him about his meeting with Cassandra after the funeral.

"Wait a minute," Chad interrupted. "The old lady's jewels are missing, and you're a suspect?"

"Yeah, I guess so." Jace had been so offended by Cassandra's implication, that he hadn't stopped to consider the ramifications of it.

"Jace, you could be in some serious shit here. You wouldn't stand a chance against a family like the Van Brodens. Doesn't matter if you're guilty or not. It comes down to who's got the best lawyer, and buddy . . . " Chad shook his head, "that ain't gonna be you."

Jace remembered his mom's warning, telling him to be careful because the Van Brodens were a powerful family. It had sounded ridiculous at the time. Now he was worried. "Shit." He slumped down on the sofa. "What am I gonna do?"

Chad sat down across from him. "Let's look at this from all the angles," he suggested. "The old gal's jewels are missing, but do they know what exactly—like how many pieces and how much they're worth?"

"I don't know," Jace shrugged. "That's the thing. I have no idea how big a crime I'm suspected of committing. It might be a trinket or two, or it might be some really old, expensive diamonds or something. Sophie was rich once; who knows what she kept from her past."

"You did have a key, but you gave it back the next day," Chad reasoned. "Still, you'd have had a whole day to go through her stuff. That won't look good. I wonder who else had a key."

"Anybody else with a key would be a suspect. Besides family, obviously."

"And Cassandra's aware that you know about the jewelry because you're the one who told her the old lady was wearing it that morning." As Chad summed up the facts, his look was discouraging. "I'm assuming she's told her family."

"She said she hadn't told anyone yet."

"But she did accuse you, right?"

"Not exactly," Jace replied. "She said the thought crossed her mind. Then she made a feeble apology, saying she knows I'd never do something like that."

"You know what?" Chad's expression brightened. "She may just be your wild card here. If she still likes you and believes you're innocent, she could be a character witness or something. If nothing else, she could try to convince her parents."

"I don't know. She'd have to go against her family if they all see me as a suspect. Plus if they think we're an item, and they don't like it . . . " Jace shook his head, "they'll come down on me even harder."

"Then you've gotta find a way to prove you're innocent," Chad maintained. "If the stuff is missing, then somebody else took it. Either that or she gave it away or something. Maybe you could . . . "

"Hold on," Jace interrupted. "We're all assuming that somebody stole it, but you're right, there has to be another explanation."

They both sat quietly for a moment, Jace thinking back to the morning of the Harbor Fair. He tried to recall what Sophie was wearing. *She had a necklace on, and she made a comment about her rings.* He smiled, remembering how she'd looked.

"You know what?" He grabbed his cell phone from his pocket. "I took a picture of her . . . when I dropped her off at her apartment." He found the photo and examined it closely. She didn't appear to be wearing any jewelry at all. "Let's view it on your computer," Jace suggested. "I want to get a better look." They downloaded the picture to Chad's laptop and then clicked on it, making it the full size of the screen. "There's definitely no necklace or earrings," Jace frowned. "Only one of her hands is showing, but it's her left, and there aren't any rings on it. That means she had the jewelry on when she left but not when she got back." He scratched his head. "What would she have done with it?"

"She could have lost it," Chad offered.

That didn't make sense. Sophie was slightly odd and maybe a bit forgetful at times, but a woman doesn't lose her jewelry. Jace shook his head.

"So she gave it away, then."

It was a definite possibility, and suddenly Jace realized he could simply ask her. *What am I doing?* He silently reproached himself. *She said she's always with me, and she knows exactly what happened.* He didn't feel comfortable having a conversation with Sophie in his head while Chad was next to him, so he quickly made an excuse to leave.

"What are you gonna do about this?"

"I'm not sure yet, but it's gonna be okay," Jace replied, confident now. The bewildered look on Chad's face made him wonder how he'd ever explain that he had regular conversations with a dead person. He still didn't understand it himself. Nevertheless, it was true, and he couldn't wait to talk to her.

CASSANDRA WAS QUIET on the ride home in the limousine. Given the somber occasion, she felt no need to explain her silence, yet her father was perceptive.

"What's wrong, kitten?"

She looked at him, knowing she couldn't lie.

"Who was that young man you were talking to?" her mother asked, her tone accusing.

"That was Jace," she stated calmly, deciding not to withhold information. She wasn't ashamed of knowing him, wasn't ashamed of how she felt about him. "He was Aunt Sophia's neighbor. He drove her car."

"How do you know him?"

"We've gone out a few times." Cassandra noticed her father's look, cautioning her to tread lightly. She disregarded it, not caring now that Jace was gone. He may never be part of her life, but she was determined to see his name upheld. She believed in him—even if it was too late to convince him of it.

"You dated him?"

The pitch of her voice told Cassandra she'd be hearing more about the subject in the future. For the time being, she decided to give her mother some assurance. "Yes, Mother, I did. But you can relax, it's over."

"What happened, kitten?" her father asked.

She told her parents about the jewelry Sophia had supposedly been wearing the morning of the Harbor Fair. She admitted she hadn't seen any on the way to the hospital, and then informed them she and Trevor had found nothing when they'd searched her apartment. "The jewelry was missing, and Jace had a key to her apartment. Her car wasn't parked out front, and Jace's neighbor said he hadn't been around for a few days." She looked at her father, hoping the circumstantial evidence wouldn't sway him before she had a chance to say more. "I jumped to conclusions, but I was wrong. Jace would never have done something like that. Aunt Sophia trusted him. I should have, too."

Helen was about to speak when Richard held up his hand. "Corruthers has the car at his office, kitten. He told me Jace met him there last Sunday. Dropped off both the car and the key to Sophia's apartment."

"That doesn't mean he didn't take the jewelry," Helen interrupted. "We really should report this, Richard. "Who knows what else he took."

"He didn't take anything." Cassandra was adamant.

"We have no proof that it was Jace," Trevor spoke up. "Look at all the people she was associated with. For all we know, others may have had access to her apartment as well."

Cassandra silently thanked her brother for his support. He had a valid point—one she hadn't considered. There was plenty more she should have considered as well. She'd assumed Jace had kept the car for his own use or worse, taken off with it, yet it had been at the lawyer's office the whole time. She desperately wished she could make him see how sorry she was.

"There's nothing we can do about it now. We'll bring it up when we meet with Corruthers, this week." The tone in her father's voice meant the subject was closed for discussion. Cassandra appreciated his strength. He was a powerful man in many ways, yet Cassandra often got to see his softer side, and she dearly loved him for it.

The subject was closed, as was the possibility of a relationship with Jace. Even friendship was out of the question at this point. Still, she was determined to see his name cleared. Jace Rutherford was a good man, and Cassandra felt honored to have known him.

I GUESS YOU heard all that. Jace addressed Sophie the instant his feet hit the sidewalk.

"Yes, I did."

I can't believe I didn't think to ask you in the first place, Jace said, still kicking himself.

"You can ask me now," she replied politely.

Okay, what happened to the jewelry? He smiled at how easy it was to go straight to the source and learn what others could only speculate about.

"I've been donating it to charity," she explained. "The community center has a silent auction every year. I've given them a few pieces each time. Like they say, 'You can't take it with you,' and I wanted it to go to a good cause."

Jace laughed. *And you just wanted to wear it one last time, right?* It all made sense now. The Harborside community center was only a block from where the fair had been set up. Sophie had dropped the jewelry off while she was down there. *I don't understand, though. Why didn't you just state in your will that you wanted it to go to a certain charity?*

"Oh, wills can be complicated," she said matter-of-factly. "It seemed easier this way . . . and more personal."

He smiled. Sophie certainly did have her own way of doing things. He appreciated that about her.

Though a huge weight had been lifted now that he knew the truth about the jewelry, Jace still had questions. *How am I going to convince the Van Brodens I didn't take it? I can't very well let them know I still talk to you.*

"That's up to you, Jace. At least you know the truth."

The truth. The words brought up Cassandra's lack of faith in him. She'd claimed she believed in his innocence, but the fact that she'd suspected him at all—that's what was eating at him. He'd never done anything to deserve her bad opinion of him. Part of him wanted to call and tell her what he'd learned, just to vindicate himself, yet he hated the idea of having to prove anything to her. He decided to let it go.

Now that he had the evidence he needed, he was feeling cocky. He dared anyone to try to pin what they saw as a crime on him. He'd simply go to the people in charge of the auction and have them verify that Sophie had made a donation on the day she passed away. It gave him a sense of power, knowing what others didn't. He could imagine proving the Van Brodens wrong in court. *I'd supply the evidence at the last minute and embarrass that high and mighty family in front of everyone. It would do them good to be taken down a notch or two.*

All of a sudden Jace noticed that his thoughts didn't feel as good as they had moments earlier. *Why is that?*

"Your feelings reflect where you are in relation to what you want," she explained. "When your thoughts feel good, you're moving toward what you want; when they feel bad, you're moving in the opposite direction. It's that simple."

So the thoughts I had about proving the Van Broden's wrong—they aren't serving me?

"Thoughts evoke emotion, and emotion can feel good or bad. It depends where you're coming from."

What do you mean?

"Remember how you felt about the rich a few weeks ago?" Sophie inquired.

Yeah..., he said hesitantly, *I think so.*

"Do you feel that way now?"

Jace had to think a minute. *No... I don't.*

"Back then, thoughts of revenge felt good. The idea of getting back at someone who was in your mind unfair or immoral was a welcome change from the powerlessness you felt most of the time. However, those thoughts don't serve you now because you're not there. You're not in that powerless place anymore."

Yeah, you're right, Jace acknowledged. *I've changed; it makes sense those old thoughts would feel different now. And you know,* he smiled, filled with new appreciation for his friend, *it feels good not to push against all that stuff. It feels good to let it go and trust that I'm heading in the right direction, that my thoughts and feelings are guiding me there.* Jace pondered his statement for a moment. *My thoughts and feelings . . . my mind. That's really where all the power is, isn't it?*

"Yes!"

Jace could hear Sophie's enthusiasm. With it came a tingling sensation that spread through his entire body. *Cool!* Jace responded. *Did you do that?*

"That's what alignment feels like."

I'm not sure what that means, but I like it.

"We're spiritual beings, Jace. The only difference between us is that you're focused in the physical and I'm not. What we just felt was an aligning of our vibrations.

"In the physical," she continued, "we often get tripped up when we experience contrast. We lose our balance for a while, and it can take months or years to find it again. But it doesn't have to. We can feel our way back into alignment."

That's the power of focus, Jace asserted, enjoying the sensations coursing through his body. It was exhilarating, and he wanted to ride it as long as possible. *Focus helps us find that alignment.*

"Exactly. Focus guides your thought, and thought evokes emotion."

He felt a down-pouring of insight. He wasn't sure whether it came from Sophie or whether he'd realized it himself or whether it even mattered, because there didn't seem to be any separation at the moment. *So emotion is an indicator of this vibration you're talking about.* Jace could feel the power of his words. *People make such a big deal of emotions, but they're really just an indicator, a road map. I like that!* Jace had never experienced anything like it. To have questions and receive insight almost simultaneously was a real rush. *So how do my desires play into this?*

"Desire is simply preference. As we focus, we learn to separate what we want from what we don't want. As creative beings we seek to create, or attract, the object of our desire. It doesn't matter whether it's money or a relationship or seeing lives transformed by the power of belief—you can choose anything you want. Once you know the object of your desire, the fun is in moving toward it, aligning your vibration with the vibration of the thing wanted. Your feelings will tell you if you're headed in the right direction."

Lights were going off in Jace's head. He felt like a pinball machine he'd played once in a retro bar in the city. Flashing lights, bells sounding, his heart pounding. As he reached his apartment, he sat down on the front step. He could tell by the position of the sun that he'd been walking awhile, yet he had no memory of getting from Chad's place to his. He let the intoxicating emotions wash over him like a soothing shower. His thoughts quieted, and for a moment all he could feel was a delicious fusion of love, exhilaration, and appreciation.

This alignment . . . he asked softly, feeling Sophie's presence so profusely that he could barely distinguish it from his own. *Is that why I can feel you here and talk to you like this?*

"Yes. The conversations we're having aren't that much different from the ones we had when I was physical, so it was natural to continue them. But you couldn't have heard me if you weren't in a vibration that was close to that of who I've become."

Is that why others can't hear you?

"It is."

Can Cassandra? Jace had to ask.

"She's beginning to receive thoughts or impulses that feel good when she follows them. She doesn't know it's me, though."

Jace's heart warmed as he thought of Cassandra again. He wasn't angry with her now. He knew more than ever that he loved her, that he'd always love her.

He didn't know when or how that could be, but it didn't matter. His mind went instead to her beautiful smile, her soft, silky voice, the heartwarming words she'd spoken at Sophie's funeral. He recalled the look in her eyes as she apologized for having doubted him.

Suddenly he longed to be with her. He wanted to go to her, accept her apology, and hold her in his arms. The inspiration was powerful, lifting him off the step and propelling him toward his apartment with one thought in mind. *I have to call and let her know how I feel.* His hand was on the heavy outer door when he heard a voice.

"Jace?"

He turned to see her standing on the sidewalk in front of his building. "Cassandra . . . " He hesitated, wanting to go to her, but needing to know the reason for her visit. In her eyes he saw love blended with regret and humility.

"Jace." The tears welled up as she began to speak. "I'm sorry. I've been so stupid. I know that doesn't change anything . . . "

He quickly removed the distance between them and wrapped her in his embrace. "I love you, Cassandra."

She held him tightly for a moment and then looked into his eyes, half laughing and half crying. "I really don't know why." She shook her head. "I've given you so many reasons to hate me."

"Maybe," he conceded, "but I have more reasons to love you."

Chapter 20

Cassandra couldn't stop the river of tears as the words she'd been dreaming of flowed from the lips of the only man she could imagine spending her life with. "I thought . . . when you walked away . . . ," she faltered. "I thought you'd never speak to me again. What made you change your mind?"

"Sophie," he said simply.

She looked at him curiously. "I don't understand."

"Do you want to go inside?"

"Yeah," she sniffed. "I'd like that."

He took her hand and, as they neared the top of the stairs, opened the door for her. It was where they'd first met. She nearly laughed as she thought of how badly she'd misjudged him. Squeezing his hand, she turned to him. "I love you, too, Jace." He kissed her in the very spot that weeks earlier he'd nearly bowled her over. She'd been in the wrong place then, but how glad she was to have been there, to have met the man who was capable of making her dreams come true.

They went up to his apartment, Jace still holding her hand. He had a look on his face that Cassandra could only describe as radiant. She still didn't understand what had caused the sudden change in him or how Sophia had been involved, but she was eager to find out. The building, the stairway, even Jace's presence seemed to make her aunt's memory come alive, and she welcomed the pleasant thoughts. With their time together cut short, she'd been feeling regret. Now she relished the idea of getting to know her aunt through the people whose lives Sophia had touched. And Jace was one of those people. Cassandra smiled, knowing that her aunt had played a part in their coming together; she'd helped make it happen. *Maybe that's what Jace was referring to. Maybe Aunt Sophia let Jace know she was in favor of us being together.*

She sat in Jace's living room while he got them a drink. As she surveyed the meager surroundings, she couldn't imagine anywhere she'd rather be. Jace caught her looking around as he returned. Their eyes held for a brief second, and she longed to read his thoughts. Their apartments were so different, as were their lives, but she truly didn't care. She hoped Jace felt the same.

"It's a work in progress," he shrugged.

What is it? Cassandra wondered. *Why does he seem so changed?* She'd rightly discerned that he was strong in character and determined, but now he possessed a confidence, an inner light she hadn't noticed before.

He sat next to her and stretched his arm behind her on the sofa. She leaned into his shoulder, savoring the intimacy. After a moment she murmured, "So what happened? You seem so . . . different. In a good way, I mean. But what does it have to do with Aunt Sophia?"

He was quiet for several long seconds, so she turned to look at him.

"She was pretty cool," he began. "We used to talk about stuff."

"Did you talk about her beliefs?" Cassandra asked, knowing somehow they had.

"Oh yeah," he grinned. "We talked about all that. But there's more. This is . . . going to sound crazy."

"What is it?"

"I've never lied to you, Cassandra. I've never deceived you in any way, and I never would."

"I know that, Jace," she frowned, wondering why he'd say such a thing. "I believe in you. I had to learn it the hard way," she added soberly. "But I do believe in you."

"Okay, good," he laughed uneasily. "Keep that in mind. Because what I'm about to tell you is pretty far out there."

"Jace," she stressed, laying her hand on his arm, "you can tell me. Whatever it is, I promise I'll believe you."

"Sophie is . . . She's not really . . . gone."

What? Her lips formed the word, but remembering her promise, she decided to let him explain.

"I know she died, but her spirit, her soul, whatever you call it—that part of her didn't go anywhere. She's still here."

"I . . . " Cassandra didn't know what to say. She'd been too focused on her loss, her dear aunt's absence, to think about where her spirit might be.

"We talk," Jace said frankly.

"Jace, wait a minute. I want to believe you; I really do. But let me get this straight. Are you telling me you've had conversations with her . . . since she passed away?"

"I know it sounds crazy, Cassandra, but it's true." He grasped her hands and looked her in the eye. "At first I thought the conversations in my head were a way of staying connected, a way of remembering what she told me because it felt good. But then they became two-way conversations." He shook his head. "I thought I was losing my mind."

The conviction in his eyes was obvious; he believed what he was saying. She couldn't say the same, and she hoped her face didn't convey what she was thinking. With his words verging on insanity, she scrambled to find an appropriate response.

"I can prove it," he insisted when she remained silent. "Ask me something, anything. Something about your family, your childhood."

Her discomfort increased. "Jace . . . I don't know . . ."

"Do this," he implored. "You won't be sorry. Just trust me." He smiled and brought her hand to his lips.

His earnest request left her no choice. If she were to have a relationship with Jace, she had to trust him. It was as simple as that. The conversation was without a doubt the strangest she'd ever had, yet she found herself compelled. Though what he was claiming sounded crazy, she wanted him to be right. "Okay," she pondered. "What's my middle name?"

He closed his eyes for a moment and then grinned. "You don't have one. But that's not hard enough. I could have found that out some other way. Ask me something more difficult."

She didn't know how he did it, but he was right. He was serious, too—not a trace of mischief, no sign of joking. Curiosity made her try again. "I had a dog when I was a little girl. What was his name?"

This time a few seconds passed before his smile reemerged. "Good one," he nodded. "Trying to trick me . . . that's perfect. But I know the answer. Your father bought a puppy for you when you were born. *Her* name was Roxy. She was an English setter, and the two of you were inseparable. She died when you were eight years old."

"Oh my God!" Cassandra's eyes filled with tears as her doubt vanished. "How . . . ? Did Aunt Sophia just tell you that? Is she here now?"

Jace nodded.

"Can I . . . talk to her?" Cassandra asked meekly, her voice nearly consumed by overwhelming awe.

"You can," Jace responded eagerly. "You have to be in a good feeling place, and you have to believe it's possible. That's all it takes. She'd love to talk to you," he added, the luminous glow having returned to his face. "She said she's got some things to tell you."

Cassandra gasped as she realized her aunt was communicating with her. "She really is here." Saying it aloud helped anchor the idea in her mind. With the revelation came relief. Not only was Jace not crazy, but her aunt hadn't gone away. Her time with the dear woman hadn't been cut short.

"Yeah." He drew her close and spoke softly, his lips nuzzling her ear. "Pretty cool, isn't it?"

Cassandra looked into his eyes, feeling that her joy was complete. Her love for Jace and her delight over what she'd just discovered took her to a new high. "Now I can learn what the fifth principle is," she exclaimed. But as the reality of it hit her, she frowned. "Do I just ask her? I mean, do I say it out loud or in my head?"

"Let's try this together," Jace suggested. "Why don't we start with something simple? Let's both think of a question and see what happens."

"Okay," Cassandra quickly agreed. "What should we ask her?"

"Ask her how she liked her funeral?" Jace grinned.

"You mean she was . . . " Cassandra stopped short, aware that she hadn't begun to think through the implications of what she'd just embraced as truth. "She was . . . at her own funeral?" She burst out laughing, then shook her head, apologizing, "I'm sorry, this is all so bizarre. I'll try to be serious. Let's ask her."

She reached for Jace's hand, liking the intimacy and longing for the connection he shared with her aunt. They both closed their eyes, and Cassandra took a minute to breathe consciously before expressing the question in her mind. The words had barely formed a sentence when something touched the top of her head and slipped down over her body like refreshing rain. As she relaxed into the comforting sensation, she heard her aunt's voice.

"It was lovely, dear."

Springing forward, she stared at Jace, eyes wide.

He kissed her softly. "You heard it, didn't you? She said it was lovely."

"Oh my God!" Cassandra had not only heard Sophia's words, she'd felt them. And the experience had been doubly wonderful because she'd shared it with Jace. "Let's ask her something else," she begged.

"Sure, what do you want to know?"

Cassandra knew in an instant. "We can ask her about the jewelry. Jace, we can find out what happened to it!" She responded to his smug look. "You already know, don't you?"

"Yeah," he shrugged. "I agonized over it for a couple of hours, until I finally remembered that I could go right to the source."

"So . . . " she poked him playfully. "What happened?"

He told her everything he'd learned. "I'm not sure anyone would believe us, though, if we told them how I found out."

"You're right."

"I do have this." Jace pulled his cell phone from his pocket and showed Cassandra the same picture he'd shown her the day Sophia died. "She's not wearing the jewelry in this picture, and I took it right after I picked her up from the fair. Cell phones store information that tells when and where pictures were taken. That should be more than enough proof to get me off the hook. If we need to, we could make an anonymous call letting them know the jewelry was donated."

She half listened as Jace laid out his defense. The picture of Sophia reminded her of her dream the night before. Again, Jace was present. *Could the dream have been Aunt Sophia's way of communicating with me?* Cassandra wondered. As she contemplated it, she realized the answer was yes. She could feel it. She'd been looking at evidence and making judgments without listening to her heart. Her heart had been telling her the truth the whole time. Her wonderful aunt had simply been showing her how to listen to it.

"I can't believe I ever suspected you of taking it, even for a second." She stroked Jace's cheek. "Can you forgive me?"

"I already have." Jace pulled her close and kissed her forehead. "I have a confession to make, too," he murmured. "I did lie to you once. I told you that we could never be together, and you asked me if that's what I wanted. I lied when I said it was. I wanted to be with you more than anything, but I couldn't see how it was possible. I still don't know exactly how it's going to work," he admitted, "but I'm starting to believe in miracles."

"Me too." Cassandra closed her eyes as tears of joy ran down her cheeks. She was in his arms, and she never wanted to leave. "We *can* make this work," she stressed. "We just have to believe in us. And if we need help, we have Aunt Sophia to guide us."

JACE AWOKE WITH Cassandra's lovely sleeping form next to him. The details of the previous night were still fresh in his mind. They'd talked late into the night and then made love and talked some more. It had been a near replica of his first dream, the one in which she was his soul mate. He understood now what Sophie meant. He and Cassandra were the same inside. It was a vibrational connection, a spiritual sameness. As strange as it sounded, it was the same kind of connection he had with Sophie.

Oneness. Jace pondered it for a moment. It seemed to be an underlying principle that held the universe together, but it could only truly be experienced by believing in it. Belief was like a master key. It determined, without fail, all that a person experienced. Jace was extremely blessed to have received that knowing. To be able to share it with Cassandra was beyond anything he could have hoped for. A relationship that was equally beautiful in the physical, the emotional, and the spiritual was rare.

He continued to gaze at her. She was more ravishing asleep than awake, if that were possible. A trace of a smile was evident as she let out a contented sigh. Jace memorized her face, the curve of her neck, and the way her satiny hair flowed onto the pillow. His eyes followed the line of her shoulder, down her arm to where her hand rested elegantly on her thigh. Her tanned body looked stunning against the white sheet that partially covered her. Her firm breasts were a shade lighter than the rest of her skin, the lines of her bikini top slightly visible. She looked like a goddess, a vision, someone da Vinci might have immortalized on canvas.

He didn't want to wake her; they'd only had a few hours sleep, but he longed to touch her, to make love to her again. As he shifted to get more comfortable, she moaned seductively and opened her eyes. When she smiled, his heart confirmed what his mind had been slow to admit. He was totally and completely in love.

"Good morning," she purred, reaching out to him.

"It is." He pulled her closer until her body molded perfectly to his.

"Mmm," she breathed contentedly. "I like it here."

It seemed obvious that she meant their physical proximity, yet deep down Jace hoped she might also be referring to his home and ultimately his heart. Her next statement confirmed it.

"I like being here with you. I like being in love with you, Jace. I've never felt this way before."

"Me neither," he smiled as he held her close. "It feels good doesn't it?"

"Mm hmm."

Chapter 21

Cassandra watched Jace as he moved about the kitchen. She was fascinated to learn that he was quite efficient. It was another one of their many differences, yet as she recalled what they'd talked about the night before, she reminded herself that they shared a common bond in areas that mattered.

He set a plate of food in front of her, and she breathed in the mouthwatering aroma. "Thanks," she smiled, enjoying the sight of him serving breakfast wearing just a pair of shorts.

As he sat down across from her at the table, their eyes met and they silently acknowledged the underlying awkwardness. They were in love, yet it was their first meal together. Much had been discussed, yet so much still needed to be said. After sharing a life-changing secret and discussing their innermost feelings, the idea of making small talk at the breakfast table seemed uncomfortable. She was glad when Jace addressed what was on both their minds.

"Last night you said you wanted to ask Sophie about a fifth principle. What's that about?"

Having temporarily set aside her quest, excitement bubbled up at the prospect of finding out. "Aunt Sophia started telling me what she believes. She had me write it down. There were five principles she lived her life by, but I only got to hear four of them before she . . . " Cassandra caught herself and grinned apologetically. "It's going to take a while for this to sink in. I mean, I believe she's still here, but . . . "

"Hey . . . " He touched her hand. "I get it. I'm just glad you're still here."

"She was very specific," Cassandra went on, "telling me a new principle each time we were together. The idea that we're one, that we're all connected somehow—that's the first principle. The second is that we're creative beings. We actually create our reality by the thoughts we think."

"We talked about that quite a bit," Jace interjected. "It took me awhile to get it, but I'm finally understanding how it works. Our thoughts aren't just random bits of information. It takes practice and determination, but we can have control over what and how we think. Creating our reality is pretty basic—at least in theory. There are two ways to think about what we want. We can think about its presence or we can think about its absence."

Cassandra's heart soared. Jace not only understood the principles, he was passionate about them. He was applying them in his life.

"It's focus," he stated confidently. "Focus puts us in control of the game. If we focus on what we want in a way that feels good, it has to manifest. I saw it happen last night." His voice softened. "I was sitting out there thinking about how much I loved you and how I wanted to be with you, and all of a sudden you were standing in front of me."

"I know," Cassandra nodded, her voice thick with emotion. She'd been thinking of Jace in the same way. The impulse to talk to him had been so strong, she'd driven over without questioning. "It really does work."

"So what's the third principle?"

"There's a source of well-being. It's like a stream continually flowing to us, and we can choose to let it in or not." Cassandra was still in awe of the powerful teaching and how deeply it had resonated with her. "It's amazing. The only reason we have sickness, or poverty, or pain of any kind, is that we aren't allowing the well-being to flow to us. We pinch it off with the negative thoughts we think."

"I learned that one the hard way," he grinned ruefully. "I was focused on lack of finances, and I didn't realize it. Sophie helped me to see how negative my thoughts were. She showed me how to think about money in a more positive way. It wasn't hard to change my thoughts once I started paying attention to how they felt. I like how our emotions guide us," he asserted. "They let us know if we're heading toward what we want or not."

"That's the fourth principle," Cassandra exclaimed. "Our emotional guidance system. Jace . . . I'm so glad you know this, too. It's such an incredible teaching."

"It is," Jace acknowledged. "I've been practicing it, and I can tell I'm heading in the right direction. I'm going to make something of my life. I'm going to be successful—even rich someday." He blushed slightly as he looked at Cassandra. "You probably can't relate to those kinds of desires."

"No," she replied honestly. "But I've experienced lack in other areas of my life. I don't exactly have a great track record when it comes to relationships." She wanted to say more, wanted to assure him that the difference in their financial situations didn't matter to her, but it was a touchy subject. "Jace." She reached for his hand. "I have no doubt you'll succeed. In fact, you already have. Happiness is the true indicator of success, and you've found that. Money is just . . . " She paused, knowing she'd sound like a hypocrite talking about money as if it didn't mean anything when she had plenty and he had very little. She decided to be honest. "Jace, I don't want money or the lack of it to be an issue in our relationship."

"Then we won't let it." He stood up, took her hand, and pulled her to him. "Cassandra, I feel so incredible right now—like I could conquer the world. I feel rich already. You're right, it isn't about the money; it's about happiness."

Cassandra melted into his arms. Her joy was full, yet every moment seemed to offer more to love, more to appreciate. It had been Sophia's encouragement, her belief in them, that made it all possible. She was the reason Jace was holding her, loving her. Cassandra silently thanked her beloved aunt.

A VOID FILLED his apartment the moment Cassandra left. It felt right having her there. It felt right being together. She'd gone to her parent's place to change clothes and pack her suitcases. She'd be leaving for the city on an evening flight. That meant they had a few precious hours to spend together before Jace saw her off at the airport.

The phone rang, startling him. Seeing his mother's name on the call display brought him back to reality. His stomach clenched. *How am I ever going to tell her that I'm in love with her employer's daughter?*

"Jace, you'll never guess what happened."

"Probably not." He tried to joke. The lightness in her voice indicated she had good news. "So you may as well tell me."

"Do you remember your father mentioning his older brother... Roger?"

"Yeah." Jace was relieved that the conversation wasn't going to be about the Van Brodens. "He was the one that left home at sixteen, and nobody's had contact with him since."

"Yes. Your father tried for years to track him down, and so did your Aunt Beth. They came to the conclusion that he must have died, or else they would have heard something over the years."

"So what about him?"

"I just got a call from Beth. Roger passed away a few months ago. Apparently, he spent the last few years of his life in an institution of some kind. He never married or had children."

The news didn't really affect Jace; he hadn't known his uncle. Still, he was his father's brother and it was disheartening to hear that he'd lived and died alone.

"He had money," Sarah informed him. "Not a fortune or anything, but since he had no family of his own, the money goes to his siblings. And since your father's no longer alive, his share goes directly to you."

Jace took a minute to digest what he'd heard. "Are you telling me a man I've never even met died and left me an inheritance?"

"Yes!" Sarah exclaimed. "Beth said the estate was worth almost fifty-thousand dollars. Of course, there'll be legal fees and taxes and all that, but it's to be split equally between you and Beth. Isn't that amazing?" She paused for a breath. "After all these years . . . "

"Mom," Jace interrupted her. "That money should go to you, not me. You were married to Dad for almost twenty years."

"I don't make the rules, sweetheart," she replied. "Anyway, it's done. You'll be getting a check in the mail anytime. Jace, I'm so excited. This will be a turning point for you. Now you can follow your dreams. You had to give up college when your dad got sick. You can use this money to go back and get your degree."

"Yeah," he responded absently, still dealing with the shock. "I could . . . I mean, I can definitely afford to take the business courses now. I checked into them, but . . . "

As he said the words aloud, he became aware that his emotions had changed. That course of action didn't line up with what he truly wanted. He'd been willing to settle when money was tight, but he didn't have to anymore. "Mom, don't be offended." He hesitated. "I took those courses for you and Dad. That wasn't what I really wanted to do with my life."

"Oh, but I thought . . . "

"I always wanted to be a pilot, don't you remember?"

"Oh, Jace . . . " Her voice was contrite. "I should have known that. That's all you talked about when you were young. Why did we try to convince you otherwise?"

"You did what you thought was best for me," he soothed. "I don't blame you guys. I may still get a business degree one day. It wouldn't be a bad thing to have. But right now . . . " He couldn't complete the sentence. It was too surreal. He needed a moment to acknowledge what had just happened to him.

"Now . . . " She finished for him. "You're going to get your pilot's license. You're going to fly one of those big commercial jets. You're going to travel all over the world. Oh Jace," she cried, "I couldn't be more happy for you!"

As he listened to his mom describe what he'd always thought was his dream job, he took note of his emotions again. They'd changed. *How come that doesn't feel like it used to?* Somehow the dream of flying felt better than the reality of it. *Maybe it's not actually what I want to do as a career. Maybe...* He noticed the tingling sensation again as his mind filled with insight. *Maybe it just represents my desire to be free.*

Free. The simple word made his heart soar. His future had opened up, and though his path was not clearly laid out, his choices seemed endless. He was free to dream now, free to become whatever he wanted. It didn't bother him that he didn't know what that was. *I did it!* he shouted inwardly. *I created my own reality.* He couldn't wait to tell Cassandra.

As she came to mind, he remembered his dilemma. Telling his mom about their relationship was something he needed to do sooner rather than later. News of it might get out, and he didn't want her to hear about it through the grapevine of gossip that went on behind the scenes at the Van Brodens. "Mom, are you going to be home tonight? I'd like to stop by. I have a dinner date, but I'll drop by later... around nine?"

"A date?" Curiosity rippled through Sarah's voice. "Is this someone new?"

"Yeah," he replied. "She's great. I'll tell you all about her tonight."

"MOTHER, PLEASE calm down," Cassandra implored. "Listen to what I have to say about him."

"He was your aunt's chauffeur, he works at a factory, and now you tell me he's the son of our housekeeper! What more do I need to know? Do you honestly see a future with someone like that?"

"Would you rather see me marry an arrogant, self-centered womanizer like Nick Hagen?"

Her mother looked shocked. "Nicholas is a fine young man. He comes from a good family . . . "

"He cheated on me, Mother." Cassandra relayed the information calmly, no longer feeling negative emotion toward him.

Helen opened her mouth in an obvious attempt to continue the discussion but closed it just as quickly. She stared at her daughter for a moment, then shook her head. "I'm sorry, I had no idea."

"Mother, I want you to trust me. I know what I'm doing. I've made mistakes. Nick was a big mistake. But you know what? I don't regret it. It's helped me know more clearly what I want in a relationship. I don't care where Jace lives or how much money he makes. I care that he's sensitive and generous and kind." Cassandra couldn't hide the love she felt. "He has the most amazing outlook on life. He's going to be successful one day—even by your standards, and it won't be because of his association with me," she added. "He's proud, and he's determined to follow his dreams.

"He didn't want to get into a relationship with me at first," she acknowledged, "because of our differences.

He was the one who was being cautious because he didn't want us to end up getting hurt. He's a good person."

Her mother remained silent. Cassandra wasn't sure whether she'd admitted defeat or was simply gathering more ammunition. Her father, on the other hand, had been sitting quietly through the whole heated conversation. Now he stood, facing the women.

"Helen," he addressed his wife, "I know you have strong opinions about the way our children should conduct their lives. And I know that your reasons are more admirable than just for the sake of appearance. I believe that deep down you want what's best for them. But I want to state *my* opinion here. We've raised two remarkable children, and I'm proud of them. They've got the sense to follow what feels right rather than what society deems acceptable. That takes courage and a depth of character that most young people don't have these days.

"If Cassandra is happy with Jace, then she has my blessing." His tone indicated there would be no arguing with his proclamation. He smiled at his daughter. "I'm looking forward to meeting Jace, kitten. He sounds like a fine young man."

Cassandra was overjoyed to have her father's approval. He'd been open-minded right from the start, not jumping to conclusions as she had. When she'd told them about the picture Jace had taken and suggested the possibility of her aunt donating the jewelry to charity, her father had accepted it without question.

Now he was more than willing to accept him as a suitor for his daughter. Cassandra was about to respond to her father's comments, but it appeared he had more to say.

"And furthermore . . . " He cleared his throat. "I want to make it clear that Trevor has my blessing as well." He fixed his eyes on his son who stood in the doorway, luggage by his side. "Son, I know I'm old school when it comes to issues like this, but times are changing, and I think . . . well, I think it's about time we change with them."

Cassandra watched her father's face as he spoke. It was clearly the most difficult speech he'd ever made, and she couldn't have been more proud of him.

"If you're happy . . . in a committed relationship," he swallowed hard while nodding his approval. "Then I'd like to meet this fellow sometime, too."

"Richard!" Helen gasped. "What will people say?"

"Damn it, Helen," he rallied. "I'm sick to death of caring about what people think. Sophia set a fine example, living her life the way she did. We could all learn a lot from that woman. You're going to have to deal with this in your own way. I've said my peace." He let out an extended breath, and with a nod to his children he headed from the room.

Cassandra waited anxiously to see what her mother's response would be. She was surprised to see tears well up in her eyes.

"You think I don't love you like he does." She addressed both her children, holding her chin up in a way only Helen Van Broden could do while eating humble pie. "Well, you're wrong. You both mean the world to me. Maybe I have cared too much about what other people think. I can see that's going to have to change. Now if you'll excuse me, I have things to attend to."

Their mother wasn't one for expressing feelings or showing physical affection, yet Cassandra had always known she was loved. Their father had more than made up for the warmth their mother unintentionally withheld. Somehow Cassandra understood and had no hard feelings toward her because of it. She turned to her brother, who was still in the doorway with a stunned look on his face.

"Did I just enter a parallel universe?"

"No," she grinned. "You've got the right universe. I think we've just witnessed the power of deliberate creation. We made the decision to change our thinking, and look what happened. We literally changed our reality. And you know what? This is only the beginning."

"I think you're right, doodlebug." He playfully twisted a strand of her hair. "So, I take it everything went well with Jace?"

"Oh, Trev, I have so much to tell you!"

They made plans to meet in the city before Trevor returned to Europe. Cassandra was glad to have more time to spend with the brother she adored, and she was thrilled to learn that she'd be meeting his partner, Maurice, who was joining him there. Right now, however, she was eager to return to Jace's apartment.

JACE HUNG UP the phone and circled the living room a couple of times before flopping down in his worn recliner. He couldn't wipe the smile off his face or keep from shaking his head in disbelief.

"It shouldn't surprise you," Sophie remarked. "You were a vibrational match to it."

I know, but an inheritance from an uncle I've never met? he laughed. *I couldn't have imagined anything like that happening.*

"The Universe is creative when it comes to your well-being," she replied. "It's not responding to your literal thoughts, it's responding to the essence of your desire. Financial well-being can come in all sorts of ways. It's fun to let the Universe take care of the details. It makes life much more interesting, doesn't it?"

You can say that again. His future had exploded into a plethora of possibilities. Nothing was out of the question. Life felt limitless. It had become a carnival ride rather than a tedious trek. Everything seemed easy and effortless. The only thing causing him angst was the unavoidable meeting with his mom, later.

"Sophie," he addressed the void in front of him. "I could use your advice. I'm not sure how to tell Mom about Cassandra."

"How would you like it to play out?"

"Okay," he nodded. "I see where you're going with this. I need to imagine it the way I want it to be. Let's see." He closed his eyes and pictured his mom's kitchen. He could smell bread fresh from the oven. He could see her smiling and hear her laugh as they joked about something. Then he thought about confessions he'd made in the past, like bad report cards or breaking a neighbor's window. Without exception, she'd listened to his side of the story before responding. She'd let him know there were always consequences for his actions but was quick to remind him how much she loved him. She was a good mother. Suddenly love and appreciation outweighed apprehension. His news would come as a shock, but she'd be okay with it. More than that, she'd find a way to be happy for him.

I did it again! Jace was ecstatic. With deliberate effort, he'd changed his emotional set point. This time he noticed something new. It was the movement itself that was exhilarating—not just the result it produced.

"Fun, isn't it?"

"I could get addicted to this!" he laughed and then thought of a new question for his nonphysical mentor. "Is this why we come here? To experience this?"

"Yes," she replied. "Desires change, manifestations vary, but the vibrational movement that brings us into alignment—that's the main attraction."

Jace contemplated the new ideas, while savoring the new high he'd achieved. When a knock on the door announced Cassandra's return, he responded by jumping up and meeting her halfway across the room. He wrapped her in his arms, burying his face in her hair. Neither of them spoke. The joy and satisfaction of being together couldn't be enhanced with words. After a moment, he led her to the sofa where the only sounds were those of passion being expressed.

Desire heightened, yet time seemed to slow as the perfection of their lovemaking revealed itself. Holding Jace's gaze, Cassandra undid her blouse, exposing breasts barely covered by a lacy bra. In one easy motion, she removed her skirt to reveal more of the tantalizing lace. Jace wanted her, and quickly, but his need for her extended beyond the physical. He had never known passion so permeated with love. He wanted all of her—body, soul, and spirit—and he was willing to give all of himself in return.

With self-control he'd never known, he kissed every inch of her magnificent body, bringing her to delirium as her need for him reached a feverish height. He watched her crest with satisfaction. Only then did their bodies unite, taking them to an ecstasy beyond anything they'd ever experienced.

Even once they'd caught their breath, it was a few minutes before they punctured the pristine silence with words. A deeper communication was taking place. Their hearts were speaking to each other in a language no words could convey. Jace didn't need to ask what Cassandra was thinking. The joy on her face, the smile on her lips, and the tears shimmering in her eyes echoed the powerful love that filled his heart and constricted his throat.

"If we have to be apart for five days . . . " Cassandra breathed, running her hand through Jace's hair. "I'm going to replay this moment every time I think of you. I love you so much."

"Me too." He laced his fingers in hers. "When I was kissing your beautiful body, I was memorizing every part of you so I could have you with me... in my mind. You're already in my soul. I think you've been there for a long time."

"No one's ever said anything like that to me, Jace." She laughed as more tears escaped. "But then, I've never met anyone like you . . . at least not in this lifetime."

"Did you tell them?" He didn't have to say who, and she didn't have to ask. His curiosity had been set aside momentarily, but now he really wanted to know how her parents had responded.

"Yeah," she nodded.

Her smile told him the encounter hadn't been too unpleasant. As she supplied the details, he was tangibly relieved to learn that her father had sanctioned their relationship.

"What about your mom? Will she be okay with this?"

"She'll love you," Jace assured her.

When it was time to go out for dinner, Cassandra smiled and handed him the keys to her rental car. He'd made a reservation at the restaurant he'd taken his mom to for her last birthday. As they pulled up, she proclaimed, "Celinos! I love this place. Good choice."

The food was excellent, though pricey, and it gave Jace satisfaction just knowing he could afford to take Cassandra there. He'd yet to tell her about the money he was to receive. He waited until the main course was served before relaying the news, trying to sound casual. He'd come to the realization that while the amount seemed like a small fortune to him, for Cassandra it was a pittance. "I know it's not a big deal," he shrugged. "I figure between fifteen and twenty-thousand after taxes. But it'll really help. I can finally do something with my life."

"Oh my God, Jace!" she exclaimed, grasping his hand. "It *is* a big deal. You created this. You changed your reality by changing your thinking. Do you know what this means?"

He was taken aback by her response. His mind sought to analyze what had just taken place. *Why did I downplay it? Why did I feel I had to make it less significant for Cassandra's sake?* By doing so, he'd removed the joy from it. Not only that but he'd let their differences, real or perceived, influence his behavior. What struck him the most, however, is that he'd made an assumption about Cassandra, about how she would react to his news, and he'd been wrong. *Sophie, I could really use your help here,* he petitioned.

"What is it?" Cassandra asked.

"You . . . us. This is going to be interesting," he sighed, still trying to sum up his thoughts.

She waited for him to explain, but she looked uneasy.

He tried to put her mind at rest. "You're amazing."

A smile formed, but concern remained on her brow. "Jace, talk to me. What's going on?"

"I thought . . . that amount of money wouldn't mean much to you. I'm sorry," he responded quickly to the look on her face. The last thing he wanted to do was hurt her. "I've judged you, and I don't want to do that."

"Jace, I know this may sound arrogant, but it's not about the money."

"I know." He caressed her hand lovingly. "You reminded me of that. Your response . . . your excitement for me . . . You're right. It is a big deal. I nearly went through the roof when I heard it. Nothing like this has ever happened to me before. The money's great. I mean, it's fuckin' incredible, but the power I feel knowing that I did this, knowing I can do it again . . . Finally feeling like I'm in control of my life . . . God, what a rush!" Jace was back to the high he'd been on earlier, and Cassandra was laughing.

"This *is* going to be interesting." She sat back with a nod. "Aunt Sophia wanted us together for a reason, and I'm beginning to understand why." Turning serious, she leaned forward again. "I think we've touched on something important here, Jace. If we can make money irrelevant, take it out of the equation . . . If we can focus on creating our reality and having fun, then we've found the secret to making this work." With burgeoning excitement, she added, "We've both got dreams, and nothing can stop us from achieving them. There's nothing we can't be or do or have."

"That's what Sophie always says," Jace grinned. "I guess somewhere along the line, I started believing it."

CASSANDRA DIDN'T want the evening to end. They sat in the restaurant until she had to leave to catch her flight. As they drove to the airport, it occurred to her that they were setting the precedent for many Sunday evenings to come. She realized, too, that the city no longer held the attraction it had in the past. As much as she liked what she did and the people she worked with, her job no longer offered the seduction it once had.

As she thought about her desire to do more with her life, she realized that Port Hayden held the potential for the fulfillment of her dreams. She couldn't stop thinking about the book she wanted to write. Ideas were forming; anticipation was growing. The woman she'd met at the funeral had inspired the vision. Rather than a biography or a self-help guide, it would be creative nonfiction, a genre that was becoming more common in her industry. It would be fact written in literary form, highlighting Sophia's life as it intertwined with others, her own included.

Cassandra couldn't wait to interview the woman, along with anyone else who would be willing to speak to her about their connection with Sophia Langdon. However, she wasn't deceiving herself. Port Hayden held an appeal for another reason. Port Hayden meant being with Jace.

She kept her musings to herself. As much as she loved Jace and felt his love in return, they had yet to talk about their future together. She had no doubt she wanted to spend the rest of her life with him, but it was too soon to be talking of marriage. She was content, for now, to get to know him better and spend as much time with him as she could.

They continued to hold each other after the announcement for her flight. Saying goodbye was harder than she'd imagined, so she avoided the words. Instead she stroked his handsome face as she gazed steadfastly into his eyes. "I love you, Jace Rutherford."

Chapter 22

A light was flashing on his answering machine as Jace arrived home from work the next day. The message was from the law office of Harmon, Corruthers & Scott, requesting a meeting with him on Wednesday at six. His stomach tightened as he considered the possible reasons for the call. *Could this be about Sophie's jewelry? What if Cassandra's family has changed their mind about her dating me and wants to make trouble?*

Thoughts of Sophie reminded him that all was well. He had proof that he hadn't taken the jewelry; there was no reason to worry. Nevertheless, he decided to pay a visit to the community center and get the name and number of the woman in charge of donations in case he needed to produce it for the lawyer.

When he arrived he was told that Mrs. Davidson, the woman organizing the fundraising, was in her office.

He hadn't anticipated talking to her, so he rehearsed a quick speech as he walked down the hallway. "Mrs. Davidson?" he asked, rapping lightly on her open door.

"Yes?" She looked up from a pile of paperwork.

"I don't want to bother you," he hesitated. "If you're busy . . . I can come back another time."

"No, please come in."

Her smile immediately put Jace at ease.

"It's been a busy week, getting ready for our silent auction this Saturday, but I can spare a minute."

"That's what I wanted to talk to you about." Jace began the story he'd come up with. "I was a friend of Sophia Langdon, a neighbor. I drove her car for her," he added, wanting to fully establish his association with Sophie. "My name is Jace. Jace Rutherford."

"It's good to meet you, Jace." She extended her hand amiably. "Sophie mentioned she had a neighbor driving her. I was glad to hear of it; I worried about her sometimes." Her face went solemn. "It was a shock to hear that she passed away so suddenly. We'll sure miss her around here."

Jace nodded while inwardly addressing Sophie. *If only she knew you were right here.*

"So what can I do for you, Jace?"

"Sophie . . . uh . . . Mrs. Langdon." He corrected himself, deciding that her formal name sounded more official given his inquiry.

"We all called her Sophie here," she responded politely. "She may have been a wealthy woman, but she was as down to earth as you or I."

Wealthy? Jace questioned the woman's words. *I guess she knows about your past.* He didn't wait to hear Sophie's response, yet he was sure it was the case. It was the only thing that made sense. "Um . . . yeah, she mentioned wanting to drop some things off here for your silent auction. I offered to drive her, but that was before . . . " His voice trailed off. "I didn't know whether she'd left instructions with her family . . . about what she wanted to donate, I mean. I just thought I should say something."

"I appreciate your thoughtfulness, Jace, but Sophie did drop off her donation. It was the same day she passed away." She shook her head sadly.

"Oh, I'm glad to hear you got it," he replied, getting into the part. "She showed me some of the jewelry she planned to donate. I know how much she wanted you to have it for the auction."

"That reminds me . . . " The woman shook her head with admonishment. "I've been so busy this week, I totally forgot. I'm glad you came in."

Jace had no idea what she was talking about. He watched as she opened a filing cabinet and rummaged through a few files before pulling out a slip of paper.

"Sophie had a ring that needed repair. She'd taken it to a jeweler, but it wasn't ready when she brought me her items, so she asked if I'd mind picking it up." She frowned. "I might have forgotten altogether if you hadn't come by.

"I'll have to call and see if the jeweler could have someone drop it off for me," she muttered, seeming to forget that Jace was still there. "I've got no time this week." She adjusted her bifocals to read the number on the claim check and then picked up the phone to dial.

"Mrs. Davidson," Jace offered. "If you'd like, I could pick it up."

"Oh, would you mind? You don't know how much I appreciate that. Thank you."

"Not at all," he replied, glad to help after she'd readily supplied the information he needed.

The ring was ready for pickup, and the store would be open for another half-hour. Jace left with the address in hand. He took a taxi for the sake of time, and as they pulled up in front of the store, he realized he'd been there recently. He'd dropped Sophie off at the hairdresser next door. *I bet you took the ring to the jewelers on the same trip.*

"Yes, Jace, I did," Sophie affirmed.

He waited at the counter while an old man went to the back to get the ring.

"I sorry to hear about Ms. Langdon," he imparted in a thick, oriental accent when he returned. "Very nice lady; one of my best customer."

The old man took the ring from the small velvet case and held it up to the light. Jace wasn't sure whether he was admiring his handiwork or lamenting the fact that it was the last job he'd ever do for Sophie. He wondered, too, about his comment. Given his age, he might have served her in her younger days when she still had money. But Jace was quite sure he hadn't seen her much in recent years.

The large stone glistened conspicuously in the bright light above the display case; it looked like a diamond. Jace decided to see whether the jeweler would offer any information. "It looks good," he remarked casually. "Was it a big job to repair it?"

"Not too bad," the man replied. "Gold getting thin on underside of shaft, so I build up; couple of claws need replace too." He pointed to the work he'd done. "Don't see wedding ring like this anymore. Ms. Langdon say it was custom design for her by late husband. Very beautiful."

Her wedding ring! Jace's mind began to work. *An heirloom like that should be kept in the family. I should probably tell Cassandra about this.* It seemed like the most reasonable thing to do, yet other thoughts clamored for his attention. *Why would Sophie include it with the items to be donated, and not leave it to her family in the will if that's what she wanted?* He didn't think to ask her directly, yet a comforting sensation told him that events were unfolding according to plan. *Maybe she wants them to bid on the ring. It makes sense. That way the family keeps the ring, and the community benefits too. But if I hadn't stopped by the center...* Suddenly he had a strange inkling that his part in it was not by accident.

His thoughts continued as he left the jewelers. A taxi was sitting out front, the driver obviously taking a break as he downed a burger. Jace hopped in and instructed him to return to the community center where Mrs. Davidson was waiting. As he sat in the back of the cab, a new idea began forming in his mind. It was accompanied by the now-familiar tingling sensation, and he was sure it had come from Sophie. Jace's pulse quickened as he considered the suggestion. *I'm part of this,* he breathed, *and so is Cassandra. This is all happening for a reason!* By the time he'd reached the community center, the idea had hatched into a plan—one he wanted to discuss with Mrs. Davidson.

THE DECISION had been easy. It was a job Cassandra had wanted more than anything; she'd worked hard to get to the place she was at. Now, suddenly, she was handing in her resignation with no regrets. She appreciated all she'd learned. The knowledge she'd acquired, the experience she'd gained—both would be valuable assets as she moved on to future endeavors.

Her plan had become clear as she sat on the airplane the previous evening. She knew what she wanted now; she'd never felt more certain about anything in her life. Port Hayden was calling her in a powerful way. She was eager to begin the research for her book, and she was excited to move forward in a relationship with the man she adored. She couldn't be happier.

She'd talked to Jace when she got home but hadn't told him about her plans, though she'd been tempted. It was a bold decision, a sudden one, and he was a big part of her reason for making it, yet she didn't want her decision to pressure him. She intended to get a place of her own, and as their relationship progressed they could discuss the possibility of living together or even more.

The idea of more occupied her mind. She could see herself married to Jace one day and hoped that day wouldn't be too far away. There was nothing to stop them now except their need to take it slow, to be sure they were both ready for that important step.

Their families supported them. Cassandra was happy to learn that Jace's mom had responded favorably. She'd been shocked, as Jace had predicted, but willing to trust that he was making the right decision. Sarah had even told him she'd seen something she liked in Cassandra the first time they'd met.

Her father called that evening to give her the details of a meeting scheduled with Sophia's lawyer. Although Cassandra knew about it, she hadn't made plans to attend. It was legal business, and probably just a formality. Her father was Sophia's closest living heir; the bulk of her estate would no doubt go to him.

"It's up to you, kitten," he maintained. "But Corruthers did say it was customary for the family to be present for the reading of the will. Besides . . . I'd like you to be there."

Cassandra couldn't object; her father rarely asked anything of her. Moreover, it would be a perfect excuse to see Jace again. She could imagine dropping by his place unannounced and seeing the surprise and, she was sure, delight on his face.

Sitting in her apartment that evening, she couldn't resist summing up all that had taken place in a few short weeks. It seemed like a lifetime ago that she'd broken up with Nick and started questioning what she wanted to do with her life. She smiled as she thought of where those questions had led her. *Aunt Sophia . . . It's because of her I know what I want.* Pleasant images of Jace filled her thoughts. *. . . and who I want.*

She'd enjoyed time spent with her wise old aunt, and Jace had shown her that talking to her was something she could continue to do. It had been thrilling to ask a question and hear the response in her head. However, there had been moments since, when she'd wondered if she'd imagined it. Logic proposed that the thrill of being with Jace along with the desire to believe him had caused her mind to formulate what would have been a typical response from her aunt.

But Jace heard it, too, she argued. *And he couldn't have possibly known the answers to those questions. It happened; I know it did.* She truly wanted to experience it again, yet something kept her from trying. *Jace said all it takes is to feel good and to believe it's possible. I've been feeling amazing,* she reasoned, *so it must be my lack of belief that's the problem.*

In the quiet of her living room she focused her mind, willing herself to allow what was lacking. Try as she might, she couldn't get to that elusive place. Finally, closing her eyes in what felt like defeat, she whispered, "Aunt Sophia, where are you?"

"I'll always be with you, dear."

The words her aunt had spoken right before she died echoed clearly in her head. Still she questioned whether it was her aunt speaking or just a powerful memory. She decided to test it further. "Are you here now?"

"Yes."

Cassandra wanted to believe, but she continued to struggle. The responses were too simple; her mind could have supplied the answers she desperately wanted to hear. "Please let me know you're here," she pleaded. "I really want to believe." As she heard her own pathetic plea, she decided to take a more positive stance. "I do believe. I believe in you, Aunt Sophia. I believe in the possibility of life after death. I believe you're here with me now." Tears began streaming down her face as she felt the almost instantaneous shift in her vibration. "I don't need to hear your voice," she asserted. "I know you're with me. I love you, Aunt Sophia." A calming warmth surrounded her, assuring her of her aunt's love as well as her presence. Cassandra was satisfied as she sat wrapped in loving arms. She no longer needed words as proof.

A noise in the kitchen startled her from her meditative state, and she went to investigate. She wasn't afraid; her building had the highest security features imaginable. Besides, it sounded like it had come from inside one of the cupboards. She opened a door cautiously to see what had made the noise, and a glass mug fell toward her. She caught it before it hit the counter and then nearly dropped it again as she heard her aunt's voice.

"Shall we have some tea, dear?"

"Aunt Sophia?" she gasped. Though she was in shock, she managed to laugh at her aunt's delightful sense of humor.

"Yes, dear, it's me."

For the next hour, Cassandra visited with her aunt. She had questions, but first needed to show appreciation for the tremendous gift Sophia had given her. "You helped me know what I want to do with my life," she gushed. "You showed me my purpose. How can I ever thank you?"

"What you're seeing as your purpose, is just an experience that's calling you in the moment," her aunt clarified. "Your true purpose will always be joy."

"My purpose . . . is joy?"

"Yes, my dear," Sophia explained. "You'll continue to have experiences from which you'll grow and expand. But expansion is inevitable. Joy is what you're really seeking."

The new insight left Cassandra tingling. "I love that. I've been feeling it, too. I knew joy was an important element, but I still thought that having a purpose in terms of action was what we were ultimately striving for. Is it because we're taught that? Because we grow up believing it?" Cassandra was silent for a moment, absorbing the new ideas. "So . . . the purpose I was seeking was really joy, and the principles you gave me allowed me to discover that."

"Yes, I had a desire to share the wonderful knowledge I'd come to know, and you had a desire to hear it," her aunt responded lovingly. "That made us a vibrational match. I suggested you write down the four principles I'd learned about living life, because writing is something you love to do. The knowledge is yours now; you get to choose what you do with it."

"But Aunt Sophia," Cassandra objected, "you mentioned five principles."

"Yes, and the fifth is the most wonderful of all; it explains how we can continue interacting in this way."

"Wait!" Cassandra cried as she caught a glimpse of what Sophia was telling her. "You said the first four principles were about living life. The fifth must be about life after death. Or is it . . . " She paused as the understanding unfolded. "Is it that we don't really die at all?"

"Yes, dear!" Sophia exclaimed. "It is. You see, we're eternal, interconnected, creative beings who come to this wonderfully diverse time-space reality to experience joy. We come knowing our power and trusting our guidance system to steer us through the contrast to the well-being that we instinctively know is ours for the having. We can't get it wrong, because every experience—whether we label it good or bad—adds to the expansion of all that is, and we never cease existing. Even when we have what humans call the death experience, we never stop being interested in the life we've created and are continuing to create.

"Those, my dear," she concluded, "are the principles of the universe. You knew them when you made the decision to come here, and you wanted to remember them now so that you could begin living life on purpose."

"And my life's purpose," Cassandra repeated the exciting truth, "is joy!"

JACE FELT PREPARED as he left for the meeting. He had proof of his innocence and could produce it if necessary. Moreover, he had Sophie as his constant companion. Whatever happened, she would be there to support him.

Arriving a few minutes before six, he pushed the button for the eighteenth floor where the offices of Harmon, Corruthers & Scott were located. When he'd dropped off Sophie's car, he'd met Mr. Corruthers in the lobby. The lavishness of the building's common area should have given him some indication of what the suites would be like. Still, he wasn't prepared for the opulence he witnessed as he stepped off the elevator and into the firm's reception area. Directly in front of him, water cascaded down a rock wall that was at least fifteen feet in height. The name of the law office stood out from the stone in gold embossed lettering.

Built into another wall was a fish tank he estimated to be at least five feet high and ten to twelve feet long. The fish, darting through mazes of artificial seaweed, underwater castles, and sunken pirate ships, were large and colorful. A seating area consisted of low-back leather chairs and ultra-glossy tables with magazines that looked as though they'd never been opened. A coffee bar housed a cappuccino machine and a crystal dome under which a selection of pastries was perfectly arranged. Jace wondered if it was all for show or if people were actually made to wait. He found out as the woman behind the reception desk called his name.

"Mr. Rutherford?"

"Yes."

"You can come right this way."

He followed her to a conference room with a large mahogany table in the center and cushiony, black leather office chairs surrounding it. The woman invited him to have a seat. On the table was a tray with a gleaming coffee decanter and another assortment of delicious-looking pastries. He accepted her offer of coffee and was told that an associate of Mr. Corruthers would be with him shortly.

Jace's mind was reeling, and questions were amassing. *What the hell am I doing here? What do they want with me, anyway?* Other thoughts vied for his attention as he took in the luxurious surroundings. *Is this what Cassandra and her family are used to?* He'd heard his mom speak of the lavish home she spent her days cleaning, and suddenly Jace wondered how he would ever fit in.

How could Sophie afford a firm like this to look after her affairs? Or did the Van Brodens pay for stuff like that? Though Sophie's answers were always forthcoming, Jace's barrage of questions and his uneasiness with the setting in which he found himself kept him from hearing them.

Before long, a man not much older than him entered the room and introduced himself. Jace shook his hand and then waited anxiously as the young man sat in a chair across the table and poured himself a cup of coffee before he spread open the large file folder he'd been carrying.

"Mr. Rutherford," he began. "I have some paperwork to go over with you before I show the reading of the will. So bear with me; we'll get through this as quickly as we can."

Jace heard the word *will* and didn't take in anything else the man said. "Excuse me," he interrupted. "Did you say the reading of the will?"

"Yes," the man replied. "You'll be viewing a taped version. We do it this way to save time, especially when it's as long and complicated as this one is. All parties view the reading in separate rooms. This way we can deal with your questions and concerns individually."

"I don't understand," Jace inquired further. "Why do I have to be here for the reading of the will?" He was still under the impression that he was there because of the missing jewelry.

"Mr. Rutherford," the young lawyer explained patiently, "all parties mentioned in the will, as well as anyone with a legal interest in the disbursement of the deceased's estate, are invited to be present for the official reading of the will."

Jace had to be sure he was hearing right. "Are you saying that my name is mentioned in the will?" he asked tentatively. "In Sophia Langdon's will?"

"Yes, Mr. Rutherford, it is."

Chapter 23

Cassandra listened somewhat removed as Mr. Corruthers went over the paperwork with her father. She was interested to hear what was contained in her aunt's final will and testament, yet her mind was on Jace and her plan to surprise him later. She found herself getting impatient as the time dragged on. Finally, the lights were dimmed and an image of Sophia appeared on the screen before them. A recorded voice began the reading of the official document.

The will held no surprises. After a lot of legal jargon, it confirmed that her father, Richard Van Broden, was the primary heir to his late aunt's vast estate. A generous sum was to go directly to both Cassandra and Trevor. As well, several charities were to receive sizable donations.

The lights went on, and Mr. Corruthers stood up to address the family. "What you just heard was the will that I executed for your aunt fifteen years ago. The will stands today, although a recent amendment has been made, and as I mentioned previously, a law suit has been filed against the estate.

The lawyer had Cassandra's full attention. She'd nearly forgotten that someone was interfering with the will. For a brief, regrettable moment she'd suspected Jace. Now she had no idea who it could possibly be.

"I'll go over the amendment first," he continued. "Approximately one year ago, Sophia purchased the building in which she was living. She also acquired the one next to it."

Cassandra and her father looked at each other in surprise but said nothing.

"As part of her assets, these properties would normally fall under the terms of the original will. However, as you'll see, the will was amended, and these properties are part of that amendment. Sophia contacted me about three weeks ago and informed me of her desire to have some of her assets bequeathed to a party that I will name shortly. She wanted it done in a way that could not be contested. I suggested transferring the properties to a holding company.

I won't get into the details of the arrangement at this time, but I will let you know that the deeds to these particular properties, as well as a car that was recently purchased through the company, are not part of the overall estate. Those assets belong to one Jace Rutherford."

Hearing Jace's name filled Cassandra with delight. "Oh my God!" she exclaimed. "The apartment building, the car—they belong to Jace now? Does he know?"

"He's being informed of it as we speak."

As her mind registered the fact that Jace was there receiving the news, she glanced at her parents. Her father smiled and nodded his approval. Her mother had a look of indifference on her face, but offered a genial remark.

"That's wonderful, sweetheart. I'm sure he'll be happy to hear it."

Knowing that Jace was present for the reading of the will, Cassandra wanted to go to him immediately. *He could be in the next room.* She bubbled with anticipation. *And he probably has no idea I'm here.* Before she could inquire about him, her father spoke up.

"So, Peter," he asked. "Who filed the law suit?"

"That brings us to our next order of business," the lawyer went on in his dry legal voice. "Several weeks ago, we were contacted by a London law firm representing one Bradford Langdon. He's a grandson of the late William F. Langdon who was a half brother to Sophia's husband, Lord Phillip."

"So he's a nephew," Richard frowned. "Sophia never mentioned any family on Phillip's side. I wonder if she knew about him. What does he want exactly?"

"The family claims to have had a verbal agreement with Sophia. Williams' son, Thomas—who was Bradford's father—negotiated the agreement on behalf of *his* father. She's been sending them a sum of money every year for the past four years. Though Thomas passed away earlier this year, the family is claiming that Sophia's promise is still binding and that the annuity should continue.

"I wanted to find out all I could before I met with Sophia regarding this. I called her the week before last, to schedule a meeting. Unfortunately . . ." He shook his head. "I suspect this nephew tried to appeal to her directly and she denied his request," Peter added. "Since learning of her passing, Bradford is claiming entitlement to part of the Langdon estate."

Again, Cassandra and her parents exchanged surprised looks. This time her mother spoke up. "You can't be serious," Helen exclaimed. "Does he really think he has a case?"

"We're still looking into it," the lawyer replied. "Apparently Phillip made several large payments to his half-brother when he was alive and a similar appeal was made after his death. All I can say at this point is that I see no grounds for contesting the will, but the claim for annuity may be more difficult to dispute. However, based on what we've learned about him, my feeling is that he'll want to avoid the inconvenience of a lengthy court battle and be willing to settle."

"Peter . . . " Richard stood up. "You may be right; I think we should look into this and consider making him an offer. Let's schedule a meeting later this week to discuss it. But right now . . . " He turned to Cassandra and smiled. "There's someone I'd like to meet."

WHEN THE LAWYER left the room, Jace sat staring, trying to absorb what he'd just heard. The image of Sophie's sweet, smiling face remained on the screen in front of him, and suddenly he was filled with a greater love and appreciation than he'd ever felt for the woman. *Sophie,* he shook his head. *I didn't know . . . I mean how can I begin to . . . ?*

"You're very welcome, Jace."

He wiped a tear from his eye. The news had left him shaken. It wasn't just the size of her estate, but that she'd cared enough to leave him any part of it when they'd only known each other a short time.

"Jace, we've known each other longer than you think. We've been together before this lifetime. We're soul mates, too."

The truth of it resounded in his heart. It was the connection she'd talked about before, the same one he had with Cassandra. He didn't understand it completely, but not knowing didn't bother him. He'd have plenty of questions for Sophie and plenty of time to ask them in the weeks and months ahead.

As Cassandra came to mind, Jace's heart filled with a love so powerful and so pure it seemed to take him to a new level of being. Not only that, but he felt her presence as if she were standing next to him. Eager to share his excitement, he considered calling her to tell her the news. However, there was something he had to do first. When he'd learned that the Van Brodens were present, he knew he had to speak to them. Despite escalating nervousness, he was determined to go and introduce himself to Cassandra's parents.

The door opened, and he was informed that the Van Brodens had finished their meeting. Jace's feet were like lead as he walked down the hallway. Before he entered the room, he took a deep breath and smiled at the image of Sophie still clear in his mind.

A man stood as he entered the room. He met Jace halfway across the large office and extended his hand. "Hello, Jace. I'm Richard Van Broden."

"Hello, sir. It's nice to meet you."

"Cassandra's told us a lot about you. It's good to finally meet."

An uncomfortable silence echoed between them, and then Richard added, "Congratulations, Jace. We were pleased to hear that Sophia included you in her will. I know she thought highly of you."

"Thank you," Jace responded with sincerity. The reality of his newfound abundance still hadn't sunk in, and he shook his head in amazement. "I didn't know why they called me here today. I certainly didn't expect anything like this." He paused as emotion squeezed his vocal cords. "She was . . . an amazing lady; I'm honored to have known her."

Richard nodded, affirming the sentiment.

In the silence that followed, Jace fought the impulse to ask the question burning within him. Though his mind argued that the timing wasn't right, his heart was hearing another voice. "Sir . . . " he began, buoyed by a confidence that surprised him. "There's something I'd like to ask you."

"Of course, Jace," Richard replied. "Go ahead."

"I want you to know how much your daughter means to me." He forced himself to speak slowly as he delivered his speech. He'd imagined the scene in his mind and had even rehearsed the words, yet he had no idea the opportunity would present itself so soon. "I know that our circumstances are different, and I may not be your idea of an ideal match for Cassandra. But sir, I'd like you to know that I love her more than words can say. Her happiness means everything to me." Jace stopped to take a breath. "I'd like to . . . ask your permission . . . to marry your daughter."

His knees went weak as he realized the question had been verbalized. He stood waiting for what seemed like an eternity as he stared into the eyes of the man who had the power to make his dream come true. A smile began to form on Richard's face. Jace's pulse slowed as Cassandra's father slowly nodded his head.

"Well, son. You have my permission, but why don't you ask her directly?"

Jace frowned at what seemed to be a strange request and then turned to see Cassandra standing in the doorway with a woman he assumed was her mother. Her hands flew to her mouth in surprise. Pure delight spread across her face as she started toward him. Before she reached him, Jace went down on one knee and reached in his pocket, pulling out a small velvet box.

"Cassandra, I never imagined meeting someone that makes me feel the way you do. We have our differences, but what we have in here." He tapped his chest. "It's the same. It's a connection of mind, body, and soul that I didn't know was possible. Most people spend a lifetime looking for what we have. I want to spend a lifetime enjoying it with you.

"Cassandra . . . " His heart swelled as he saw the answer in her eyes. "Will you marry me?"

THROUGH satin tears, Cassandra gazed into the eyes of the man she loved. She'd already given Jace her heart, now she was thrilled to give him her hand. She responded to his proposal with a passionate yes.

Jace slipped the ring on her finger and stood to his feet, still holding her hand. She glanced at the sparkling gem, but didn't really see it. Her eyes were clouded, her mind busy taking everything in. Seeking his arms and then his lips, she celebrated the special moment with Jace.

Then she turned to her parents, beaming with never-before-known happiness. As she met her mother's eyes and saw the uncharacteristic smile on her face, Cassandra was overcome with emotion. Jace had not only received her father's blessing, he'd received her mother's approval as well.

After more hugging and drying of tears, Cassandra took a closer look at the ring. "Jace," she gushed, "this is exquisite! Wherever did you get . . . ?" She stopped mid-sentence, knowing the answer to her question. "Is this . . . Aunt Sophia's ring?"

He nodded, smiling.

"But how . . . ?"

After telling her how he'd discovered it, Jace added, "An heirloom like this . . . well, it should stay in the family. I discussed it with Mrs. Davidson at the community center. When I told her about us . . . I mean, when she understood my intentions," he explained awkwardly, "she suggested I make a donation to the center in exchange for the ring."

"You made . . . a donation?" Cassandra repeated haltingly. She couldn't imagine what Jace could donate in exchange for a valuable piece of jewelry like that. To her knowledge he had no assets before today, no money saved. Then she remembered the inheritance he was to receive from his estranged uncle. "Jace." she cried, "you didn't!"

"EVERYTHING WORKED out the way it was supposed to," Jace assured her, thinking of the synchronistic flow of events that had led up to that moment. When he'd told Mrs. Davidson about the money he was to receive, she agreed to set the ring aside. Though it was appraised considerably higher, she felt it wouldn't bring more than ten-thousand at the auction. Therefore they'd agreed to that amount.

After that, everything unfolded so perfectly he could only attribute it to Sophie's loving intervention. The certified check arrived in the mail, Tuesday afternoon. Jace was able to pick up the ring on his way to the meeting with the lawyer. And Cassandra just happened to be there for him to give it to. He couldn't have planned it any better. "I have all I need." He kissed her softly. "And now that you've agreed to marry me, I have all I want."

"I guess when you put it that way . . . who am I to object?" Cassandra grinned playfully. As she looked at the treasured piece again, she sighed with delight. "Having Aunt Sophia's ring means a lot to me, Jace. But having you in my life—that means everything. I love you so much."

Jace felt the same. All else paled in comparison to his love for Cassandra. Though his unexpected inheritance had for a brief moment offered to change the course of his life, he'd gladly exchanged a good portion of it for the ring he knew Cassandra would cherish. Now Sophie's extremely generous gifts had catapulted him to a place of financial security. That, he realized, was only the beginning. There was a huge, swirling vortex filled with abundance, ready for him to allow into his experience. There was no shortage, no lack. Not any more. However, it was about more than just money. He'd learned how to create his own reality. He'd learned how to guide his thoughts deliberately. He was in control of his life now.

Both he and Cassandra had Sophie to thank for helping them find the pathway to their dreams. He'd found the key to attracting financial abundance, and she'd found the passion missing in her writing career. Not only that, but they'd found each other. As Jace left the lawyer's office with Cassandra by his side, he glanced one more time at the image of Sophie still on the screen. *You knew this would happen all along, didn't you?* he accused lovingly.

"It seemed like a nice idea." she replied.

"The standard of success in life isn't the things. It isn't the money or the stuff. It is absolutely the amount of joy that you feel."

--- Abraham-Hicks

CPSIA information can be obtained at www.ICGtesting.com
Printed in the USA
LVOW050337120313

323735LV00001B/3/P